P9-BIB-207

The Immigrant Heritage of America Series

Col. Com. Michael Kovats de Fabriczy
(Painting by Zoltán de Bényey)
Reproduced by permission of the Col. Com.
Michael de Kovats Historical Society

The Hungarian-Americans

By Steven Bela Vardy

Duquesne University, Pittsburgh

Twayne Publishers • Boston

The Hungarian-Americans

Steven Bela Vardy

Copyright © 1985 by G.K. Hall & Company
All Rights Reserved
Published by Twayne Publishers
A Division of G. K. Hall & Co.
A publishing subsidiary of ITT   any
70 Lincoln Street
Boston, Massachusetts 02111

Book Production by Lyda E. Kuth
Book Design by Barbara Anderson

Printed on permanent/durable acid-free
paper and bound in the United States of America.

Library of Congress Cataloging in Publication Data

Várdy, Steven Béla, 1935-
   The Hungarian-Americans.

   (The Immigrant heritage of America series)
   Bibliography: p.
   Includes index.
   1. Hungarian Americans—History.   I. Title.
II. Series.
E184.H95V37 1985   973'.0494511   84–20526
ISBN 0–8057–8425–X

To: *Ági*
Attila Nicholas
Zoltan Alexander
Laura Agnes

Contents

About the Author

Born in Hungary, educated in Hungary, Germany, Austria, and the United States, S. B. Vardy, Ph.D., is a professor of East European History at Duquesne University, Director of the University's Forum, and adjunct professor at the University of Pittsburgh. He is also the current president of the American Association for the Study of Hungarian History, an affiliate of the American Historical Association. Professor Vardy's scholarly articles have appeared in many national and international periodicals throughout Europe and North America, and he has also contributed to such major reference works as the *Encyclopedia Americana,* the *World Book Encyclopedia,* the *Academic American Encyclopedia,* and the *McGraw Hill Encyclopedia of World Biography.* His books include *History of the Hungarian Nation* (coauthored, 1969), *Hungarian Historiography and the Geistesgeschichte School* (1974), *Modern Hungarian Historiography* (1976), and *Clio's Art in Hungary* (1985). He has coedited *Society in Change* (1983), and two other forthcoming books on East Central European history. His interest in Hungarian-American history reaches back to the early 1970s, and he has already authored well over a dozen articles in that field, published both in the United States and in Hungary. In 1984 Professor Vardy was also chosen to be the recipient of Duquesne University's "Excellence in Scholarship Award"—an honor that is bestowed only occasionally by the university.

Preface

This work presents an account of the history and every-day life of those Americans whose roots reach back to their millennial homeland: Hungary. The Hungarian immigrants to America came sporadically from the late-sixteenth to the mid-nineteenth century, and then in ever-increasing numbers in the decades that followed. Their migration reached flood proportions during the two decades before World War I, climaxing in 1907, and then coming to an abrupt halt in 1914. Hungarian immigration resumed after the war, but only on a modest scale, with a new but much less pronounced peak in the 1950s. The interwar years, but especially the post–World War II decades, saw the arrival of new types of immigrants who were distinguished from their pre–World War I predecessors both by the cause of their emigration (political rather than economic) and by their social, cultural, and educational background. Whereas the turn-of-the-century immigrants and a sizable portion of the interwar immigrants were peasants, small farmers, and unskilled or semiskilled workers with rural backgrounds, many of the interwar and most of the post–World War II immigrants came from the middle and upper layers of Hungarian society. As such, their adjustment to American society was different.

In summing up the developments of the post–World War II period I had no models to follow, and thus produced a scheme of my own. Understandably, it is the chapters dealing with this period that will be the most controversial. As is the obligation of every professional historian, my aim was to write *sine ira et studio* ("without anger and prejudice"). But however carefully written, these chapters deal with a period and touch upon problems that are filled with emotions and overshadowed by the struggle of conflicting ideologies.

As befits a short history, I have documented in my notes the most essential data and direct quotations. Whenever possible, I have cited English-language works but in many instances refer to Hungarian-language publications. The sources cited in the notes in an abbreviated form are all listed in the bibliography.

In the course of researching and writing this work, I received help from many sources. Some people sent me materials; others called my attention to additional sources. The list is so long that it would be impossible to mention them all. While I am grateful to everyone, all I can do here is to cite a few institutions, including the American Hungarian Foundation of New Brunswick, New Jersey (headed by Professor August J. Molnar), the Department of Uralic and Altaic Studies of Indiana University–Bloomington (headed by Professor Denis Sinor), and my own institution, Duquesne University, which has twice awarded me Hunkele Foundation Research Grants to facilitate the completion of this work. I am also grateful to many of my colleagues in Hungary, especially to those at the Institute of History of the Hungarian Academy of Sciences and the Széchényi National Library of Budapest. Most of all, however, I am grateful to my wife, Agnes Huszar Vardy, of Robert Morris College and the University of Pittsburgh—a scholar in her own right— who was an ever-present help and a constant source of inspiration during the writing of this work; and to my son Nicholas A. Vardy of Stanford University, who has read and commented on my manuscript at all stages of its preparation.

S. B. Vardy

Duquesne University

Chapter One
Hungary and the Hungarians

Although Hungarian adventurers, travelers, missionaries, and political immigrants have been coming to North America ever since the sixteenth century, their mass immigration to the United States did not begin until the 1880s. But when it did, it soon became a flood, eventually landing perhaps 850,000 or more Hungarians in this country. They became part of American society, but knowledge about their origins, language, and culture did not become widespread, and is limited even today. This still holds true, even though during the past three decades the study of Hungarian history and culture at American universities has increased dramatically.[1] Yet, even today, many Americans—including some well-educated persons—routinely classify the Hungarians as Slavs and confuse their capital, Budapest, with the Rumanian capital of Bucharest. In light of the above, a brief summary of their past and a few words about present-day Hungary should not be in vain.

Hungary Today

In the course of the past eleven centuries Hungarian influence and political control extended throughout and even beyond the Carpathian Basin—an area that is basically identical with "Historic" or "Greater Hungary." Yet, today Hungary is only one of the small states of East Central Europe. Since Historic Hungary's dismemberment after World War I (Treaty of Trianon, June 4, 1920), the country has shrunk to about one-third of its former size. Today its area is only about 36,000 square miles (roughly the size of Indiana), with a population of less than eleven million people. Of these, over 95 percent are Hungarians and thus belong to the so-called Magyar linguistic stock. The rest are composed of Germans, Croats, Slovaks, Serbs, Rumanians, gypsies, and a few smaller ethnic groups.[2]

Who Are the Magyars?

The world today is inhabited by four and a half billion persons who belong to a wide variety of ethnic and linguistic groups and

1

who speak about four thousand languages and many more dialects. These languages are all different from one another, but most of them can be classified into one of eight to ten linguistic groups or "families of languages." This means that most of the nations and ethnic groups of the world speak languages that are related to numerous other languages in the same group, although this relationship may be a very close one (e.g., Czech and Slovak), or a rather remote one (e.g., English and Persian).

Linguistic relationship does not always mean ethnic relationship, either because occasionally people change their languages or because they alter their ethnicity through intermarriage with other ethnic groups. There are also instances of people who go through a gradual and partial ethnic transformation, but do so without losing their original language.

A good example of the latter phenomenon is the case of the Hungarians or Magyars. Since their conquest of the Carpathian Basin in the ninth century, they have intermarried with Germans, Slavs, Turks, and various other peoples who preceded or followed them into the area. As such the Hungarians of today are certainly different in appearance from their conquering ancestors eleven hundred years ago. Yet, except for the incorporation of certain Germanic, Slavic, Latin, and Turkic words, their language is basically identical with that of their forefathers. Thus, while transformed ethnically, and as such at least partially related to the people around them, linguistically the Hungarians are totally different from their neighbors. As opposed to the latter—all of whom speak one of the related Indo-European languages—the Hungarians speak a Finno-Ugric tongue. The most distinguishing mark of the latter—which are probably part of the larger so-called Ural-Altaic family of languages—is the system of "agglutination," i.e., a heavy reliance on prefixes and suffixes. The closest linguistic relatives of the Hungarians are the Finns and the Estonians, and somewhat more remotely the Turkic-speaking peoples.

The Origins of the Magyars

The roots of the Hungarians are lost in the mist of history. All we know is that these roots are in the East and perhaps—according to some recent theories—in the Near East. The traditional view holds that the Hungarians conquered their present homeland in the late ninth century, but nowadays a number of scholars believe that they came in several waves, predating by several centuries the time of the traditional conquest.

The Hungarians call themselves Magyars—after the dominant tribe of the ninth-century conquerors—but the outside world knows them by one of the many variants of the Turkish word *Onogur* ("Ten Tribes"), e.g., Hungarian, Hongrois, Ungar, Ungharese, Vengri. While we know very little about the history and activities of the early waves of Hungarians, we know that one of the leading princes of the ninth-century conquerors was a certain Árpád, who had established a royal dynasty that ruled Hungary for over four centuries (896–1301).[3]

The Medieval Hungarian Christian Kingdom

In the century that followed the Árpádian conquest the Hungarian tribes were molded into a nation. One of Árpád's successors, King St. Stephen (897–1038), Christianized his nation and also laid the foundations of a kingdom that dominated the region for well over five centuries. In the course of the twelfth to the fifteenth centuries Hungarian power extended into the Balkans (over Croatia, Dalmatia, Bosnia, Serbia, Wallachia, and Moldavia), and internally Hungarian society underwent a significant transformation. The Golden Bull of 1222 (Hungary's Magna Charta) obliged the king to share some of his powers with the emerging nobility and thus laid the foundations of Hungarian constitutionalism. In this way Hungary was transformed from a "patrimonial kingdom" (regarded by the king as his private preserve) into a "feudal kingdom," where political, economic, and military powers were shared by the king and the landowning nobility.

Although devastated by the Mongols in 1241, Hungary was soon rebuilt and repopulated. Moreover, in the course of the next two centuries it emerged as one of the significant powers in Central and Eastern Europe. King Louis the Great (1342–1382) also gained control over Poland (1370), while King Matthias Corvinus (1457–1490) conquered Moravia, Silesia, and during the final years of his reign made Vienna (1485–1490) into the capital of his expanding realm. King Matthias's reign also saw the influx of Italian influences into Hungary, and the royal court of Buda soon emerged as the most important center of East Central European Renaissance. This same period also saw the foundation of Hungary's third university (Pécs in 1367, Óbuda in 1389, and Pozsony in 1465), as well as the establishment of the country's first printing press, at Buda (1473)—the latter being the first of its kind east of the Germanic world.

King Matthias's death was followed by a rapid decline of Hungarian power, which was the result of the lack of effective leadership and the consequent feudal anarchy. This anarchy and the subsequent exploitation of the population soon led to a major peasant uprising in 1514, which in turn resulted in the enserfment of the Hungarian peasantry. In the absence of an effective central leadership, and with much of the political and military power in the hands of the various feuding regional lords, the internally weakened country was unable to withstand the increasing Ottoman Turkish pressure from the Balkans. This was all the more so, as no effective help was extended by the Christian West. In 1526, at the fateful Battle of Mohács, the Hungarian royal army was defeated, the young King Louis II was killed, and Hungary fell victim to its covetous neighbors, both from the South as well as from the West.

Under Ottoman and Habsburg Rule

Although defeated by the Turks in 1526, Hungary could still have had a chance to recover, had the country's leaders been one in purpose. But not even that great national catastrophe was able to bring them together. Thus, instead of uniting their efforts against the Turks, the Hungarians added to the nation's problems by electing two rival kings: John Zápolya (1526–1540), the former governor of the province of Transylvania, and Ferdinand of Habsburg (1526–1564), the Grand Duke of Austria and the brother of Emperor Charles V. These elections soon produced a fratricidal struggle between the two factions and gave the Turks the chance to consolidate their hold over south and central Hungary. In 1541 the Turks also conquered the royal capital of Buda, which for the next 145 years became the administrative center of their ever-increasing holdings in Hungary. Thus, after its initial twofold division, the country now came to be trisected, and this situation lasted until the very end of the seventeenth century.

This state of national disunity came to an end at the turn of the seventeenth to the eighteenth century, when Hungary was freed from the Turks, and the whole country was reunited under the rule of the Habsburgs. During the eighteenth century, the Habsburgs tried to impose their centralized absolutism on Hungary, but they never fully succeeded. Early in the century the Hungarians rose in rebellion against this absolutism, and under Prince Ferenc Rákóczi's leadership they fought for eight long years (1703–1711) against the Habsburg imperial armies. Although eventually overwhelmed, the strength of their uprising persuaded Vienna that it would be much wiser to compromise with the Hungarians. Thereafter the Habsburgs tried to achieve their end not by the force of arms but by gaining the support of the Hungarian aristocracy through favors and titles. They also tried to bind the nobility to the dynasty and to the imperial idea by cultural and family ties. Much of this effort proved to be successful. Yet the nation's independent spirit was still maintained by the members of the lower nobility. The latter constituted a sizable class (about 5 percent of the population), whose members continued to function according to the old constitution and the traditional political system, within the confines of the autonomous counties. The leaders of the Hungarian linguistic, cultural, and national revival also came from their ranks; and they even managed to regain many of the alienated aristocracy for the Hungarian national cause.

The Hungarian National Revival

Similarly to developments in Central and Western Europe, the Hungarian national revival also began in the eighteenth century. Initially it did so largely in the linguistic and cultural field, and then it moved to the political arena.

Although this national revival was an eighteenth- and early nineteenth-century development, the Hungarians had been conscious of their national identity long before this period. This was a natural by-product of their unique position among the nations of Europe. But this traditional national consciousness was widespread only among the nobility, who retained the use of the term *Natio Hungarica* ("Hungarian Nation") only to themselves. With the birth of modern nationalism, however, the walls between the nobility and the people at large began to break down, and the concept of *Natio Hungarica* came to be extended to everyone who spoke the Magyar language.

The rise of this modern cultural and political nationalism went hand in hand with the rise of liberalism. These two ideas came to be the driving force behind the changes in the Era of Reform (1825–1848), which climaxed in the Revolution of 1848 and swept away the remnants of feudalism.

The Revolution of 1848 and the War of Liberation that followed (1848–1849) are among the most glorious and romanticized events in Hungary's modern history. For the first time the ideas of liberty, equality, and fraternity were being implemented on a mass scale, and absolutism was pushed into a defensive position. True, the Hungarians were eventually defeated, but many of the achievements of the revolution could not be undone. Moreover, because Habsburg victory was achieved through a massive Russian intervention, the victory itself revealed the weakness of the absolutistic state structure. Thus, even though the Hungarian defeat was followed by the reintroduction of absolutism, there was little chance for it to succeed. Many of Hungary's political leaders who remained at home were fully aware of this and were convinced that change was inevitable. They were proven to be correct. After a number of foreign-policy reverses in the 1850s and 1860s, the Habsburgs were forced to come to terms with the Hungarians. The result was the transformation of the Habsburg or Austrian Empire into the dualistic state of Austria-Hungary in 1867, and a new chance for the Hungarians to play a significant role in European history.

The Austro-Hungarian dualistic arrangement satisfied many of the demands of the Magyars, yet it was far from a perfect solution, for it gave relatively little recognition to the other nationalities. Even so it was a definite improvement, for it replaced absolutism with two constitutional regimes. Moreover, with the internal peace reestablished, the two governments could turn their attention to the pressing social and economic problems. Of these there were many. But they could at least now be attended to. Economic progress during the next half a century became increasingly rapid, and at times even phenomenal. Even so—because of centuries of stagnation—it was still largely these economic problems, coupled with increasing opportunities abroad, that drove millions to leave their country and to seek out their fortunes in the United States.

This so-called "great emigration" of the dualist period had often been castigated by the spokesmen of the Magyar nation, who regarded it as a national catastrophe. Recent research by Julianna Puskás, however, has proven that "neither in rate nor in intensity is this Hungarian emigration comparable to the outflow from Ireland."[4] In other words, in contemporary European terms, the Hungarian emigration was only of "medium intensity"; and it also displayed the increasing tendency of repatriation before the First World War. Thus, if we accept the thesis that the primary cause of emigration from Hungary was economic—and all serious contemporary and recent studies come to this conclusion—then we must also accept the view that Hungary's economic plight during those decades of the late nineteenth and early twentieth century was also less severe than that of a few other areas, such as Ireland and southern Italy.

Twentieth-Century Developments

World War I is a significant watershed not only in the history of Hungary but also in the history of Hungarian emigration. Following the war, Austria-Hungary as well as Hungary itself was partitioned in the name of the principle of national self-determination. But in Hungary's case this dismemberment was so punitive that fully one-third of the Magyar nation found itself beyond the new frontiers in such newly created or newly enlarged states as Czechoslovakia, Rumania, Yugoslavia, and even the radically reduced Austria. This development was soon followed by the introduction of various immigration laws in the United States that placed a very low quota on Hungarian immigration. Thus, while the humbled Magyar nation struggled to face its bleak future within its much reduced frontiers and limited economic potential, and while their brethren across the new frontiers were confronted with the new reality of having become minorities in the lands of their ancestors, they also had to face the fact that the American safety valve had been virtually closed. Even so a number of them managed to make it to the "Land of Promise"; but many of them did so only as "Czechoslovaks," "Rumanians," or as "Yugoslavs." Moreover, soon even these new immigrants saw their dreams evaporate in the Great Depression of the 1930s.

Hungary became involved in World War II largely because of her geographical position. But this involvement was on the side of the Axis powers primarily because Germany and Italy were the only great powers who were willing to listen to Hungary's claims for the revision of the frontiers of 1920. The prospects of this involvement drove many progressive intellectuals out of the country already during the 1930s. Their ranks were further increased by several major waves after World War II. These included the participants of the exodus of 1944–1945, those of 1947–1948, and those of the Revolution of 1956. A sizable portion of these emigrants landed on the American shores, as did the steady if small stream of emigrants during the 1960s and 1970s. This stream is still flowing today, notwithstanding the political liberalization and the general improvement of the quality of life in Hungary. The reasons for this continued exodus are many, including intellectual dissent, personal dissatisfaction, or the simple desire to see the world beyond.

The situation is totally different with those Hungarians who flee from the surrounding states. With the exception of those who live in Yugoslavia under relatively acceptable conditions, most of them leave because of political and economic reasons; and more recently and even more importantly, because of the increasingly anti-Hungarian nationality policies of the governments of Rumania and Slovakia (within Czechoslovakia). The combination of political pressure and nationality oppression makes these Hungarians much more daring than their brethren in the comparatively liberal Hungary in finding ways to reach the West and then to settle in the United States.[5]

Chapter Two
From Early Adventurers to Nineteenth-Century Political Immigrants

Being originally horsemen and living in a basically landlocked country prevented the Hungarians from ever developing close affinity to the sea. As such they never had any meaningful role in the geographical discoveries and explorations of the fifteenth to the nineteenth centuries. Yet, some of them did reach the Americas as early as the sixteenth century, with others coming in increasing numbers in the centuries that followed.

As in the case of most nationalities there is even the story of an alleged pre-Columbian Hungarian in America. His name is Tyrker (Turk), who accompanied Eric the Red on his expedition to North America in A.D. 1000. (It is to be noted here that in the ninth to the eleventh centuries the Hungarians were often referred to as "Turks," and the Byzantine Emperor Michael Dukas even addressed one of them, Géza I, as the "King of Turkia.") The first historically verifiable Hungarian, however, was not Tyrker but the classical scholar and poet Stephen Parmenius of Buda (ca. 1555–1583), who participated in Sir Humphrey Gilbert's expedition to Newfoundland in 1583 and then died on the way back. The next visitor with Hungarian connections was the well-known Captain John Smith (1579–1631), the founder of Jamestown in Virginia (1607). Before his coming to the New World, Smith had traveled through Hungary and Transylvania (1601–1603), where, because of his military exploits against the Turks, Prince Sigismund Báthory raised him to the ranks of the Hungarian nobility.[1]

In the two centuries that followed Parmenius's tragic adventure in Newfoundland and Captain John Smith's excursions to Hungary and Transylvania, few Hungarians appear to have had the desire and the daring to face the challenges of the high seas to see the world beyond. Those who came were driven by *Wanderlust*, the desire for religious freedom, or by the zeal to Christianize the natives of the New World. Some of the latter included the Reformed clergyman István Zádor, who reached Boston in 1682; the Pietist Johannes Kelp, who brought a group of Transylvania Saxons to Pennsylvania in 1694; the teacher Izsák Ferdinánd Sárosy, who in 1695 settled for a while in Germantown, Pennsylvania; and the two Jesuit missionaries Johannes Rátkay (1647–1683) and Ferdinánd Konság (1703–1759). Both of the latter visited and explored the southwestern region of what later became the United States, and both of them wrote reports about their travels and experiences.

The members of the Jesuit order were also responsible for preparing the earliest Hungarian geographical and ethnographical descriptions of the New Continent. These included Ferenc Szdellár, whose *Itinerarium* (1720) contained a detailed description of North America; István Vecsei-Pap, whose *Hungarian Geography* (1741) also contained references to the future United States; and Pál Bertalanffi, whose *A Short Description of the World's Two Orders* (1754) is really a detailed description of New England, Canada, and much of the southern United States. Being a zealous Catholic, Bertalanffi was naturally very critical of the Protestant colonies, referring to Boston as a "Calvinist humbug" and decrying the fact that Virginia was "infested with Calvinist colleges."[2]

From the American Revolution to the Hungarian Revolution

The dissolution of the Jesuit order in 1773 ended most of the Hungarian missionary activities, but it did not end Hungarian interest in America. Being under even more exacting "colonial rule," the Hungarian educated classes naturally felt a great deal of sympathy for the American colonists and their struggle with the British. As expressed by Professor J. K. Zinner of the Imperial and Royal Academy of Buda (Budapest) in a letter to Benjamin Franklin, "all the chiefs of your new republic [are viewed by the Hungarians] as angels sent by Heaven to guide and comfort the human race."[3]

But Hungarians went much beyond the simple expression of sympathy for the American cause. A goodly number of them also joined the colonial armies to fight the British. The best known among these are Colonel Michael Kováts (1724–1779) and Major John Ladislaus Pollereczky (1748–1830).[4] The first of these became the Master of Exercises of the famous Pulaski Legion, which was America's first hussar regiment. Although underarmed and underequipped, the Pulaski Legion fought a number of successful encounters with the British, including the Battle of Charleston on May 11–12, 1779. It was in this battle that Kováts died while leading a charge against General Prevost's forces on the first day of the encounter. As recorded by the Charleston physician Dr. Joseph Johnson, "the British buried him where he fell. . . . He was an officer of great merit and experience, a Hungarian by birth."[5] Like Colonel Kováts, Major Pollereczky was also a cavalryman. He was the commander of Duc de Lauzun's French auxiliary forces, a sizable portion of which consisted of Hungarian hussars. Although a member of the Hungarian nobility whose descendants still live in Hungary, Pollereczky himself remained in the United States. He lived and died in Dresden, Maine, where his grave can still be found today.

Almost simultaneously with Kováts and Pollereczky, the great Hungarian traveler and adventurer Count Maurice Benyovszky (1741–1786) also spent some time in America. But as his offer to fight for the American cause was declined by Washington for want of a position "suitable to his rank," Benyovszky soon left and became involved in numerous unusual adventures bordering on the incredible. Going through the Russian Empire from Poland to the Kamchatka Peninsula, he eventually ended up on the island of Madagascar, where in 1777 the natives elected him their *"king."* After many more adventures Benyovszky died on May 23, 1786, while trying to defend his "kingdom" against a French expeditionary force.[6]

After the success of the American Revolution, Hungarian interest in the new republic became even more intense. This is evidenced both by the increased number of Hungarian publications about the United States as well as by the coming of an ever greater number of travelers to the American shores. The most influential of the former was a translated version of William Robertson's *History of America* (1807), which portrayed American society in an idealized and most favorable manner. Of perhaps even greater importance were some of the travelogues published by Hungarian travelers during the 1830s and 1840s. They were instrumental in pushing Hungary's political leaders in the direction of social and political reform. The most significant and epoch-making of these travel accounts were Sándor Bölöni-Farkas's *Journey to North America* (1834),[7] which described his experiences during his 1831 visit to the northeastern states, and Ágoston Haraszthy's *Journey in North America* (1844),[8] which related the author's American adventures in the early 1840s. Bölöni-Farkas was both awed and inspired by what he had experienced in the "happy country" across the sea, which he saw as a "stern warning to the despots" and an "inspiring beacon to the oppressed." He was equally impressed with America's well-functioning democracy, as well as with the learning and culture that he witnessed in Benjamin Franklin's Philadelphia.

Haraszthy's sojourn lasted considerably longer than that of Bölöni-Farkas. Moreover, he was so impressed with the new country that he soon returned as a settler, bringing his family along. After founding a settlement in Wisconsin (today's Sauk City), he moved on to California's Sonoma Valley, where he introduced the Tokay grapes and thus became one of the founders of that state's now famous wine industry. In the course of the next few years he served in various public functions (e.g., Sheriff of San Diego County, State Commissioner for Viticulture) and also authored the first American handbook on the art of grape culture and wine making (1862).[9]

These laudatory descriptions of the United States in Hungarian publications were largely responsible for the initiation of cultural and scientific exchanges between the American Philosophical Society of Philadelphia and the Hungarian Academy of Sciences. Begun with the visit of the mathematician and astronomer Károly Nagy to Philadelphia in 1832, these exchanges continued throughout the nineteenth century, with only a slight decline during the Hungarian Revolution of 1848–1849 and the years of repression that followed.[10]

These early nineteenth-century writings about the United States and about the functioning of democracy in the new republic had an incalculable influence upon developments in Hungary during the 1830s and 1840s. They had sown the seeds of social and political discontent, and thus aided the triumph of liberal and democratic ideas. They had also opened up new possibilities by pointing to the almost limitless freedom and opportunities in the United States. It was this freedom and opportunity that brought Haraszthy to America, to be followed later by hundreds of thousands of others.

Kossuth and the First Political Immigrants: The Forty-Eighters

The 1830s and 1840s were years of reform in Hungary that culminated in the Revolution of 1848 and in the abolishment of the remnants of feudalism. The long Austro-Hungarian war that followed, however, resulted in Hungary's defeat with the aid of Russia and in the flight of many thousands of Hungarian revolutionaries to various Western lands. In the course of 1849–1851 the United States received perhaps as many as 4,000 of these emigrants. They constituted the first of several successive waves of Hungarian political emigrants whose lines stretch through 130 years right to our own days, even though the great majority of those who came— particularly around the turn of the century—did so for economic, and not political, reasons.

The most famous of these 48-ers was Louis Kossuth (1802–1894) himself, the leader of the revolution.[11] He arrived in New York in December 1851 but stayed only for seven months, returning to Europe to continue his agitation there. Although his seven-month tour took him through much of the eastern United States from New York to St. Louis and from Buffalo to New Orleans, and he was received with much acclaim everywhere, ultimately it still ended in disappointment. Nothwithstanding the public enthusiasm for this imposing champion of national independence and political liberalism, the United States government refused to depart from the principle of nonintervention as formulated by Washington and as codified by the neutrality laws of 1818. President Fillmore, who was totally ignorant of Hungarian affairs, was "unequivocal in his defense of Washington's principle of neutrality." But this principle was also adhered to scrupulously by the much more knowledgeable Daniel Webster, who, as Secretary of State, promised "to treat him [Kossuth] with respect," but also indicated that he would "give him [Kossuth] no encouragement."[12]

In addition to encountering this policy of nonintervention, however—which doomed his whole purpose for coming to the United States—Kossuth also found himself in political difficulties because of his inability, or rather unwillingness, to take sides in the abolition controversy that plagued contemporary American politics. His heart was naturally with the supporters of emancipation. But to have declared this openly would have been interpreted as a foreign exile's intervention in the host country's politics and would also have invited the attacks of southern political interests. His efforts to stay out of the slavery controversy, however, did not save Kossuth from attacks by the radical abolitionist Lloyd Garrison, who castigated him for refusing to take sides openly, or from criticisms by the proslavery circles for his hardly veiled sympathies for emancipation.

In light of the above, Kossuth left the American shores on July
14, 1852, with much disappointment. He failed to achieve his goal
of securing immediate United States help for the cause of Hungarian
independence, and he also realized that such support would not even
be forthcoming in the future. True, because of his imposing personality and his great oratorical skill, he left a deep impression upon
the contemporary American mind, but this impression proved to
be largely ephemeral, with no meaningful and lasting consequences
upon United States–Hungarian relations. Notwithstanding the virtual "Kossuth craze" that swept through American society in those
days, American policymakers basically agreed with Ambassador Abbot Lawrence in London, who wrote to Washington that "we [Amer-
icans] have enough agitators of our own, without having to depend
on foreigners to explain our political obligations to us."[13]

When Kossuth returned to Europe, some of his fellow emigrants
followed him, hoping to find more sympathy and help in some of
the European countries. Many others, however, stayed behind. The
latter were convinced that the cause of Hungary's independence
could not be resurrected in the near future, and they were determined
to make it in the United States. In addition to nameless thousands,
the latter included László Újházi (1795–1870), the founder of the
Hungarian settlement of New Buda in Iowa, who eventually settled
and died in Texas; Major János Prágay (?–1851), one of the most
radical of the 48-ers, who died in an anti-Spanish invasion of Cuba;
Frigyes Kerényi (1822–1852/53), a noted romantic poet who, unable to adjust to the New World, went insane and then disappeared
on the vast American prairie somewhere between Iowa and Texas;
Nicholas Fejérváry (1811–1895), the founder of the Hungarian
colony in Davenport, Iowa; Captain Márton Koszta (1819–185?),
whose abduction by Austrian agents in 1853 in Turkey almost led
to a military encounter between United States and Austrian naval
units in the eastern Mediterranean; the explorer, geographer, and
naturalist János Xanthus (1825–1894), whose explorations and
writings about the American West created quite an impression in
Hungarian scholarly and scientific circles, which eventually led to
his appointment as the first director of the Hungarian National
Museum's Ethnographical Collection (the future Hungarian Ethnographical Museum); and many scores of other notable personalities
who in one way or another have made their mark in American
society.[14]

In addition to making their mark in American society, these political immigrants were also responsible for establishing the first Hungarian-American organizations, as well as the first Hungarian-American newspaper. The former included the ephemeral "Hungarian Sick Care Society" *(Magyar Betegápoló Egylet)*, which existed for about three or four years after the revolution, and the much more substantial "New York Hungarian Society" *(New Yorki Magyar Egylet)*, founded in 1865; while the latter was the *Magyar Száműzöttek Lapja* (Hungarian exiles' news), established by one of Kossuth's more radical followers, Károly Kornis (1822–1862) in the fall of 1853.[15] This first attempt at Hungarian-American journalism, however, was printed only in one hundred copies and ceased publication after the sixth issue. The time was simply not ripe as yet for a Hungarian-language paper in the United States. There were too few readers and most of them were still in a transient status, unable or unwilling to support a permanent periodical.

Hungarians in the Civil War

Being political immigrants and consisting largely of intellectuals and professionals, most of the 48-ers found it difficult to adjust to the conditions of this country of self-made men, where practical achievements were valued much more highly than birth, past careers, or titles. Of those who did make it, however, many made significant careers in such diverse fields as the military, the diplomatic corps, journalism, and publishing. But given the background of the 48-ers and the opportunities presented by the outbreak of the Civil War, it was especially in the first of these fields where they made their mark.

While no reliable data exist on the number of Hungarians in the United States at the time of the Civil War, past historians have estimated their number to have been somewhere between three to five thousand, with four thousand being an acceptable compromise. Of this number about eight hundred served in the Union Army, among them nearly a hundred officers. The latter ultimately included two major generals, five brigadier generals, fifteen colonels and lieutenant colonels, thirteen majors, twelve captains, and several dozen first and second lieutenants.[16] There were also several scores of noncomissioned officers. Their rapid promotion was the direct result of their military experiences in Hungary and in western Europe, as well as the lack of sufficient number of seasoned military leaders among the Northerners. By way of comparison we may cite the case of the Czechs, who, although perhaps five to six times as numerous as the Hungarians in the United States, were unable to produce even a single officer above the rank of a colonel, and their lower-ranked officers were also fewer in number.[17] The Germans, on the other hand, were much more numerous (216,000 served in the Union Army) and had many high-ranking officers, but not even they could compete with the Hungarians in proportion to their numbers in the country.[18]

In addition to being few in number, the Hungarians were also scattered through much of the country. This prevented them from establishing separate Hungarian regiments in imitation of the Germans and the Irish, but not from joining other nationalities in their localities. Thus many of them joined the so-called "Lincoln Riflemen" of Chicago, the 8th Volunteer Infantry Regiment of New York, and the "Garibaldi Guard" and the "Black Riflemen" of the same city and state. Others who were far away from such major immigrant centers simply joined one of the local regiments in such states as Iowa, Missouri, Ohio, Indiana, Kansas, Wisconsin, West Virginia, Illinois, Nebraska, California, and Florida.

The best known of the Hungarian officers who fought in the Northern armies included Major General Julius H. Stahel (1825–1912)—the former Gyula Számvald of Hungary—who was the only one to receive the Congressional Medal of Honor; Major General Alexander Asboth (1811–1868), who for a while was General John C. Fremont's chief of staff and ended his days as the United States Minister to Argentina; Colonel Géza Mihalótzy (1825–1864), the commander of the "Lincoln Riflemen" of Chicago, who died in an encounter near Chattanooga, Tennessee, and had a fort named after him on Cameron Hill; Colonel Charles Zágonyi (1824–1867?), the commander of General Fremont's personal bodyguards; and Major Julian Kuné (1831–1914), one of Colonel Mihalótzy's fellow officers with the "Lincoln Riflemen," who later published his memoirs under the title *Reminiscences of an Octogenarian Hungarian Exile* (1911).[19] The five Hungarians who reached the rank of brigadier general were Frederick Knefler, Eugene Kozlay, Charles Mundee (formerly Mándy), George Pomutz, and Albin Schoepf. The ranks of the Hungarians in the Northern armies also included two of Kossuth's nephews, the Zsulavszky brothers (Sigismund and Ladislaus), both of whom were officers, as well as the young Joseph Pulitzer (1847–1911), the future American newspaper magnate and the founder of the prestigious Pulitzer Prize, named after him.

While the large majority of the Hungarians in the United States served in the Union Army, a number of them also found their way into the ranks of the Confederates. This was usually the result of family connections, since some of them married into prominent Southern families. The best known and the highest ranking among them was Colonel Béla Estván (1827–1864?) of the Virginia Cavalry. By 1863, however, even Estván became disenchanted. He resigned his post and left for England, where he wrote and published his memoirs, *War Pictures from the South* (1864). Later that year he left for Hungary, but upon reaching Vienna he was arrested and then disappeared from history.[20]

The general support given to the Northern cause by Hungarians in the United States was also reflected in the pro-Northern sympathies of the Hungarians at home. This is amply reflected in the contemporary Hungarian press, even though much of the news to Hungary had been filtered through various German, French, and English newspapers, the majority of which had anti-Union bias. Hungarian public opinion, however, was instinctively pro-North, both because Hungarians regarded the North as a depository of human freedom and also because they instinctively drew a parallel between its struggle against the slave-holding South and their own recent struggle for freedom against Habsburg Austria.[21] Thus they rooted for Northern victory, and when it came, they characterized it as a "triumph for freedom and progress."[22] At the same time, however, they called upon the victors to refrain from retribution, which, in their view, would stain the moral purity of that victory.

Chapter Three
The Great Mass Migration: Its Causes and Composition

Most Hungarians who reached the American shores up to the 1860s and 1870s were either travelers, adventurers, or political immigrants. True, there were a few exceptions to this rule, for even in the late eighteenth and early nineteenth century we find those who came simply because of the unique economic opportunities offered by the young American Republic. But the number of these were few and far between. Thus, as late as the 1870s, the Hungarian-American community scattered throughout this land consisted almost exclusively of the political emigrants of the Revolution of 1848–49 and of their native-born descendants. Few would have thought even then that within less than a decade a new wave of Hungarians would hit the American shores and inundate this land in such great numbers that their predecessors, who numbered four to five thousand, would simply lose themselves in this sea of compatriots.

This new wave of Hungarian immigrants, however, was made up of a totally different kind of people than those who came between 1849 and the Civil War. The new immigrants came not for political but almost exclusively for economic reasons. The majority of them were young men of peasant stock who took to the sea simply to escape from the economic hardships of their native land. They were determined to return to Hungary with sufficient money to be able to buy land and to resume their lives as peasants and farmers. Some of them did return to the mother country, but most of them—for various economic, political, and social reasons—remained in the United States. And in this way, although unintentionally, they became the founders of the sizable Hungarian-American community, which even today numbers close to 780,000, and two and a half times as many (1,776,902) when including those of mixed parentage.

The great Hungarian emigration during the three and a half decades between 1880 and 1914 was a phenomenon that was not unique to Hungary. It was part of the general intra- and intercontinental migrations that characterized Europe and much of the Western world during that phase of the industrial revolution and the rising free economic system or capitalism. Moreover, within its European context, the Hungarian migration was only of a medium intensity. Of course there had been mass migrations before. But during the previous three or four centuries these migrations were usually the results of religious persecutions and the search for new frontiers. Nor were they on a scale as extensive as the migrations of the nineteenth and the early twentieth century, when the growth of industrialization and the spread of the free economic system produced increasing disparities between the industrially advanced states and the traditional agricultural countries. After a period of painful readjustment, the former were able to increase wages much more rapidly than the latter and thus improved significantly the quality of life for their workers. Consequently, they began to serve as magnets for the underpaid and often underutilized workers of the less-industrialized states.

During the nineteenth century, this phenomenon of mass migration was basically limited to the Europeans, whose primary destination was the United States, which appeared increasingly as the most viable and promising among the new non-European countries. Thus, between 1820 and 1914 the United States received over thirty million immigrants, nearly 93 percent of whom were Europeans. During the first and middle part of the nineteenth century these immigrants came largely from western and northern Europe, but by the last third of that century the southern and eastern Europeans began to outnumber them, and in the first decade of the twentieth century the latter came to constitute 70.8 percent of the European immigrants to this country. The majority of these "new immigrants" were peasants and farmers who, upon leaving their countries, also left their traditional way of life. Upon their arrival in the United States they usually settled in urban centers and in the industrial-mining regions of the country, and thus joined America's industrial labor force.[1]

This basic trend also holds true for the majority of the Hungarian immigrants, not all of whom were of Magyar linguistic stock. During the late nineteenth and early twentieth century altogether about

1.7 million Hungarian citizens immigrated to the United States (i.e., 430,000 up to 1899 and 1,260,000 between 1899 and 1914). The peak year of this immigration was 1907, when their numbers reached 185,000, i.e., close to 1 percent of Hungary's population.[2] Migration on such a mass scale was a phenomenon that was bound to affect the position and attitude of all Hungarians at home or abroad.

Although coming in unprecedented numbers, most economic immigrants did not come with the intention of staying permanently. For this reason, until World War I repatriation was also common among Hungarian immigrants. A number of them actually emigrated and repatriated several times, which makes it even more difficult to calculate the number of those who stayed permanently. On the basis of Hungarian statistics for the years 1899 to 1913, however, we can safely assume that about 25 percent of the immigrants repatriated to their mother country, of whom one-fifth returned once more to these shores. This means that of the 1.7 million immigrants who came from Hungary up to 1914, about 80 percent (i.e., 1,360,000) ultimately settled in the United States.[3]

The National Composition of the Immigrants

While we know that up to July 1914 about 1.7 million Hungarian citizens immigrated to this country, we are also aware that a sizable portion of them were not real Hungarians, i.e., they were not of the Magyar-speaking group. This was a natural by-product of historic Hungary's multinational composition.

As revealed by contemporary statistics, in the period under consideration Magyar-speaking Hungarians made up only about half of the country's population, although their share in Hungary proper (without the associated state of Croatia) was about 54.5 percent. At the same time the shares of the other nationalities were as follows: 16.1 percent Rumanians, 10.7 percent Slovaks, 10.4 percent Germans, 2.5 percent Rusyns or Ruthenians, 2.5 percent Serbians, 1.1 percent Croats, and the remaining 2.2 percent divided among all of the other smaller nationalities.[4]

Hungary's multinational character was naturally also reflected in the ethnic-linguistic composition of its citizens who emigrated to the United States, although not necessarily in direct proportion to their relative size in the mother country. Contrary to earlier views, we now believe that the share of the Magyars in this emigration was considerably less than their share in the country's population. The specific percentage is unknown, although recent calculations have pushed these estimates to as low as 31.8 percent and even 28.9 percent. The latter figure, however, appears to be far too low, for the United States census of 1910 clearly shows that the Magyar immigrants in that year made up 46 percent of the nationalities stemming from Hungary.[5] This is all the more likely as immigration statistics do not really reflect the actual number of those who entered the country. We now believe that one-fourth to one-third of the Hungarian citizens left Hungary illegally, and that within their ranks there were many more Magyars than non-Magyars. The reason for this was that Hungarian authorities were generally more reluctant to grant exit permits to Magyars than to non-Magyars, for the emigration of the latter was often viewed as desirable from the vantage point of Hungary's national unity and territorial integrity.[6]

If we accept the figure of 1.7 million as the number of those Hungarian citizens who immigrated to the United States prior to 1914, then the number of Magyars among them must have been somewhere between 500,000 and 780,000. Because it is really impossible to come up with a completely reliable figure, we shall accept the compromise figure of 650,000. This is really a conservative figure, and it is significantly below many of the earlier estimates. If we add to this the approximately 200,000 Magyar Hungarians who came to the United States between 1914 and 1984, then we have a total Magyar immigration of 850,000.

Although various economic considerations were the primary and almost exclusive causes of emigration from Hungary, a few other factors may also have played a role. One that has generally been overemphasized in the past was the so-called "nationality question." While we are now well aware that this factor had very little to do with the mass migration at the turn of the century,[7] the relative high percentage of the non-Magyars among the immigrants still compels us to look at this problem. In doing so, the first thing we find is that the emigration curves of all of the nationalities from Hungary are virtually identical. In other words, the levels of their respective exodus all peaked and all had their low points at about the same time. Simultaneously, however, a much larger percentage of the Slovaks (20.2 percent), Ruthenians (11.6 percent), Germans (11.5 percent), and Rumanians (6.8 percent) emigrated than of

Magyars (3.8 percent). Contrary to the tendency to do so, this should not be attributed to their alleged or real economic and political plights as compared to the Magyars. The best proof for this is a comparison between the Germans and the Ruthenians, both of whom emigrated in the same percentage, even though there was a great deal of disparity in their respective socioeconomic positions and political influence in Hungary. As a matter of fact, the Germans were the wealthiest of Hungary's nationalities (considerably above the "ruling" Magyars), and their political influence was also extensive. The Ruthenians, on the other hand, were on the lowest social, economic, and political rung in the country. In light of these facts, therefore, the answer to this puzzle must be sought not in the "nationality problem" (which was almost exclusively the "problem" of the very small intelligentsia and not of the peasantry, which in most instances was still on a very low level of national consciousness), but rather in what one researcher had recently called the "differences in [the] attitudes [of the individual nationalities] to emigration."[8] In other words, because of their different historical traditions, ways of life, and economy, compounded by the impact of geographical-topographical factors, some nationalities—such as the Slovaks, Ruthenians, Germans, and Rumanians—were more prone to periodic and seasonal migrations. As such, for them coming to America was simply another step in their accepted way of life. To the Magyars, on the other hand, leaving their homeland was a new and strange idea, and as such much less acceptable.

In addition to the causes discussed above, some of the other factors that induced turn-of-the-century Hungarians (and other East Europeans) to leave their native land included the agitation of the ticket agents of various shipping companies, the personal letters of earlier immigrants, which portrayed unheard-of opportunities in America, the inflated stories of the temporary repatriates, and the visible success stories of those who returned permanently and became persons of means.

The Social Composition of the Immigrants

Contrary to the political emigrations that preceded and followed the great economic emigration of the late nineteenth and early twentieth century, the latter was primarily a peasant migration. In other words, the great majority of the Hungarian immigrants of whatever mother tongue who came to this country between 1870 and 1914 were largely of peasant stock, perhaps even more so than revealed by official statistics. They were the people who had been displaced from their traditional agricultural pursuits by the dislocations that accompanied the economic changes following the Compromise of 1867. Having been made superfluous in their native village, and finding no meaningful employment opportunities in the country's industrial centers, they were forced to seek their fortunes abroad, particularly in the United States.[9]

Although neither American nor Hungarian statistics are fully reliable, we nonetheless have sufficient data to come up with an acceptable consensus on the percentage of those immigrants who were basically of the peasant class. According to Hungarian statistics concerning the peak years of 1905–1907, for example, we know that 17 percent of the immigrants from Greater Hungary (including Croatia) were small landholders and 51.6 percent were landless agricultural workers, making a total of 68.6 percent. To this must be added such other categories as "day laborers" (9.5 percent) and "household servants" (5.2 percent), who are known to have been in contemporary Hungary almost exclusively of peasant background. And this also applies to a sizable portion (perhaps half) of the category of "unskilled industrial workers and day laborers" (11.3 percent), many of whom were only recent immigrants from the villages. All this adds up to about 89 percent (i.e., 68.9 + 9.5 + 5.2 + 5.7) of all of the immigrants. For Hungary proper (without Croatia) this same ratio is 88.3 percent, while for Croatia alone it is 92.3 percent.[10]

To a number of researchers these figures may appear to be too high. (István Rácz, for example, believes that only 75 to 80 percent of the immigrants were of peasant stock.[11]) But this disagreement is more apparent than real. It is simply a question of what made one a "peasant" versus an "industrial worker" in contemporary Hungary. In this connection one should note that, because of Hungary's relatively late industrialization drive, a great majority of the country's industrial day laborers, and even many of its industrial workers, were really ex-peasants, who were only a few years removed from their peasant past. As such, their way of life and their mentality were hardly different from those of a typical Hungarian peasant, all the more so as a good number of them were only seasonal industrial day laborers. Thus, even if they appear in contemporary statistical tables in columns other than those reserved for the peasantry, in reality we should still deal with them as with peasant immigrants, i.e., ex-villagers who were totally alien to America's large urban centers, and who thus displayed all the fears and basic attitudes of the unsophisticated peasants of contemporary East Central Europe.

The Emigration of the Urbanites and the Intellectuals

While close to 90 percent of the Hungarian immigrants were peasants or near-peasant urban day laborers and household servants, at least 10 percent or more were of the nonpeasant category. As a matter of fact, the same Hungarian statistics for the years 1905 to 1907 on which the above calculations are based categorize 15 percent of the emigrants under various nonpeasant headings. These categories include miners (1.2 percent), independent craftsmen (2.2 percent), independent merchants (0.3 percent), and unskilled industrial workers and day laborers (11.3 percent). But if we deduce half of the latter category as being essentially peasants or near-peasants (5.7 percent), then the above "industrial-merchant-worker" category is reduced to a mere 9.3 percent. The remaining 1.7 percent (if we accept the "peasant" category as being 89 percent) was made up of intelligentsia (0.5 percent) and of various other persons of unknown occupations (1.2 percent), some of whom were doubtlessly also of peasant background.[12] On the basis of the above figures we can safely assume that of the nearly 1.7 million Hungarian citizens who emigrated to and settled in the United States prior to 1914, about 90 percent were basically in the "peasant" and 10 percent in the "nonpeasant" categories.

The question that still remains to be discussed in this connection is the basic social composition of those in the nonpeasant category. United States statistics concerning the years 1900 to 1913 identify forty-nine different occupational skills among the Magyar-speaking immigrants. The emigration of independent craftsmen and industrial workers affected the whole of Hungary. Yet, proportionately many more craftsmen emigrated from Transylvania and from sections of northern Hungary than from the country's other regions. We believe this to be the result of the fact that Hungary's nascent industry was more able to absorb the underutilized representatives of the traditional crafts in the country's central and western regions than in its eastern and northern reaches, where industrialization was proceeding at a slower pace.

While the great majority of the nonpeasant immigrants from Hungary were in the craftsmen–industrial workers category, both American and Hungarian statistics also speak of a small category of "intellectuals." This was a very small group, whose numbers in the course of the half-century preceding 1914 were no more than six to seven thousand, i.e., less than 0.5 percent of the total number of immigrants. According to the United States census of 1910, for example, in that year there were only 1,739 persons in the category of Hungarian-born intellectuals. That was less than 0.4 percent of those 495,609 persons who were born in Hungary, although nearly 0.8 percent of the Magyar-speaking among these foreign-born Hungarian immigrants. [13]

In assessing the meaning of the low percentage of so-called "intellectuals" among the Hungarian immigrants, one should keep in mind that in those days the United States and American society in general had very little drawing power for educated Europeans. Thus, unless forced by circumstances—such as political or personal reasons—they would seldom opt to come to this land of the hardy self-made men, where a person's stature and position in society depended not so much on one's diplomas or titles but rather on what one could make of oneself through one's own abilities.

The situation was different for those who came to the United States to serve their fellow countrymen. Most of these were preachers or priests who had their goals and their dedication to the cause. Notwithstanding the many difficulties they had to face, their lives were filled with sufficient self-satisfaction and they were generally able to escape most of the spiritual self-torments suffered by those whose lives remained unfulfilled and whose past continued to haunt them, at least in the form of pangs of conscience.

Gender, Age, and Literacy of the Economic Immigrants

When we examine the male-female ratio of the immigrants in the years between 1899 and 1913 as reflected in the Hungarian statistics, we find that men made up over two-thirds (68.2 percent) and women less than one-third (31.8 percent) of their numbers. [14] These figures reassert our earlier conclusion that this migration was basically of a temporary nature, motivated by economic considerations. More specifically, it was a search for work by men, who intended to return to their country and to their families as soon as economically feasible.

While men undoubtedly dominated this economic migration, during the final few years the ratio of women began to increase. Thus in 1908 they passed the 30 percent mark, and by 1913 they outnumbered men 52.1 to 47.9 percent. This seems to indicate a gradual change in the attitude of the immigrants toward returning to their native country. For whatever reasons their resolve to return was weakened in the period before World War I, and this was accompanied by the growing desire to marry and to establish families in their new country, or, if already married, to have their wives and children brought over to them. It was this change in attitude that forced the ratio of women up to a point where by 1913 they exceeded the number of male immigrants.

Although the relevant statistics for the period before 1899 are missing, in light of our knowledge of the nature of early economic immigration we can safely assume that in those decades the ratio of men was even higher. Thus, in the course of the whole period of economic emigration from the mid-nineteenth century to 1914, the ratio of males among the immigrants must have been somewhere between 70 and 80 percent. In fact, in the case of Croatia alone, this ratio was even higher: in the period between 1899 and 1907 it was always above 80 percent, and between 1908 and 1913 it was about 71.6 percent.[15] This again shows a declining tendency during the final years of the period.

Closely connected with the originally temporary nature of Hungarian immigration to the United States was the age bracket of the immigrants. Those who came in search of temporary employment were largely men (and to a lesser degree women) of the young working age category. Thus, for the peak years of 1905 to 1907 73.3 percent of the immigrants were in the twenty-to-forty-nine-year-old category, 24.1 percent in the below-twenty-years-of-age category, and only 2.6 percent in the fifty-years-and-older category. But even in the first of these categories the heaviest representation came from the ranks of the twenty- to twenty-nine-year-olds, who made up over one-third (35.4 percent) of the immigrants. All in all at least 90 percent of the immigrants of the late nineteenth and early twentieth century were in the working-age category, with at the most only 10 percent being composed of nonworking dependents.

Although perhaps nearly 90 percent of the immigrants came from the ranks of the peasantry or near-peasantry, they did not represent the least able or the least educated segment of Hungary's population. As a matter of fact, the literacy rate among the immigrants was higher than the literacy rate within Hungary's total population. Thus, whereas the country's literacy rate in 1910 (for those over six years of age) was 68.7 percent, this rate among the immigrants varied between 89 percent for the Magyars and 70 percent for the Ruthenians.[16] These figures, however, represent some improvement over those reflected in United States statistics for the years 1899 to 1910, when the literacy rate among the various nationalities from Austria-Hungary above fourteen years of age was as follows: 98.3 percent for the Czechs, 94.8 percent for the Germans, 88.6 percent for the Magyars, 76 percent for the Slovaks, 74 percent for the Jews, 65 percent for the Rumanians, 64.6 percent for the Poles, 63.9 percent for the Croats, 59 percent for the Dalmatians and Bosnians, 58.9 percent for the Bulgarians and Serbians, and 46.6 percent for the Ruthenians.[17] In light of the above, there is much to be said for the view that, while driven primarily by poverty and economic need, the immigrants of the pre-1914 period did not necessarily represent the most forsaken or the most underprivileged segment of Hungary's lower classes. Their very decision to face the perils of emigration singled them out as perhaps the hardiest and most determined group among the population, who had more willpower and more daring than most of the others of their own socioeconomic class. And much of this boldness was undoubtedly connected with the fact that they were also the most literate and therefore the most informed among their own kind.

In light of what has been said above, we can safely reassert our earlier contention that those who decided to emigrate to America— whether temporarily or permanently—did so almost without exception with the intention to work so as to improve their economic positions. And they did work, giving their sweat and blood— although as yet little of the brainpower—to the land of their choice. The age of the "Hungarian brainpower" was still in the future. It came only during the later part of the interwar and during the post– World War II periods, when "the mystery of the Hungarian tal-

ent"—to quote Laura Fermi[18]—both enriched and puzzled the
American mind.

Hungarian Settlements in the United States

Although—as we have seen—by far the greatest number of the
Hungarian immigrants of the pre–World War II period were peasants or near-peasants, very few of them chose to continue agricultural
labor in this country. Rather, they settled mainly in the industrial
centers of the Northeast. According to a contemporary calculation
by József Szász, in 1920 there were about 450,000 Hungarians in
the United States, of whom a mere 1,000 were engaged in farm
labor.[19] While these figures are perhaps too low both with respect
to the number of Hungarians and the number of farmers and farm
workers among them, the unusually low percentage of those engaged
in agricultural work (0.2 percent) does tell us something. Most
importantly it reinforces our basic assertion that the original cause
of this mass migration was simply the immigrants' desire to earn
money and then to return to Hungary with enough capital to be
able to buy farms for themselves. They could hope to fulfill this
goal, however, only if they chose to work in industry, which paid
much more than farm labor. As such, virtually all of the Hungarian
immigrants gravitated toward America's major industrial regions,
more specifically to the large cities and mining areas of the Northeast.

According to the United States census of 1910, there were 710,904
persons in the United States who were born or whose parents were
born in Hungary. By 1920 their number had increased to 935,801.
These same census figures tell us that of these "Hungarians" 320,895
(45.1 percent) and 495,845 (52.9 percent) were Magyar speaking,
that is, real Hungarians.[20] Augmented by the calculations of the
above-mentioned József Szász, these statistics also reveal that in
1920 the Magyar-Hungarians were settled primarily in about a dozen
northeastern states. Thus, in that year 78,000 lived in New York
State (with 64,393 in New York City), 73,000 in Ohio (with 29,724
in Cleveland), 71,000 in Pennsylvania (with 11,519 in Philadelphia
and about 26,000 in and around Pittsburgh), 40,000 in New Jersey
(mostly in Perth Amboy, Newark, Passaic, New Brunswick, and
Trenton), 34,000 in Illinois (with 26,106 in Chicago), 22,000 in
Michigan (with 13,564 in Detroit), 20,000 to 25,000 in Connecticut (mostly in Bridgeport, Hartford, and South Norwalk),

12,000 in Indiana (mostly in South Bend, Gary, and East Chicago), 10,000 in Wisconsin (with 4,803 in Milwaukee), close to 10,000 in Missouri (with 6,637 in St. Louis), 6,200 in West Virginia (with 4,000 in Pocahontas), 5,200 in California (with 1,706 in Los Angeles and 1,390 in San Francisco), and the rest of them scattered throughout another dozen or so states.[21]

In the course of the next few decades the number of Hungarians in the United States fluctuated, but their geographical distribution remained basically unchanged right up to the 1960s and 1970s. Only in the 1960s was there a gradual shift away from the Northeast, largely in the direction of Florida and California. Those moving to Florida were mostly retirees, whose numbers were and are being replenished continuously by newer waves of the elderly population. The majority of those settling in California, on the other hand, were and are young working-age people who are drawn to the Pacific Coast by the tremendous economic opportunities offered by the Golden State. The story of their lives and achievements, however, belongs in a later chapter of this work.

Chapter Four

Hungarian-American Society and Social Organizations

Hungarian emigrants of the late nineteenth and early twentieth century set out to America under the assumption that it was a "land of promise" and the "country of unlimited opportunities." Once reaching the American shores, however, they found themselves confronted with the realities of a society in the process of rapid industrialization and modernization. True, the opportunities for advancement and material enrichment were there and expanding, and the peasant immigrants from eastern Europe had the chance to earn four to five times (occasionally ten times) as much as in their native lands. But the cost of these opportunities was also great. In addition to higher prices, which deprived them of a sizable portion of their earnings, they were forced to live and to work under the most miserable conditions. They also had to face the harsh realities of a society that barely tolerated them.

The majority of the immigrants were unskilled or semiskilled workers of peasant stock, and as such they were forced to accept the most menial and most dangerous jobs that urban and industrial America had to offer. These were usually in the mines, iron and steel mills, and factories of the industrialized Northeast. They worked long hours for relatively low pay, in abysmal surroundings, under adverse safety conditions. Their unfamiliarity with American society, the overabundance of cheap labor, the weakness of the American labor movement, and the indifference and even hostility of the American public toward them all combined to make their position difficult and to prevent them from trying to do anything about it. They simply had to accept what was offered to them and hope that the three to five years they had originally alloted to themselves in this country would be sufficiently rewarding financially to make their stay and privations worthwhile. They were able to tolerate the difficulties of their existence because they were simply postponing their rewards. This "ability to postpone enjoyment of rewards" was a necessary common phenomenon among the turn-of-the-century economic immigrants from central and eastern Europe.[1] With the exception of the unassimilated Yiddish-speaking Jews, "who really had no homeland to return to," they all wanted to return to their native countries.[2] To claim, therefore, that "the cause of . . . their migrations was a lack of national sovereignty" or nationality oppression—as is still done occasionally—is not only the repetition of the old philiopietistic views of the amateur "ethnic historians" of the first half of this century but is also outright incorrect.[3] This claim is belied both by the heavy emigration of the "dominant nationalities" from similar socioeconomic backgrounds as well by the equally heavy remigration of the so-called "oppressed nationalities," with the exception of homeless Jews.

Not being interested in staying permanently, the majority of the pre–World War I Hungarian immigrants failed to acquire American citizenship. Nor did they become involved in the American labor movement, except as strikebreakers brought in by the unscrupulous industrial magnates or as participants in spontaneous, unorganized strikes. The latter were usually violent and bloodily suppressed work stoppages in the coal fields and steel mills of Pennsylvania and West Virginia. A case in point is the infamous Homestead Strike of 1892, which produced an armed clash between the strikers and three hundred hired Pinkerton guards and resulted in the loss of thirteen lives. Another case was the bloody "Lattimer Massacre" of 1897, where nineteen Hungarians, Poles, and Slovaks died and thirty-nine others were seriously injured. This massacre, by the way, has gained new currency and significance through Michael Novak's recent work, *The Guns of Lattimer,* on this classic confrontation between the exploited immigrant workers of eastern Europe and the unscrupulous apostles of unhindered capitalism in this country in the age of America's Manifest Destiny.[4]

Life-styles: Boarding Houses

Although occupying the lowest levels of the social and economic scales in contemporary America, Hungarian immigrants were still better off than some of their fellow immigrants who settled in the southern states, where they were subjected to agricultural peonage (virtual serfdom). The Hungarians were able to escape such a fate because, although largely of rural background, very few of them

were willing to engage in agricultural labor in the United States.
Even so, their initial years in the squalid tenements of the immigrant
quarters of America's burgeoning industrial cities and mining towns
were very tough, cruel, and unenviable. Most of them lived in
vermin-infested, dilapidated boarding houses, under conditions that
were unequivocally condemned by most contemporary observers—
even though this condemnation was not necessarily done from the
correct perspective and for the right reasons. As a matter of fact,
the primitive life-styles, unhealthy living and dietary conditions,
and the apparent lack of real cultural needs among the immigrants
were often interpreted by native Americans as signs of the newcomers' fundamental primitivism and their inability to appreciate the
finer aspects of life.

Of the many contemporary accounts about life in late-nineteenth-
century boarding houses, one of the best is the 1890 report by a
Special Commission of the United States Department of Labor,
which deals with the life-styles of sixteen Hungarian and Slovak
iron and steel communities:

The workers employed here are almost all Hungarians, and the majority
of the married ones left their families in Europe. They are unassuming.
They generally keep 40 dollars in ready cash on themselves for times of
sickness or other unexpected occurrences. They send their savings back to
their families regularly. They resolve their lodging collectively: 20–45
men find a suitable house together and elect a *burdos gazda* (usually a man
with a wife). His job is to get provisions, pay the rent, and keep the
accounts. At the end of each month all members of the group pay their
part of the total expenses, plus 1.5 or 2 dollars for the wife of the *burdos
gazda,* who cooks and cleans. Besides this, they pay 50 cents to the *gazda*
if he spends all his time taking care of the business of the collective; but
if he is a worker who lives on his wages, then he too is a member of the
collective and pays his part in the common expenses. The aim is not to
exceed 9 dollars a month as the total expense for food and lodging per
capita, and if, at the end of the month, they find that they have overstepped
this sum, they have a meeting and cut the food, in order to reduce expenses.
Everyone provides his own bedding. The furniture is poor, consisting of
home-made tables, benches instead of chairs, and beds fabricated out of
old boards, and the only well-equipped piece of furnishing in the entire
house is the stove they cook on. The houses are chock full: those working
the night shift alternate in using the same rooms with those working the
day shift; 4–10 men sleep in a room. Once a month, on pay day, they
collectively buy a barrel of beer for 3 dollars, if there are 20 of them to

do so, and drink it up together. But if there are fewer than 20 men, then they do not buy together, because then the expenses for each is too much. They usually have one decent suit besides their work clothes; each spends an average of 18 dollars on clothes annually.[5]

This system of boarding houses among the immigrants resulted in the birth of an unusual communal way of life, in which one-dozen, two-dozen, or even more men shared a house with one of their married companions, whose wife had the responsibility of keeping the community going. Her regular obligations consisted of cleaning, washing, ironing, mending, cooking, preparing and packing the lunch buckets, keeping records of the boarding house's finances, and generally also keeping the boarders' savings, in lieu of banks. Her life was harsh and unenviable. As observed by one of the keepers of such boarding houses *(burdos gazda)* in his later years, "the present generation [1941] can hardly imagine the work entailed in cooking and washing for 15–20–25 laboring men. . . . One wonders at the fortitude and hardyhood of those pioneer immigrant women."[6]

But this was not all. In some places, the feminine duties of the wife of the *burdos gazda* also included the washing and rubbing down of the backs of the returning workers, and at times even of serving as the mistress of one or several of the boarders. As described by an acute observer in 1909, a boarding house is "the strangest community, the most unusual republic, whose president is the boarding mistress, whose subjects enjoy completely equal privileges [with the husband]—usually with his knowledge and in front of him."[7]

While this practice may not have been as common as intimated by this description, it must have been widespread, as was also the custom of providing the special sexual favors only to a "highly favored and privileged lodger," usually known as the *főburdos* or "star-boarder." The latter practice was partially an outgrowth of the same conditions that produced the widespread custom of sexual promiscuity ("communal sex") in the boarding houses—i.e., the lack of sufficient number of women among the immigrants—and partially the result of the need to keep the other boarders in check while the husband was doing his shift in the mine or in one of the nearby mills or factories. The husband may or may not have known of this liaison, but—as revealed by immigrant folklore—he often accepted it, because he had no alternatives. On many occasions the "star-boarder" was physically stronger than he. The husband could, of course, have walked out as an alternative, but that would have resulted both in the loss of certain social and economic benefits and the loss of his sex partner. And in those years when in these enclosed immigrant communities men outnumbered women three or four to one, the latter consideration was also of utmost importance. Thus the "risk of losing his wife and his privileges" and "end[ing] up as a *burdos* [boarder] himself" often forced many a husband to swallow his pride and accept the idea and practice of sharing his wife with at least one other partner.[8]

On many occasions, however, such matrimonial infidelities— even if tolerated for a while—often led to violent family tragedies, including murders and suicides. As a matter of fact, contemporary observers linked most of the murders among turn-of-the-century Hungarian-Americans to jealousies and to the resulting brawls and fights in the boarding houses.[9]

In studying this phenomenon of "communal sex" in the turn-of-the-century boarding houses of immigrant America, one of the researchers compared the system of "star-boarder" to the eighteenth-century Italian custom of "cicisbeoism"—i.e., the custom whereby ladies of contemporary high society officially accepted younger lovers, whose "duties and rights . . . were sometimes incorporated into the marriage contracts." Although motivated by different considerations, the revival of this phenomenon in the immigrant communities of late-nineteenth and early-twentieth-century America can hardly be denied. Similar to its predecessor, this neo-cicisbeoism also involved various economic and sexual relations, and it was governed by generally accepted though "unwritten regulations." Or to put it more simply and more bluntly, quoting one of the former successful star-boarders: "While the landlord was working in the factory [or in the mine], the *főburdos* [star-boarder] filled his place."[10]

Target Areas and Domestic Migration

When departing for the United States, most immigrants had a target area, a city, town, or mining community where friends, relatives, or hometown acquaintances were waiting for them. Once there, virtually all of them joined the industrial labor pool. Over 90 percent of them ended up in such northeastern states as Pennsylvania, New York, Ohio, New Jersey, Illinois, Indiana, and Michigan. Their settlements were either on the fringes and within the slums of large industrial cities (e.g., New York, Cleveland, Chicago, Detroit, Pittsburgh, Philadelphia) or in one of the many small mining and steel towns of the same states and West Virginia. None of their communites was a homogeneous Hungarian settlement, although most of the larger cities had one or more Hungarian quarters. But even these quarters were generally mixed through the settling of many other East Central Europeans among the Hungarians.

Upon arrival at their destinations, the immigrants usually began their new lives and careers in close proximity to their relations and Old World acquaintances. This was particularly true for those with peasant or near-peasant backgrounds, who preferred to stay close to one another. Contrary to earlier assertions by scholars, however, very few of the Hungarian immigrants remained in one place. They changed jobs very frequently, and in search of better opportunities and improved pay they often wandered from settlement to settlement. Their almost wholesale movings-about are amply documented in the pages of the contemporary Hungarian-American newspapers as well as by the lives and careers of those among them who made their marks in Hungarian-American society and thus had their deeds chronicled (e.g., poets, writers, clergymen, artists). Their wanderings carried them through thousands of miles in the region between New York and Chicago, and between the Great Lakes and West Virginia. This same wandering spirit, coupled with the strong drawing power of their homeland, often compelled them also to return repeatedly to Hungary. But such returns, whether permanent or temporary, were also motivated by their difficulty to adjust to a society that refused to accept them as equals. Often their search did not end until old age, when they finally settled down permanently either in the United States or in their native countries.[11]

In the light of these mass-scale wanderings, some researchers have rightfully abandoned the idea so popular in American ethnic studies that East Central and Southeast European immigrants from the same village or locality tended to emigrate to the same town and even the same city quarters in the United States and stay there permanently. While this may be true for the Italians and the Slovaks, it certainly is not true for the Hungarians. As demonstrated recently by Julianna Puskás, this "staying together" was only temporary. The constant wanderings of the immigrants from city to city and from region to region soon mixed persons from diverse regions of Hungary into an amorphous group of Hungarian-Americans.[12]

Working Conditions

Like their fellow immigrants from southern and eastern Europe, most turn-of-the-century Hungarians were employed only in jobs that no native American wanted. These were generally the hardest, dirtiest, and most dangerous jobs that America's industrial society could provide. They were usually in mining or in the iron or steel industry, and almost exclusively in the category of "unskilled" or "semiskilled" work. As an example, in Steelton, Pennsylvania— where the Hungarians constituted about 18.5 percent of the Steelton Steel Plant—in 1905 84 percent were in these two categories, with 79 percent being unskilled and 5 percent being semiskilled.[13] Ten years later this percentage even increased to 85 percent, although the ratio between the unskilled (76 percent) and the semiskilled (9 percent) did improve slightly. In this same period their daily wage was well below $1.50 per day, for a working day that consisted somewhere between ten and twelve hours. Counting six working days, this added up to less than $9.00 per week.

The situation was similar in many of the large cities. Thus, in the early 1910s, the average Hungarian day laborer in Cleveland earned about $10.55 per week, and in New York only about $8.70. In New York's case this meant $1.45 per day at a time when the average daily wage for all New York workers was $3.79 per day. The Hungarians were at a disadvantage both because they were foreigners and because they worked mostly as unskilled laborers. The difference in pay between skilled and unskilled workers was substantial and increasing at the turn of the century. Thus, while in the period between 1890 and 1914 the wages of the skilled workers increased by 79 percent, those of the unskilled grew only by 31 percent.

Although underpaid and exploited, most Hungarian immigrants were still making much more than they could have earned at home. Thus, if they were able to endure the harsh working conditions for seven to ten years, while at the same time denying themselves almost everything beyond the bare essentials for survival, they could return to Hungary and buy sufficient land for themselves (twenty to thirty *holds,* i.e., twenty-eight to forty-three acres or eleven to seventeen hectares) to become well-to-do farmers. Many did so. Others never made it, if for no other reason than because the returning immigrants' land hunger drove the price of the land up to a point where it was beyond the reach of many of the later returnees.

The immigrants earned more in the United States, but they also had the tendency to overestimate their earnings. This was largely the result of their custom of calculating primarily in their native currency, the Hungarian *korona* or crown (1 *korona* = 20¢), without taking into consideration the cost differences. In this way they deceived themselves, often knowingly, but it gave them a feeling of satisfaction. The self-inflated value of their earnings gave them the feeling that they were doing much better than they actually were, and made their sacrifices appear worthwhile. And this feeling that they had made the right decision in coming to America was also increased by the more democratic nature of American society, i.e., the informal relationship between the workers and their immediate superiors, and the workers' total freedom of action once having finished their work. Nor should one forget that psychologically the immigrants lived *in* and *for* the future, and expectations from the future made their lives much more bearable.[14]

While the immigrants' working and social conditions lacked the humiliating relationships that infested the more traditional society of their homeland, their American environment was filled with many more physical dangers, the direct result of the complexities of their industrial workingplaces and the relative lack of safety measures. Not being familiar with their new environment, and unable to read notices or understand verbal warnings, they were often victims of shocking industrial accidents. This was all the more so as not even the few existing safety regulations were enforced. Being maimed or killed, therefore, was an ever-present prospect for every Hungarian and East European immigrant—as described, for the Slovaks, in Thomas Bell's novel *Out of this Furnace*.[15] This inordinate high rate of severe and fatal accidents among them is also illustrated by the fact that between 1907 and 1910 approximately 25 percent of the new immigrants at the Carnegie Steel Works in Pittsburgh were either injured or killed.[16]

Contemporary Hungarian-American newspapers, almanacs, and memorial albums are likewise filled with reports of fatal mine and steel-works disasters. As an example, the tenth anniversary memorial album of the *Amerikai Magyar Népszava* lists three major and nu-

merous minor catastrophes for the years 1907 and 1908, involving
the death of twenty-four (Fayette City), fifty (Monongahela), and
ninety-five (Jacobs Creek) Hungarians. But it also claims that "catastrophes are daily events—especially in the mining regions. And
cases are rare where at least one or two Hungarians would not die."[17]

The many violent deaths of the Hungarian immigrants were also
recorded in some of the church registers. Thus, as recorded by the
minister of the Hungarian Reformed Church of Homestead, Pennsylvania, between 1903 and 1914 the most frequent causes of death
among the members of his congregation—most of whom were young
men—were mine explosions, burns, deadly injuries, being run over
by a train, or contacting typhoid or dysentery.[18] These same tragedies are also chronicled in contemporary Hungarian-American prose
and poetry. Although this literature is generally lacking in aesthetic
merits, it can and does serve as a mirror of the lives and personal
tragedies of the unfortunate immigrants.

Immigrant Organizations: Sick-Benefit Societies

Life of the turn-of-the-century peasant immigrants was harsh and
often brutal. Yet most of them survived and most of them managed
to keep their sanity. This "success" was partially the result of their
belief of being "better off" than in the Old Country and of the
gradual improvement of their social and economic circumstances in
the early part of this century. On the whole, however, this emotional
survival was primarily the direct consequence of the enormous help
and moral support they received from their own people, largely
through the various Hungarian fraternal, religious, and cultural
associations.

These organizations were called into being to fill the void left by
the loss of the traditional life-style and patriarchal social order of
the Hungarian village. These institutions gave a feeling of belonging
and a measure of security to the lonely immigrants, who had been
torn away from their families and their traditional life-styles. Moreover, as already pointed out, life in the New World was much more
dangerous than life in the Hungarian village or rural town. Work
in the mines and factories was filled with many unknown dangers,
and the Hungarians and their fellow "New Immigrants" were maimed
and killed by the thousands. Those who died during the early years
of this great immigration could not even expect a decent burial.

Those who were maimed, on the other hand, were left totally helpless, with no one to take care of them. It was the fear of such a possible fate that prompted some of the Hungarian immigrants of the late nineteenth century to consider the establishment of sick-benefit and burial associations.

The first of these societies—including the Hungarian Sick-Benefit Society of New York (1852), the Cleveland German-Hungarian Aid Society (1863), and the First Hungarian Sick Care Society of New York (1865)—were all founded before the flood of the economic immigrants began to hit the American shores. They were established by the Kossuth immigrants and their descendants, or by the German-speaking Hungarian Jews who began to trickle into this country already during the 1850s and 1860s. But these early welfare organizations were generally shortlived and did not really fulfill the role for which they had been founded. The sole exception appears to have been the Cleveland German-Hungarian Aid Society, which was reorganized in 1881 as the Hungarian Benevolent and Social Union and then took its place among the more comprehensive rival organizations established by the New Immigrants during the 1880s and 1890s.

Of the latter organizations, the first to be established was the "First Hungarian Sick Benefit Society" of Newark, New Jersey (1882). This was followed by several others founded in such diverse places as Freeland, Pennsylvania (1884), New York City (1884, 1892), Scranton, Pennsylvania (1886), Cleveland (1887, 1894), Hazleton, Pennsylvania (1886), and Brooklyn, New York (1898). Soon Hungarian sick benefit societies proliferated all over the northeastern United States and by 1910 there were over a thousand of them (according to one source, 1,046) scattered all over Hungarian-America. In the course of the first quarter of the twentieth century a number of these grew into large federations, with scores and even hundreds of branches in as many Hungarian settlements. By 1921 the largest and most significant of these federations included the Verhovay Aid Association, with 295 branches; the American Hungarian Aid Society, with 198 branches; the American Hungarian Reformed Federation, with 145 branches; the Workers Sick-Benefit and Self-Culture Association, with 83 branches; and the Rákóczi Aid Association, with 54 branches. By 1940 this sequence was somewhat rearranged and the four largest of these federations were the Verhovay Aid Association, with 44,367 members and capital of $4,732,000; the American Hungarian Reformed Federation, with 20,344 members and capital of $1,800,000; the Rákóczi Aid Association, with 19,969 and capital of $3,003,000; and the American Hungarian Aid Society, with 13,110 members and capital of $1,861,000. In 1955 the two wealthiest of these federations, the Verhovay and the Rákóczi, merged, and, in line with the general tendency toward Americanization in those years, assumed the name William Penn Fraternal Association.[19]

From its humble start in the late nineteenth century the Verhovay Aid Association had grown into the largest and most successful of the Hungarian-American fraternal associations. Yet its history is typical and characteristic of most of its hundreds of rivals founded around the turn of the century. According to the "Verhovay Legend," the initiative for the foundation of the Verhovay Aid Association on February 22, 1886, in Hazleton, Pennsylvania, came from a young Hungarian worker by the name of Mihály Pálinkás, who was moved by the plight of one of his compatriots. Although red with fever and visibly suffering from pulmonary tuberculosis, an elderly Hungarian worker was simply ejected from one of the boarding houses because the owner wanted the space for "a healthy boarder who could pay the rent."[20]

Pálinkás and his fellow founding members were all typical representatives of the turn-of-the-century economic immigrants from East Central Europe. They were simple, straightforward people, with minimal education, who were forced to struggle for their existence both in their homeland and in the United States. Although economically a disadvantaged lot, they were proud people who were willing to take on the challenges of human existence and wanted to make it on their own. The fraternities were the direct results of this aspiration.

In addition to this strong desire to succeed on their own, these immigrants had also brought with them a deep-seated distrust and dislike of educated middle-class types. This dislike was so thorough that during their early years in the United States they generally refused to have any close relationships with the latter. The constitutions of a number of their early fraternities actually barred anyone from holding office who had not been a physical worker in Hungary.

In the case of the Verhovay Aid Association, this strong "anti-intellectualism" or distrust of the educated class (*úri osztály*) was manifest already in 1887, when the association's first general secretary, Károly Juhász, was replaced for no other reason than for being too learned and having too beautiful a handwriting. The delegates to the early national conventions of the Verhovay Association also reasserted regularly that their association should always represent "the interests of the laboring working class." Their bias against intellectual labor was so pervasive that during the first two decades of their existence they refused to grant decent salaries to their officers. Not until 1907 did the delegates finally agree to raise the general secretary's annual compensation to $800 "so as to make his salary equal to that of the lowest paid laborers."[21]

In the course of time, this strong anti-intellectualism of the Hungarian-American fraternities did wane somewhat, but elements of it survived even into the post–World War II period. While it was basically a negative attitude, it did have certain positive results. It prevented these associations from falling into the hands of "city slickers" of dubious character, a number of whom also ended up in America. But what was perhaps even more significant, this attitude also nurtured a considerable amount of personal and class pride among the working-class immigrants, who gradually came to the realization that, notwithstanding their lack of learning, they too were capable of founding and leading complex social organizations. In other words, these fraternities fulfilled the very important civic function of transforming the timid peasant immigrants into self-conscious, civic-minded citizens who for the first time began to think of themselves as worthy human beings with the same rights and privileges as those enjoyed by their social superiors in their native country. This change of attitude was naturally also reflected in the behavioral patterns of those who returned to Hungary. The once-humble peasants returned as self-conscious workers who, from the vantage point of the local authorities, were "difficult to handle." And much of this change was the direct result of their civic experiences in America.

The Ideological Orientation of Immigrant Associations

The sick-benefit societies were among the very first associations organized by the economic immigrants. They were soon followed by a number of other types of organizations as well. These included a wide variety of social, cultural, athletic, and pseudopolitical organizations, which mushroomed rapidly in Hungarian-America. Many of these were ephemeral organizations whose exact numbers are unknown. The available statistics, however, still tell us a great deal about the organizational zeal of the immigrants. According to one set of statistics, for example, in 1910 Hungarian-Americans had 1,339 associations. Of these associations 888 were fully and 158 partially sick-benefit societies, while the remaining 293 fulfilled various other social and cultural functions. Most of these associations were small, local, and scattered through hundreds of settlements in twenty-eight states. Some of the larger Hungarian communities, however, had dozens of associations of various types. The leading cities included Cleveland, with eighty-one associations; New York City, with seventy-eight; Chicago, with forty-one; Bridgeport, with twenty-seven; and Pittsburgh, with twenty-five. Among the states Pennsylvania led, with 461 associations. It was followed by Ohio, with 251; New Jersey, with 147; New York, with 142; Illinois, with 84; and Connecticut, with 64 organizations.[22]

While the mass immigration from Hungary to the United States came to a virtual halt by 1914, Hungarian-American associations continued to increase and by 1920 their number reached 2,092. One of the current researchers of Hungarian-American immigrant life divided these associations into three separate categories: religious associations (both local and regional), which catered largely to the membership of specific denominations; secular associations, which included various social, cultural, athletic, and "patriotic" societies; and socialist workers' organizations, which generally allied themselves with their American counterparts. While one may disagree with the validity of this categorization, if we apply this threefold division to the 1,339 associations listed for 1910, we find that 766 of them were in the secular, 382 in the religious, and 191 in the socialist category. Most Hungarian-Americans joined several associations in the "religious" and "social" groups, but not in the "socialist" category. The latter were basically in a world of their own, generally outside the main current of Hungarian-American life. Numerically their organizations constituted about 17 percent of all Hungarian-American organizations in 1910, and they themselves probably hardly more than 10 percent of the immigrants. The beliefs and attitudes of the hard-core socialists were certainly far removed from those of the large majority of Hungarian-Americans, most of whom were basically traditional, religious, and nationalist individuals. Moreover, their nationalism and attachment to their homeland became even more pronounced after emigration. True, this nationalism was rather unsophisticated and emotional, nurtured by the overromanticized traditions of the Hungarian Revolution of 1848–1849 and its idealized leader Louis Kossuth. Its most visible manifestations included an almost irrational anti-Habsburgism and a sincere but somewhat shallow national exhibitionism (e.g., the wearing of national costumes, the flourishing of national colors, the indulgence in emotional and flowery oratory, the tendency to blame others for the misfortunes of the Magyars, the making of exorbitant claims for Magyar achievements). Yet it was still this nationalism—however showy, naive, and superficial—that was the primary ideological nourishment and guiding force of most Hungarian-Americans. This force retained much of its vitality throughout the interwar period and beyond, and for a while it was even strengthened by the national reaction to the injustices of Trianon. In the face of this broad current of Kossuthist nationalism, the socialist trend without nationalist content—however appealing to some current historians and literary historians—represented a relatively minor tendency that had little influence on Hungarian-American life in general.[23]

The Search for Unity

Next to the sick-benefit societies, some of the most typical early Hungarian-American societies included the so-called "self-culture societies" *(önképzőkörök)*, singing societies and glee clubs, professional and semi-professional associations (e.g., university circles, scholarly associations, physicians' associations, social clubs), as well as innumerable religious societies connected with specific parishes or congregations. There were also some politically oriented associations, but these were found almost exclusively among the ranks of the socialists. For a while, these societies and associations functioned completely independently, without even taking note of one another. With time, however, the increasing need to coordinate their efforts and resources compelled the widely scattered Hungarian-American organizations to seek out the means of this unity. The goal was to establish an umbrella organization that would be the voice of the Hungarian-American community vis-à-vis the United States government and American society in general. Although this goal was never fully achieved, these efforts did produce some partial results. The most notable of these was the foundation of the still-functioning American Hungarian Federation.

The first call for the establishment of a United States—wide Hungarian-American organization was made on December 10, 1887. But this first effort, undertaken by Mór Weinberger in Cleveland, met with no success. The reason given by one of the chroniclers of this effort was that it proved to be impossible to unify into a single representative organization the widely scattered Hungarian-Americans, "who were of diverse educational background, represented divergent cultural levels, professed a wide variety of political ideologies and religious creeds, belonged to many different social classes, aspired toward divergent goals in life, and represented the most diverse kinds of occupations." While this assessment is perhaps more reflective of a later period of Hungarian-American history, it explains the relative lack of success in creating a "United Hungarian Front" in the United States. This earliest effort at Hungarian unity, however, was undercut by two factors: the rising rivalry between two major centers of Hungarian-American life: Cleveland and New York, and the deep-seated distrust of the educated by the uneducated Hungarians.

Four years later a new call for unity went out, this time coming from the pen of Árkád Mogyoróssy (1851–1935), the editor of the periodical *Önállás* (Independence). This call was supported by the Hungarian Association of Philadelphia *(Philadelphiai Magyar Egylet)*, and despite some bickerings by rival cities and rival organizations, the "First Hungarian Congress of Unity" did take place in Philadelphia on March 12–15, 1892. Although the congress was punctuated by personal clashes and emotional debates, a new organization was in fact founded under the name Hungarian National Federation *(Magyar Nemzeti Szövetség)*. Its alleged primary goal was to enhance cooperation and to aid the exchange of moral and material help among Hungarian-Americans. But its several other main goals also included "the nurturing of the Hungarian national spirit [and] the defense of the good name of the Hungarians." In line with this proclaimed spirit of nationalism the founders of the federation also declared Magyar as the official language of the new organization, although they were realistic enough to add that its officers would have to be United States citizens.

The founding of the Hungarian National Federation appeared to be a step in the right direction, yet it hardly lasted two years. Within less than a year it already had to contend with two rival federations: the "Federation of Hungarian Sick-Benefit Societies" and the "Hungarian Christian Workers' Federation." The resulting rivalries of these aspiring umbrella organizations soon brought this second attempt at unity to a halt.

These pioneer efforts were followed in a few years by several similar abortive attempts. Thus in 1903 a group of associations, under the leadership of Árkád Mogyoróssy and historian Jenő (Eugene) Pivány, established the "Hungarian Cultural Federation" in Philadephia. This was followed in the fall of the same year by the foundation of the "American Hungarian National Federation" in Cleveland. But again the results were the same, and Hungarian-Americans remained once more without a central organization. The forces of division and the power of personal rivalries were simply too strong to permit the rise of a truly representative body for Hungarian-Americans. It was in wake of these failures and defeats that the cause of unity was picked up by one of the towering figures of pre–World War I Hungarian-American society, whose efforts eventually led to the foundation of the first permanent and still functioning Hungarian umbrella organization. The man in question was Tihamér Koháyi (1863–1913), the founder of the largest and most influential Hungarian-American newspaper, the *Szabadság* (Liberty) of Cleveland, and the organization was the American Hungarian Federation, founded in the same city in 1906.[24]

The American Hungarian Federation

Although the primary force behind the establishment of the American Hungarian Federation (February 27, 1906) was Tihamér Koháyi, the conditions that made this possible were connected with developments in Hungary. Following violent anti-Habsburg demonstrations in the Hungarian Parliament that paralyzed the Hungarian government, Emperor Francis Joseph appointed a non-partisan prime minister without taking into consideration the wishes of the individual party leaders. He did this on the basis of the rights granted to him by the Hungarian Constitution, yet this imperial act appeared too arbitrary to the Hungarian public, and it inflamed even further the already burning Hungarian nationalism. The spirit of 1848 was once more revived, and anti-Habsburg demonstrations swept through the whole country. Soon this revived spirit of nationalism also came to affect Hungarian-Americans, who joined the popular cry demanding total independence from Austria. Given this situation, it was now much easier to rally the immigrants around a common cause, and to carry through the foundation of an umbrella organization that could serve as the collective voice of all Hungarian-Americans. Thus, when the American Hungarian Federation (AHF) was finally called into being on February 27, 1906, its primary goal—in addition to the establishment of Hungarian-American unity—was defined as "the promotion of Hungary's independence [from Austria] through all possible means." In point of fact, the key watchword of the founding congress of the AHF was: "Away from Austria! Long live independent Hungary!"[25]

Contrary to its predecessors, the AHF did survive as the most important umbrella organization of Hungarian-Americans. Yet not even the AHF became very significant until the interwar period, when it did so largely because of developments in Hungary (i.e., Hungary's postwar dismemberment), rather than any change of heart among Hungarian-Americans. The shock of Hungary's dismemberment affected the immigrants almost as much as it did their brethren in the mother country, pushing them in the direction of political activism under the flags of a representative and recognized organization. It was under these circumstances that the AHF suddenly emerged as the voice of the Hungarian-American community. It tried to live up to this image by organizing rallies protesting Hungary's dismemberment, by collecting monies for various Hungarian national and social causes, by observing Hungarian national holidays (often with the participation of local politicians in search of votes), and by sending occasional memoranda to the United States Congress, the White House, and the State Department. Such memoranda, which detailed some of Hungary's grievances, were often connected with the American tour of a prominent Hungarian personality or delegation, who also made efforts to present their nation's cause to the political leaders of the United States.

Although the representation of Hungarian national interests remained in the forefront of Hungarian-American political activities, by the 1930s immigrants and their native-born children also began to express concern for domestic political issues. Even so, however, the local committees of the AHF continued to remain under the control of those who were more interested in Hungarian than in American political issues. Moreover, this Hungary-centered approach dominated even the national conventions, where calls for "justice for Hungary" and for the "just revision of the Treaty of Trianon" took precedence over all other issues. And this approach remained unchanged even during the Second World War, when the AHF and the Hungarian-Americans in general faced an unusual problem in explaining Hungary's affiliation with the Axis powers.[26]

Cultural Societies and Glee Clubs

The large majority of Hungarian-American organizations during the pre- and interwar periods were sick-benefit societies (78 percent in 1910). By the end of the latter period, however, the number of various cultural, social, and professional organizations increased, while sick-benefit societies decreased both through attrition and through mergers. (Strictly political organizations did not come into being until World War II and after.)

Of the traditional non–sick-benefit societies, the most common were the so-called "self-culture societies" and glee clubs. Both of these were rather widespread in Hungary, their goal being to advance the cause of mass culture and to encourage the development of the hidden talents of the nation's youth. Abroad, these associations assumed the additional task of perpetuating Hungarian language and culture among the immigrants. They were to be instruments of national self-preservation by infusing national consciousness into the minds of second- and third-generation Hungarian-Americans. This was the primary motive behind the immigrants' efforts to establish self-culture societies and glee clubs at the very outset of mass immigration.

The pioneer among Hungarian-American self-culture societies was the First Hungarian Self-Culture Society of New York. This society was founded in 1888 by a group of Hungarians under the leadership of Joseph Cukor and his son Mór Cukor, who were dissatisfied with the feeble activities of the New York Hungarian Society, founded over two decades earlier (1865) by some of the Kossuthist immigrants. While the latter organization was backward-looking (i.e., dreaming about past glories), the Cukors wanted a forward-looking association that would devote its attention to the training of present and future generations.[27]

The New York Self-Culture Society soon infused a new spirit of vitality into the cultural life of New York Hungarians. It sponsored scholarly lectures, literary readings, theater performances, commemorations of national holidays, and it even supported financially the publication of Hungarian literary works (e.g., William Loew's translation of Petőfi's poetry). The elected presidents of the society included some of the most distinguished intellectual leaders of the New York Hungarian community, and many of its youth members also achieved prominence in Hungarian-American life.

The example of the New York society was soon followed by other cities, and similar self-culture societies were also established in Chicago (1890), Cleveland (1902), Pittsburgh (1904), and elsewhere. This also holds true for the glee clubs, which were founded side by side and often bound to these self-culture societies.

Professional and Literary Associations

In addition to sick-benefit associations, self-culture societies, and glee clubs, the decades before and after World War I also witnessed the foundation of a number of professional and student organizations. The purpose of these organizations was to satisfy the special needs of the relatively few, but growing, number of educated Hungarians in the United States. Initially most of these educated persons were individuals with academic degrees from Hungary, who, while perhaps employed in fields inconsistent with their education, still needed the company of their own class. In addition to priests and clergymen, this class included an increasing number of engineers, lawyers, physicians, artists, and teachers, whose numbers were increasing by the gradual influx of the native-educated second-generation Hungarian-Americans.

The pioneer among these professional societies was the Chicago Hungarian University Circle. Founded in 1912 by a dozen intellectuals at the urging of the local Austro-Hungarian consul, János Pelényi, the proclaimed goal of this association was to foster friendship among the educated Hungarians in the Chicago area. Its actual goals, however, also included the promotion of Hungary's national interests, which was a constantly recurring theme with most Hungarian-American organizations. As a matter of fact, the Chicago Hungarian University Circle soon became embroiled in Hungarian domestic politics by openly supporting the political program of the anti-Habsburg and antimilitarist Count Michael Károlyi (1875–1955), whose tour of the United States in 1914 turned into a triumphant exposition of his political goals.[28]

Although none of the other Hungarian-American centers established organizations similar to the Chicago Hungarian University Circle, in several of the major cities a number of professional associations were established. These included the narrowly professional Hungarian Pharmacists' Circle of New York (1891), the American-Hungarian Engineers' and Architects' Club of New York (1909), the Hungarian Club of Cleveland (1922), the Hungarian Professional Society of Pittsburgh (1922), the New York Association of Hungarian Physicians (1926), and an increasing number of other similar organizations founded before and after World War II by the growing number of professionals among Hungarian-Americans.[29]

The interwar period also saw the establishment of a number of literary associations by the highly educated political immigrants of the postwar revolutions in Hungary. These left-leaning, highly sophisticated, urbane intellectuals sorely missed the unique intellectual atmosphere of the Budapest that they were forced to leave behind. Thus they established associations in which they tried to re-create that intellectual world. The best known among these were the Ady Endre Society *(Ady Endre Társaság)* and the Cultural Federation *(Kultúr Szövetség)* of New York, which brought together the literary and artistic connoisseurs of old Budapest.[30] But as these societies were kept in existence only by the members of the old generation (their native-born children opting for Americanization), they were all doomed to failure. This was all the more so as the new breed of political immigrants, who came after World War II, were representatives of radically different political views, and as such opted to found their own political and cultural organizations.

Chapter Five

Hungarian-American Churches and Religious Organizations

Next to the associations, and in particular the sick-benefit societies, the most significant social and psychological props of Hungarian-American life during the age of the great economic immigration were the immigrants' religious organizations. Perhaps even more than their fraternal associations, their churches gave them a feeling of security. In most instances these churches also served as centers of the immigrants' cultural and social lives. This was all the more so as the Hungarian-American churches and congregations combined the functions of the two most significant institutions of the Hungarian village: the church and the inn.

In Hungary, the former of these was—and still is—simply a place of worship, presided over by the village priest or preacher, who is the unquestioned leader of his folk. The church basement—if it existed at all—was a crypt, the mysterious and forbidden resting place of the mighty, who in all probability used to be the feudal lords of the peasants' ancestors. These crypts and the village churches in general were sources of strange "apparitions" that were generally believed to exist and dreaded even by the grown-ups of the village, most of whom were superstitious.

Much of the social life of the villagers revolved around various religious festivities connected with the church. For the menfolk, however, this social life also centered on the village inn. It was a place of relaxation and a place for letting off steam after the long days of arduous physical labor. It was in the village inn that the peasants exchanged local gossip, discussed local and national politics, and vented their pent-up personal and class emotions, which often led to physical confrontations and at times even to bloodletting.

In the new and strange world of America, these two institutions—the village church and the village inn—were merged. Unable to blend into urban American society, their new surroundings forced the immigrants to create a separate world for themselves. In this "world within a world" the functions of the two most important village institutions were merged into one, transferring much of the functions of the village inn into the church basement. Thus the crypt of the village church was replaced by the social club–like church basement of the American congregations. They prayed and sought spiritual salvation above, and they played and brawled below. But the merging of these two institutions still had a civilizing effect on their activities. Drunkenness and man-to-man combats, prevalent at the village inn, declined, although at the expense of the prestige of the church, which lost some its sanctity and mystery. This transformation also served as a catalyst in the "modernization" of the immigrants' mentality, i.e., in making them more up-to-date persons in an industrialized society and in making their lives more bearable in a world that was both better and worse at the same time—although at the expense of a relative decline in their naive and simple religiosity.

The Role of the Churches and the Clergymen

Although it is extremely difficult to document the extent of this decline in the immigrants' religious devotions, all authorities agree that this decline had no adverse effect on the special and powerful role that the immigrants' churches played in their lives. Aside from the extremely significant role of the clergymen, who often were the only really educated persons able to represent the immigrants' interests in American society, the church in the New World also represented a portion of the lost homeland. There the newcomers could feel at home, could participate in the customs and rituals of their people in their own native tongue, could meet their own kind, and could relieve their souls to persons who felt like them, spoke like them, and faced similar social and personal problems. The Hungarian-American churches, therefore, were really "Hungarian" churches in the midst of an alien world. For this reason they also became "national" and at times "nationalistic" churches and displayed characteristics that in the homeland were usually reserved for nonreligious patriotic organizations. In this way Hungarian-American churches became instrumental in merging religiosity with patriotism and in perpetuating Hungarian patriotic feelings among the immigrants. This was particularly true for the Protestant—especially Calvinist—churches, whose history was more intimately connected with Hungarian national traditions than that of the much more universalist Hungarian Catholic Church or that of the recently assimilated Hungarian Jewry.[1]

The establishment and leadership of the Hungarian-American churches were closely tied to the presence of Hungarian clergymen, most of whom came from Hungary with the intention of preserving the language and nationality of their immigrant countrymen. Moreover—as we shall see later—many of them came with the approval and encouragement of the Hungarian government, whose national and economic interests demanded the preservation and eventual repatriation of most of the Magyar-speaking immigrants. As a result, the role and influence of the Hungarian priests and preachers were even more pervasive in the United States than in Hungary. As the Hungarian-American churches became the centers of the social, cultural, and national life of the immigrants, so their priests and preachers became their social, cultural, and national leaders. And this was true even though these clergymen depended exclusively upon the financial support of their congregations. But their moral influence, as the "fathers" of their flocks, was very extensive. In fact, their presence and participation was almost a precondition for the success of any movement or collective action. As such, they also exerted a phenomenal influence on the general course of Hungarian life in America; and were therefore largely responsible for the relative successes and failures in this life.

The Origins of the Hungarian-American Churches

Hungarian religious life in America reaches back to 1852, when Kossuth's self-professed preacher, the Rev. Gedeon Ács, held the first ecumenical service in New York City for Hungarians of all faiths. As revealed by his diary, Rev. Ács's congregation was a rather mixed lot. In his own words, "The majority of them were Catholics, but there were also a few Calvinists, Lutherans, Greek Catholics, as well as those of Moses's faith; the latter being the most faithful members of the Hungarian Congregation."[2] Apparently, some of this ecumenical spirit of the immigrants was preserved as late as the early twentieth century, as revealed by the experiences of the

Hungarian-American poet László Pólya (1870–1950) in Garnerville, Ohio, where he encountered a Hungarian congregation where all Hungarians worshiped in common, including "Calvinists, Catholics, Russians [i.e., Greek Catholics], Lutherans, and even Mr. Schwartz [i.e., a Jew]."[3]

While the religious activities of the Hungarian immigrants reach back to the mid-nineteenth century, the first Hungarian churches were not established until the early 1890s, with Cleveland leading the way both among Catholics and the Protestants. Prior to the establishment of these early Hungarian congregations, however, the Hungarians were even compelled to prove their separate national identity to the uninformed American ecclesiastical authorities.

As a matter of fact, to most secular and ecclesiastical authorities in late-nineteenth-century America, all immigrants from Hungary were "Hungarians." While this general lack of understanding concerning Hungary's multinational composition may have appealed to the Hungarian authorities, in this country it worked against the interests of the Magyar-speaking immigrants. The reason for this was that the early mass migration from Hungary was made up largely of Slovaks, who therefore represented most of the so-called "Hungarians" in late-nineteenth-century America. Thus, when the first Magyar-speaking immigrants began to arrive, they were routinely assigned to Slovak parishes founded earlier. But this resulted in a twofold problem: on the one hand, the Magyars who did not speak Slovak (and very few of them did) were unable to communicate with their fellow parishioners or participate in many of the social-cultural activities of the parish; on the other hand, they suddenly found themselves in a subordinate position to a nationality that for a thousand years had occupied a secondary position in the Magyar-founded and Magyar-led Hungarian state. Nor was the situation helped by the fact that the local bishops, who had already established some rapport with the Slovaks, were neither able nor willing to appreciate the special problems of the Magyars.

A good example of this lack of appreciation was the situation in Cleveland in the late 1880s. When the Hungarians asked for permission to establish a Hungarian parish and to build a Hungarian church, they were promptly told to join forces with the Slovaks. Having no alternatives, they did so. But the church they built and named after Hungary's canonized monarch, St. Ladislas, was from the very beginning dominated by the Slovaks, who were in the majority. Their strongly anti-Magyar priest, John Mártvony—whom the Hungarians called "Pán Márton"—although equally fluent in Slovak and Magyar, refused to speak Magyar even when dedicating the flag of the Hungarians' St. Emeric Association in 1891. This was simply too much for the Hungarians. They rebelled against this Slovak dominance, which eventually persuaded the administrator of the Diocese of Cleveland, Msgr. Felix Boff, that they were really not Slovaks. He eventually wrote to Hungary's Prince Primate, Cardinal Kolos Vaszary, asking him to send some Magyar-speaking priests to serve the Hungarians of his city. But the Latin-language letter of this apparently well-meaning clergyman—in which he beseeched the Hungarian Primate to dispatch a priest to the "forsaken Huns" of Cleveland—reveals not only Msgr. Boff's desire to help but also the universal ignorance about Hungary and the Hungarians.[4]

The Catholic Church

The man Cardinal Vaszary selected, who thus became the founder of Hungarian Catholic life in America, was a middle-aged parish priest from Márianosztra, the future Msgr. Charles (Károly) Bőhm (1850–1932). His arrival in the United States in December 1892 was a milestone in Hungarian-American Catholicism. In less than a year after his arrival, the foundations of the first and still-functioning Hungarian Roman Catholic church in the United States—the St. Elizabeth of Hungary Church—were laid. This was followed in rapid succession by the establishment of dozens of Hungarian Catholic parishes and churches throughout Hungarian-America, including two more churches in Cleveland (St. Emeric's, 1914; St. Margaret's, 1918) and at least one each in most larger Hungarian settlements (Hazleton, Pa., 1893; Toledo, 1898; Bridgeport, Conn., 1899; McKeesport, Pa., 1899; South Bend, Ind., 1900; New York City, 1901; Chicago, 1904; Detroit, 1904; Pittsburgh, 1914; etc.). As a result of these foundations, by 1927 Hungarian-American Catholics had fifty-nine different parishes and churches scattered throughout the northeastern United States. By the 1960s this number had grown to seventy-six, with an additional twelve parishes in Canada. Most of these parishes and churches fulfilled the double function of being both the religious and cultural-social centers of Hungarian-Americans. As such they also became the sources of national pride and the perpetuation of national consciousness in an age when being "different" was generally viewed with scorn and dislike by most Americans.[5]

In addition to being the founder of the first Hungarian Catholic church in the United States, Msgr. Bőhm was also responsible in 1894 for the establishment of the first fraternal association for Catholic Hungarians. Although the American Hungarian Catholic Society *(Amerikai Magyar Katolikus Egylet)*—a name it assumed only in 1942, after several changes—was never able to compete with some of the other, more successful "national" associations, it did emerge from the ranks of the multitude of local fraternities and is even today one of the broadly based Hungarian-American associations.[6]

In giving solace to and instilling pride in the souls of the immigrant Hungarians, the role of Msgr. Charles Bőhm can hardly be overestimated. But this also holds true for the Rev. Kálmán Kováts (1863–1927), the founder of St. Stephen's Hungarian Catholic Church in McKeesport, Pennsylvania, whose powerful personality and intransigent nationalism were particularly instrumental in perpetuating national pride and the desire to survive among Hungarian-Americans.

Rev. Kováts came to the United States in 1899 from a Slovak-inhabited section of former northern Hungary. This factor was of utmost significance in shaping his mind and in determining the role he was to play in the United States, where Slovak immigrants preceded the Magyars, and where the rising Slovak nationalism immediately assumed a strongly anti-Magyar flavor. Having been confronted with some of this antagonism already in Hungary, and then witnessing the continued anti-Hungarian manifestations of the Slovaks in the United States, Rev. Kováts immediately took the offensive. He did this both in his sermons and his writings. Thus, only a year after his arrival, he launched the weekly *Magyarok Csillaga* (Hungarian Star), which immediately became a voice of both militant Catholicism and Hungarian nationalism. The Catholic-Hungarian profile of his paper was all the more pronounced as the Slovak national cause was promoted most vocally by the Slovak Lutheran Church and Slovak Lutheran clergy, whose center was Pittsburgh. Their fiery call for historic Hungary's dismemberment was the primary cause of Kováts's own militancy, which led, among other things, to his many disagreements with the much more sedate Msgr. Bőhm of Cleveland.[7]

During his twenty-eight years in McKeesport (1899–1927) Rev. Kováts was responsible for many Hungarian-related developments, including the transplanting of the first Hungarian female religious order—the Daughters of the Divine Redeemer—to American soil (1912).[8] It is an irony of fate that in the post–World War II period Rev. Kováts's church in McKeesport was among the first of the well-to-do and still functioning Hungarian Catholic parishes to switch from Hungarian to English and to end instruction in Hungarian. These changes naturally became a source of dissent among the parishioners, particularly at the time of Cardinal József Mindszenty's visit to the United States in 1974, who, like Rev. Kováts, was a strong advocate of Hungarian patriotism.[9]

Although Hungarian nationalism and a continued emotional attachment to the homeland were significant factors among all Hungarians during the pre- and interwar years, contrary to Hungarian Protestantism, the Catholic Church of Hungary displayed relatively little interest in the fortunes of the Hungarian immigrants in the United States. This lack of attention may have been the direct result of the universalist tendencies of the Catholic Church, but it still made things difficult for most Catholic Hungarian-Americans. Not until after World War I did the leaders of the Hungarian Catholic Church discover their forsaken brethren across the sea, and then only because of their own need and bewilderment following historic Hungary's dismemberment. The psychological shock that followed the Treaty of Trianon (1920) compelled all Hungarians to reach out for help and sympathy to whoever was willing to listen. Soon Hungarian-Americans were inundated with pleas for help. They were also visited by delegations, some of them led by high church dignitaries, who naturally appealed first of all to their own co-religionists among the immigrants. These visiting Hungarian Catholic dignitaries included, among others, Hungary's Prince-Primate, the Cardinal-Archbishop János Csernoch (1852–1927), who came on the occasion of the Eucharistic World Congress in 1926; the prolific Jesuit orator and journalist Béla Bangha (1880–1940), who visited the Americas in 1922 and 1934; and the fiery nationalist army bishop István Zadravecz (1884–1965), whose extremist views were too severe even for Hungary, yet served as a source of inspiration for many Hungarian-Americans unaware of the implications of these views.[10]

In light of the new post-Trianon perspective concerning the future of their nation, these Hungarian Catholic Church leaders also took up the cause of the national preservation of the new generation of Hungarian-Americans. While their newly found interest and encouragement did help somewhat, ultimately the foundations of this preservation (Hungarian schools, language classes, cultural institutions, etc.) were laid by the pioneers of Hungarian-American Catholicism, including Msgr. Bőhm, Rev. Kálmán Kováts, and those who came in their wake. As a matter of fact—largely as a result of the efforts of these pioneers—by the mid-1920s Hungarian Catholic life and Hungarian national consciousness were being perpetuated in the United States in nearly sixty churches and twenty parochial schools. The nationalist spirit of these institutions was being expressed even in their names, most of them carrying the names of Hungarian or "Hungarianized" saints, including King St. Stephen (fourteen churches), King St. Ladislas (six churches), The Blessed Lady of Hungary *(Nagyboldogaszony)* (five churches), St. Emeric, St. Elizabeth and Our Lady of Hungary (four churches each), and St. Margaret, who was not even canonized officially until 1939 (three churches).[11]

The work of the patriotic Hungarian Catholic priests was aided by the increasing number of Hungarian nuns, who settled in the United States to teach and to do social work among Hungarian-Americans. The first of these goals was particularly important, for it was only with the help of Hungarian schools that the Magyar language could be perpetuated among the native-born generations.

The first Hungarian order of nuns to settle in the United States was the already-mentioned Daughters of the Divine Redeemer, who arrived in McKeesport, Pennsylvania, in 1912. From there they spread out to such other Hungarian-American centers as Toledo (1921), Cleveland (1922), and Elizabeth, Pennsylvania (1924). They were followed by the Daughters of Divine Love, who settled in New York City (1913); the Sisters of Social Mission, who took charge of Cleveland's St. Margaret Church School in 1922; the Society of Social Sisters, who began their activities in 1923 in and around Buffalo; and then after World War II by the Daughters of the People of Jesus's Heart (1949) and the Sisters of Mercy of Szatmár (1950)— the latter being transplanted from China following the Communist victory there. All of these orders spread out to several Hungarian centers in North America, and the Society of Social Sisters even to Cuba and Puerto Rico. They took charge of schools, founded social missions and old-age homes, and generally spread the Christian ideals of love in combination with the Hungarian language and culture. Without the dedication of these Hungarian nuns, the preservation of this language and culture in North America would have been much more difficult. [12]

The Calvinist or Reformed Church

Following Rev. Gedeon Ács's somewhat premature attempt to found an ecumenical congregation for the Kossuthist political immigrants in New York in 1852, the first serious efforts to establish Hungarian Protestant congregations in North America were initiated only in the early 1890s. The pioneer of this effort was the Calvinist clergyman Rev. Gustav Jurányi (1856–1940), who came to the United States in 1890 and founded the First Hungarian Reformed Church of Cleveland (May 1891)—the very first Hungarian-American congregation of any denomination.

Jurányi was followed a year later by the Rev. János Kovács, the founder of the Hungarian Reformed Church of Pittsburgh (September 1891); by the Rev. Ferenc Ferenczy (1893), who also settled in Pittsburgh and soon became Kovács's successor after the latter's return to Hungary (1894); by the Rev. Sándor Harsányi (1894), who took Jurányi's place in Cleveland after the latter's move to Trenton, New Jersey; by the Rev. Bertalan Demeter (1895), who was responsible for the second Hungarian experimentation with an ecumenical congregation in America; and by the Rev. Sándor Kalassay (1895), who, after a brief period in Mount Carmel, Pennsylvania, settled in Pittsburgh and soon became one of the dominant figures of Hungarian Calvinism in the United States. It was Kalassay's call for unity among the Hungarian Calvinists in America that resulted in the foundation of the American Hungarian Reformed Federation (AHRF) in 1896, a still-existing organization that soon became the second-largest Hungarian-American fraternal association. But in addition to playing the role of a major fraternal association, the AHRF also served as a factor of unity among Hungarian-American Calvinist congregations whose leaders became increasingly involved in personal and ideological rivalries, leading to the fragmentation of Hungarian Calvinism in America. [13]

In addition to the lack of a clearly defined central authority—such as is the case with the Catholic Church—the primary reason for the prolonged fraternal struggle that rocked the history of Hungarian Calvinism in the United States was the result of disagreements concerning the relationship between the Reformed Church of Hungary and its congregations in America.

Hungarian Calvinism, which in 1910 was the second-largest church in Hungary (14.3 percent Calvinists versus 49.3 percent Roman Catholics, 12.8 percent Orthodox, 11 percent Greek Catholics, 7.1 percent Evangelicals or Lutherans, 5 percent Jews, and 0.4 percent Unitarians), [14] had for centuries been regarded as a powerful exponent of Hungarian patriotism. This view and mission remained unchanged even among the immigrant Calvinists (Reformed), whose congregations continued to be exponents of the Hungarian national spirit. Thus, even though the early Hungarian Reformed churches (congregations) in the United States were aided financially either by the Reformed Church of the United States (1890 onward) or by the Presbyterian Church (after 1898), most Hungarian Calvinists and their clergymen wished to retain close ties with the Reformed Church of Hungary.

This unanimous and unquestioned attachment to the Hungarian Mother Church among Hungarian-American Calvinists was shattered between 1898 and 1903, when several Hungarian-American clergymen were ordained by the American Presbyterian Church and began to establish congregations under the latter's auspices. On the one hand, this pitted the pro–Reformed Church Hungarians against the pro–Presbyterian Church Hungarians; on the other hand, the increasing involvement of these two American churches in Hungarian affairs also began to aggravate the relationship between Hungarian-American Calvinists and the Universal Convent (Synod) of the Reformed Church of Hungary.

The most vocal exponents of these two orientations, i.e. pro–Reformed Church and pro-union (pro-Hungary) versus pro-Presbyterian and anti-union (anti-Hungary) orientations, were the Rev. Zoltán Kuthy and the Rev. Géza Kacziányi. Their ideological struggle—fought in such papers as the pro-union *Heti Szemle* (Weekly review) and the anti-union *Magyar Reformátusok Lapja* (Hungarian reformed review)—eventually led to bitter personal recriminations and even legal battles. As such, it divided further the fragile unity of the Hungarian-American community, which was already racked by many dissensions, including the rivalry of the two most influential newspapers, the New York–based *Amerikai Magyar Népszava* (American Hungarian people's voice) and the Cleveland-based *Szabadság* (Liberty). Although all three of the churches were amenable to a compromise, and although they arranged a number of meetings and conferences to iron out their differences, ultimately no permanent solution was found, and Hungarian-American Calvinists continued their seemingly inevitable move toward fragmentation. By 1908 they were firmly divided into three main groups, with twenty-one congregations controlled by the Reformed Church of Hungary, ten by the Reformed Church of the United States, and twenty by the American Presbyterian Church.[15]

The situation was further complicated by World War I, when, in light of Hungary's role as one of the enemy states, there was a growing danger that the property of the pro-union churches (i.e., those controlled by the Reformed Church of Hungary) would be confiscated as enemy property. This danger did not pass until after the war, when—on the basis of the so-called Tiffin Agreement of October 7, 1921[16]—the two American provinces of the Reformed Church of Hungary were released by the Mother Church and permitted to join the Reformed Church of the United States. This agreement was concluded with the approval of most Hungarian-American Calvinists, yet it failed to bring about the desired unity. There were those who, under the leadership of the Rev. Endre Sebestyén, wished to establish an independent Hungarian-American Reformed Church. A number of other clergymen, on the other hand, remained with the Presbyterian Church or joined various other American Protestant churches. The result was an even further fragmentation of Hungarian-American Calvinism. Thus by 1926 Hungarian-American Calvinists were divided among seven different churches and groups, including the Reformed Church of the United States (fifty-one congregations), the Presbyterian Church (thirty-two congregations), the Independent American Hungarian Reformed Church (eleven congregations), the Protestant Episcopal Church (three congregations), the Reformed Church of America (three congregations), the Southern Presbyterian Church (three congregations), and an unaffiliated group of three congregations.[17] Subsequently these congregations shifted back and forth, altering their allegiances, merging, and separating, but were never able to come to terms with each other. By 1940 there were 140 congregations, bound together only by the knowledge of their common origins[18] and by the Hungarian American Reformed Federation (soon renamed Hungarian Reformed Federation of America), which served as a bond of unity among all Hungarian-American Calvinists. Based on the HARF's financial might, in 1921 they were even able to establish an orphanage and an old-age home in Ligonier, Pennsylvania, which were soon joined by a school and a printing press—all of them named after the famous Hungarian Calvinist ruling prince of Transylvania, Gabriel Bethlen (1613–1629). Under the leadership of the Rev. Sándor Kalassay (1921–1941), Ligonier, with its Hungarian institutions, soon became the cultural center of Hungarian-American Calvinism and remained so right into the 1970s. While the orphanage and the printing press were liquidated in the late 1970s, the old-age home still stands as a monument to the achievements of the pioneer immigrants. Moreover, there is the hope that Ligonier will also house the Archives of the HRFA with its huge collection on the lives and achievements of these pioneers.[19]

The Lutheran or Evangelical Church

The Catholics and the Calvinists together constituted nearly 64 percent of Hungary's population, and they were also the bastions of Hungarian (Magyar) nationalism. This was much less true for some of the smaller denominations, which were also present among the immigrants, although not necessarily in direct proportion to their numbers in Hungary. Discounting the Orthodox Christians (who were not Magyars, but Rumanians or Serbians), the most significant of these denominations were the Lutherans, the Greek or Byzantine Catholics, and the Jews. The remaining, constituting less than 0.5 percent of the population, were members of such smaller sects as the Unitarians, the Baptists, and the Pentecostals or Seventh Day Adventists. Of all of these smaller denominations, it was perhaps the Lutherans who had played the most significant role in Hungarian-American life.

The Lutherans of Hungary have traditionally been closely associated with the Calvinists. Being 7.1 percent of the country's population, numerically they were about half as strong as the Calvinists. In terms of their historical role and institutional strength, however, they carried much less weight. Moreover, they constituted an even smaller percentage of the immigrants, which placed them at a distinct disadvantage when compared to their Calvinist brethren, not to speak of the Roman Catholics.

Prior to 1907 there were no Hungarian Lutheran churches and institutions in America. Consequently, many of the Hungarian Lutherans were compelled to attend religious services in Slovak churches, most of whose clergymen also spoke Magyar. The coming of the young István Rúzsa (1883–1940) in 1907, however, changed all this. After being ordained into the ministry by the United Lutheran Church of America, Rúzsa went to work quickly to lay the foundations of Hungarian Lutheranism in America. The first congregation was his own First Hungarian Lutheran Church of Cleveland (1906), which was soon followed by the establishment of several others in such cities as Detroit, New Brunswick, Allentown, Buffalo, Pittsburgh, and others. By 1927 there were nine Hungarian-American Lutheran congregations, with a number of others founded in the 1930s and the post–World War II period.

Throughout this period Cleveland remained the center of Hungarian-American Lutheranism. In addition to two congregations (the second having been founded in 1938), that city also became the seat of a shortlived Hungarian Lutheran orphanage (1914–1920).[20]

Following World War I Hungarian-American Lutherans were also discovered by their brethren across the sea. In contrast to the Reformed Church of Hungary, however, the Lutheran Church of Hungary never attempted to extend its control over Hungarian congregations in America. The latter placed themselves immediately under the control of the United Lutheran Church of America and thus avoided the fratricidal struggle and rivalry that plagued Hungarian Calvinism in the United States and Canada.

The Byzantine or Greek Catholic Church

At the turn of the century, the Greek or Byzantine Catholics constituted about 11 percent of Hungary's population, but their proportion among the immigrants was somewhat higher. This was true because many of them lived in the heavily emigration-prone northeastern section of Hungary, where social and economic conditions were such that many more people chose emigration as a solution to their problems.

The majority of these Byzantine Catholics were not really Magyars but Ruthenians or Rusyns. They spoke a language that was closely related to Ukrainian, but their national consciousness was on a very low level. In fact, similarly to many of the Slovak immigrants, most of them did not even become conscious of their nationality until coming to the United States, where they fell under the influence of a number of their increasingly nationalist intellectuals, many of whom were priests.

The rise of Ruthenian national consciousness gradually drove a wedge between the Magyar-speaking minority and the Rusyn-speaking majority. This was all the more true as a portion of the Ruthenians fell under the influence of the Russian Orthodox Church of America, and another portion under that of the Galician Ruthenian (Ukrainian) Church. Both of these churches had already established themselves in America, with bishoprics in San Francisco and Shenandoah, Pennsylvania, respectively. Their influence among the Hungarian Ruthenians was also aided by the American Catholic Church's refusal to accept married priests as Catholics, even though married priesthood had been a rule, rather than an exception, in Byzantine Christianity from its very inception. Moreover, the Galician-Ukrainians could also appeal on the basis of their ethnic and linguistic relationship to the Carpatho-Ruthenians.[21]

The leader of the pro-Russian faction among the Ruthenians was the Rev. Elek Tóth of Wilkes Barre, Pennsylvania, who was aided in his anti-Hungarian crusade by the increasingly anti-Hungarian Slovak nationalists. As a result of these activities (whether pro-Russian, pro-Ukrainian, or pro-Orthodox), many of the Ruthenians found themselves in a defensive position both with respect to their Byzantine Catholic faith as well as with regard to their newly found Ruthenian-Rusyn national identity.

After various attempts by the Hungarian government to intervene in this struggle (which—rightly or wrongly—was viewed in Hungary as a Russian-led Pan-Slavic political activity), in 1907 the Vatican finally decided to create a separate Byzantine Catholic Church in America and appointed the Rev. Stephen Sótér Ortinsky as its first bishop. This was done through the so-called *Ea semper* decree of 1907, which ended the jurisdiction of both the Hungarian and the Galician bishops over their faithful in America and at the same time also proposed the imposition of celibacy on the Byzantine Catholic clergy in the New World. The first of these decisions was generally welcomed, but the celibacy issue incensed both the clergy and the faithful. The situation was further complicated by the fact that Bishop Ortinsky turned out to be an advocate of Ukrainian nationalism, which was generally rejected not only by the Magyars but also by most of the Ruthenians.

Following Bishop Ortinsky's death in 1916, the situation improved somewhat. The two factions of the Byzantine Catholic Church received two separate administrators: Gabriel Martyak for the Hungarian Ruthenians, and Peter Ponyatyshyn for the Galician Ukrainians. The controversy between the two groups, however, was not solved until 1924, when Rome created two separate bishoprics, appointing Bishop Basil Takách to head the Ruthenian Church and Bishop Constantine Bohachevsky to oversee the Galician Ukrainian Church. [22]

With the establishment of the Ruthenian Exarchate in Munhall, Pennsylvania, under Bishop Takách in 1924, order gradually returned to the ranks of the Byzantine Catholics. This order, however, was soon shattered once more by the celibacy question, which was reopened by Pope Pius XI's *Cum data fuerit* decree of 1929, and which in effect did lead to the abolishment of married priesthood in America. The resulting turmoil continued throughout the episcopacy of Bishop Takách (1924–1948) and resulted even in a number of schismatic movements. Order gradually returned to the Church under Bishop Daniel Ivancho (1948–1955), who also established the first Byzantine Catholic Seminary for his people (1950), while at the same time fending off all attempts at the Ukrainization of his church and the Ruthenians. This policy was upheld by both of Bishop Ivancho's successors: Bishop Nicholas T. Elko (1955–1967) and Bishop (1967), later Metropolitan-Archbishop (1969–   ), Stephen Kocisko—the latter of whom now presides over his own archdiocese, three other dioceses (Passaic, New Jersey; Parma, Ohio; Van Nuys, California), and about 250 parishes. [23]

Being a small minority among the Ruthenians, the Magyar-speaking Byzantine Catholics have played a relatively minor role in all of these controversies within their church. And this was true even under the episcopacy of the Hungarian-born Bishop Takách, when about 9 percent of the parishes were Magyar-speaking (i.e., 14 out of 155 in 1924), [24] scattered in and around such major northeastern centers as Cleveland, Chicago, Detroit, Pittsburgh, Toledo, New Brunswick, and Trenton. Although the number of parishes has almost doubled since Bishop Takách's appointment, this does not hold true for the Hungarian congregations. Their number is small, and for this reason their leadership role in the Byzantine Catholic Church is also minimal. For all practical purposes that Church today is associated almost completely with the Ruthenian or Rusyn nationality.

Jewish Congregations

Although Hungarians of the Jewish faith were perhaps the earliest immigrants from Hungary (starting as early as the 1850s and 1860s), and although they have played a most significant role in Hungarian-American cultural life, their synagogues and other religious organizations were unable to retain for long their Hungarian national characteristics. This may have been due to a number of factors, including the well-known fact that many of the early Hungarian Jewish immigrants spoke German or Yiddish rather than Magyar and many of them were only at an early stage of assimilation into Magyardom. Moreover, being more intimately involved in business and manufacturing activities than their Gentile counterparts, they were more willing and more able to learn English, which in turn made them more prone to rapid Americanization. Even so, Hungarian Jews did establish a number of Magyar-speaking synagogues in such major Hungarian centers as New York, Cleveland, Pittsburgh, Chicago, Detroit, St. Louis, and Bridgeport—the first of these being the B'nai Jeshurum Hungarian Jewish Orthodox Synagogue of Cleveland, founded in 1866.[25] But in light of the members' proneness for assimilation, none of these congregations preserved its Hungarian character beyond the first generation. In point of fact, a number of them began the process of Americanization already during the life of the first generation.

True to their traditions in Hungary, most of the Hungarian-American Jewish congregations represented various shades of conservatism and even ultraconservatism (e.g., Rabbi Philip Klein). Others, such as Rabbi Alexander Kohut and Rabbi Stephen S. Wise, gradually moved toward reform. In fact, in 1907 Rabbi Wise founded the first Hungarian Reform Synagogue in New York City (the so-called "Free Synagogue") and then rapidly emerged as one of the leaders of Reform Judaism throughout the world. As an advocate of Zionism, he also became the founder of the American Jewish Congress as well as the World Jewish Congress. (This is all the more meaningful, as both of the "fathers" of the Zionist move-

ment—Theodor Herzl and Max Nordau—were Hungarian-born.)
The majority of the Hungarian and Hungarian-American Jews, how-
ever, failed to embrace this movement right up until World War
II, when they did so largely under the influence of Nazism and the
Holocaust.[26]

In light of the above, we have to agree with one of the earlier
chroniclers of the Hungarian-American past, Emil Lengyel, that "as
a national religious community the Jews of Hungary did not play
an important part in the United States."[27] Even so, when conditions
in Hungary in the late 1930s forced many fully Magyarized Hungarian Jews to emigrate and to settle in the United States, a modern
Magyar-speaking Jewish congregation was in fact established in New
York City. Founded by Rabbi György Lányi of Nagyvárad (now
Oradea in Rumania), the *Új Fény* (New light) Congregation was the
first synagogue in America that represented the religious traditions
of the Hungarian Jewry exclusively in the Magyar language.[28] Post—
World War II developments, however, also ended gradually the
Magyar character of Rabbi Lányi's congregation.

The Baptists, Unitarians, and Pentecostals

As seen above, Hungary was a predominantly Christian country,
with the majority of the latter belonging to one of the mainline
Christian denominations. Less than 0.5 percent of its population
belonged to such smaller sects as the Unitarians, the Baptists, and
the Pentecostals—even though the first of these was virtually born
in Hungarian Transylvania in the sixteenth century.

Because of their small numbers in Hungary, very few of the
immigrants belonged to any one of the above denominations. Once
in the United States, however, their numbers generally increased
through conversions. This was particularly true for the Baptists,
who found here several major Baptist churches with thousands of
congregations and millions of members. But as very few of the
Catholics, Jews, or traditional Protestants (i.e., Calvinists and Lutherans) ever converted to these denominations, which were barely
tolerated in Hungary, converts to the Baptists and other "non-
Hungarian" religions must have come from the ranks of those former
agnostics and unbelievers who suddenly found themselves in need
of a personal religion in their new surroundings.

Like their Catholic, Calvinist, Lutheran, and Jewish brethren, Hungarian Baptists also founded their first congregation in Cleveland. This took place in 1902 or 1903 under the leadership of the Rev. Michael Fábián, who was ordained into the ministry of his faith at the Baptist Theological Seminary of Rochester, New York. In 1908 a second Cleveland congregation was started by the Rev. Stephen Orosz, who also became dean of the small Hungarian Baptist Seminary, founded a few years later in the same city. In 1948 the two Cleveland-based Hungarian Baptist congregations merged and established the Shaker Square Hungarian Baptist Church, which, until the congregation's move to the suburbs in the late 1970s, was the most beautiful among the Hungarian Baptist church buildings in the United States.

The Cleveland example was followed by Hungarian Baptists in a number of cities, and by 1924 about forty-eight Baptist congregations were scattered throughout Hungarian-America. But as Baptist congregations were generally very small—usually containing only a fraction of the number of families in a Catholic parish—the large number of their congregation does not really reflect a large Hungarian Baptist population in the United States.[29]

Even though the Hungarian Baptists prospered in America, their influence in Hungarian-American life was minimal. This situation did not change until the 1960s and 1970s, when under the leadership of the Rev. Alexander Haraszti of Atlanta (a close confidant and adviser to Billy Graham), the Hungarian-American Baptists took a number of new initiatives that propelled them into the forefront of Hungarian activities in the United States. The most significant of these initiatives was their search for a new, more amiable relationship with socialist Hungary, which was only a part of Billy Graham's own search for new frontiers and new opportunities in the socialist-communist world.[30]

During the same eight decades, when the Baptists made themselves increasingly visible, Hungarian-Americans also established a few Pentecostal and Unitarian congregations. But unlike the Hungarian Baptists, neither of these two churches was able to increase their almost nonexistent influence on Hungarian-American life. The Pentecostals generally lost themselves among the myriad American fundamentalist churches, while the majority of the Unitarians functioned without any formal attachments to an organized congregation or church.

Conclusions

Religion and religious congregations have played a most important and determining role in Hungarian-American life. True, in light of the tendencies of our age, their influence is declining, but they still carry much weight. They still count among their membership the large majority of Hungarian-Americans; they still serve as important focal points for many of the social and cultural activities of those who live in or close to large Hungarian-American settlements; and their clergymen still enjoy the trust and respect of most of those who regard themselves as members of the Hungarian-American community in the United States. The future of these churches, however, is somewhat bleak, for most of the major Hungarian-American settlements are in the process of dissolution. But whatever their future and destiny, no one can deprive them of the great role they played in the lives of the immigrants and their descendants for nearly a century.

Chapter Six
Hungarian-American Journalism and Publishing

Fraternities and churches were the primary cell organizations of the Hungarian immigrants in the United States. They served as the centers of the immigrants' social, cultural, and religious activities and gave them the psychological prop needed to survive in a strange and alien world. This same need also produced the Hungarian-American press, which became a bond of unity among the immigrants and their communities while at the same time giving them direction and serving as a source of Magyar-language information.[1]

Craving for the latter was particularly great among pre–World War I immigrants, few of whom ever became fluent in English—particularly in reading and writing. Living in Hungarian communities, residing in Hungarian boarding houses, working among their own kind, belonging to Hungarian churches and fraternities, purchasing their immediate needs in Hungarian stores, etc., many of the immigrants never learned any English at all, or if they did, it was basically a simple "pidgin English"—hardly sufficient to read anything beyond road signs, business signs, and perhaps some headlines. Their ability to write in English was even more limited, and then usually conformed to Hungarian orthography according to the Hungarian pronunciation (e.g., "twenty" became *tóni,* "good-bye" became *gud báj,* and "Mrs." became *Miszisz*). Given these limitations, combined with the immigrants' need to be informed about the "outside world" as well as about Hungary and the Hungarian-American community, the birth of the Hungarian-American press was inevitable. To these must be added the problems stemming from the great distances among the various Hungarian-American communities and the special needs of each of these communities.

For this very reason, the content and the quality of these newspapers were determined by the personal-social-political needs and by the intellectual-cultural level of the immigrants as a whole. And because their needs were very local and very Hungary-oriented, and their cultural level was of a rather low quality, the main features of Hungarian-American journalism throughout the six decades between the 1890s and 1950s were localism, ethnocentrism, and provincialism.[2]

As Hungarian-American newspapers were born in response to the needs of the Hungarian-American community, and as regional loyalties and ideological variations were among the dominant features of that community, these variations also showed up in the profile of the ever-increasing number of Hungarian-American newspapers. Even so it is still possible and desirable to place these dozens of papers into several major groups, without which it would be impossible to characterize them. Perhaps the easiest way of categorizing them is from an ideological point of view, where we can discern three major orientations. These include the liberal-nationalist tendencies of the majority of the papers, the socialist-internationalist orientation of a strong but rather segregated minority, and the religious orientation represented primarily by the two major Christian faiths: Catholicism and Calvinism.[3]

Of the many dozens of Hungarian-American newspapers founded before and after World War I, the great majority were local, or catered to special audiences. They were generally semiweeklies, weeklies, biweeklies, or monthlies, or appeared irregularly depending on the financial and other resources of their respective publishers-editors. The exceptions to this rule were the three "flagship" papers that achieved "national" stature before or immediately after World War I, which also managed to transform themselves into dailies for a considerable length of time. These were the Cleveland-based *Szabadság* (Liberty), the New York–based *Amerikai Magyar Népszava* (American Hungarian people's voice), and the similarly New York–based *Előre* (Forward)—the first two of these being national-liberal in orientation and the last being socialist-internationalist.

In addition to these three major dailies, by the early 1920s Hungarian-Americans had at least seventy other papers, which can be divided roughly into the following categories: religious, fraternity, political-literary, and papers of humor.[4] With the exception of fraternity papers, which catered specifically to the membership of the sponsoring associations, most of these periodical publications (even the religious papers) were founded and kept in existence by the work and willpower of a single individual, who usually served as the publisher, editor, and printer.

The Origins

The very first of the Hungarian-American newspapers was the already-mentioned *Magyar Száműzöttek Lapja* (Hungarian exiles' news), which appeared in New York City at the end of 1853 (October 15–November 30), under the editorship of Károly Kornis. This paper, however, failed after only six issues and had barely eighty-five subscribers.

The next attempt came twenty-six years later in 1879, when two literary men—William Loew and Árkád Mogyoróssy—began to publish the highly literate *Magyar Amerika* (Hungarian America) in New York. Its founders were motivated by the desire to aid the cause of Hungary in the United States and to serve as a link between the two countries (the latter goal being promoted through some English-language articles). Yet this paper also failed after only a few issues. The primary reason for its demise was that it was simply too intellectual and therefore far removed from the simple tastes and local interests of the equally simple economic immigrants of that period.[5]

Four years after the demise of this second Hungarian-American paper was born the first successful venture into Hungarian-American journalism, the *Amerikai Nemzetőr* (American national guardian) (1883–1897). Founded and edited through most of its existence by Gustav S. Erdélyi (1852–1895), the weekly *Nemzetőr* established the content, set the tone, and became the guide for all Hungarian papers in America right into the post–World War II period. Erdélyi realized that the primary reason for the failure of the *Magyar Amerika* was its editors' inability to gear the content of their paper to the needs of the immigrants, and he avoided making the same mistake. Thus he brought the literary level of his paper down to the cultural-educational level of the average immigrant, and filled it with news items that were of interest to his readers. One of his innovations, for example, was the addition of a permanent column on the Hungarian fraternities and other organizations, where he dutifully listed the names and titles of the officers of these organizations, and also reported on their social and cultural activities. Erdélyi was also careful to concentrate on "outside news" that was of special interest to his readers. Thus, instead of writing about international affairs, he zeroed in on home county and hometown news, and on news about Hungary in general. (He was also the man who popularized

the word *óhaza,* which is the Hungarian equivalent for Old Country.)
All this did not add up to a very sophisticated form of journalism—
and the *Nemzetőr* was often the object of condescending smiles in
Hungary—but it did make Erdélyi's paper into an almost indis-
pensable component of Hungarian-American life throughout its decade and a half of existence. Moreover, the *Nemzetőr* also came to
serve as a model for most of its successors, including the two largest
and most successful and influential dailies, the *Szabadság* and the
Amerikai Magyar Népszava.

The *Nemzetőr's* success in New York soon prompted several other
journalists and aspiring journalists to follow Erdélyi's example by
establishing similar papers in a number of Hungarian-American
centers. Among the first of these were the *Önállás* (Independence)
of Hazleton, Pennsylvania (1890), and the *Szabadság* (Liberty) of
Cleveland (1891). These were followed by the *Amerikai Magyar
Hírlap* (American Hungarian news) of Cleveland in 1893, the *Magyar
Híradó* (Hungarian news) of New York in 1894, the *Amerikai Népszava* (American people's voice) of Cleveland in 1895, the *New Yorki
Napló* (New York diary) in 1902, etc. By 1903 Cleveland alone had
four newspapers, with the increasingly influential *Szabadság* having
to contend with the *Magyar Hírmondó* (Hungarian chronicler), the
Magyar Napilap (Hungarian daily), and the *Katolikus Magyarok Vasárnapja* (Catholic Hungarians' Sunday). The majority of these papers
and their successors, however, proved to be shortlived. A number
of them were absorbed by their more successful rivals, while others
simply ceased to exist—at times after only a few issues.[6]

The *Szabadság:* The Dominant Hungarian-American Daily

The most successful of these pioneer Hungarian-American newspapers was the Cleveland-based *Szabadság* (Liberty), which first appeared as a semiweekly on September 12, 1891, under the editorship
of the energetic Tihamér Kohányi. It was published every Wednes-
day and Saturday for fifteen years, until in 1906 it was finally
transformed into a daily paper. In terms of its content, the *Szabadság's* news section was simply a summary of the news found in
the contemporary American press; although this news was naturally
presented from the point of view of the editor, who was a strong
Hungarian nationalist in the Kossuthist tradition. It was the news

from Hungary, and the news concerning Hungarian-American life and organizations, that made it into a paper other than simply a Magyar-language American newssheet. And it was precisely this emphasis of Hungarian and Hungarian-American news (with the generous listing of the names of all local activists) that made the *Szabadság* into a success story and kept it going for many decades as one of the two "flagships" of the Hungarian press in North America.[7]

In addition to the actual or presumed needs of its reading public, the basic political-ideological orientation of the *Szabadság* was determined by the background and philosophy of its founding editor, Tihamér Kohányi (1863–1913). As a typical representative of the recently impoverished landed gentry of northeastern Hungary, Kohányi possessed and displayed all the well-known characteristics of his class. These included a powerful and somewhat sloganistic Magyar nationalism, an equally powerful anti-Habsburgism, a staunch attachment to the ideals of nineteenth-century liberalism as interpreted in Hungary, an intense dislike of all forms of radicalism, and a somewhat condescending attitude toward the non-Magyar nationalities of Hungary, as well as toward their brethren in the United States. Among all these characteristics, it was perhaps Kohányi's anti-Habsburg nationalism that appeared to be the strongest, and thus determined the ideological orientation of his paper. In light of these factors (and discounting its special Hungarian-American features), under Kohányi's editorship the *Szabadság* simply became another Hungarian newspaper pursuing the policy of national independence, which just "happened to be published in the United States."[8] But in his dislike of the Habsburgs, Kohányi went even beyond most of the domestic Hungarian newspapers. As an example of this phobia of his, in 1910 he broke permanently with the equally nationalistic Rev. Kálmán Kováts of McKeesport, Pennsylvania, simply because the latter had sent a telegram to Francis Joseph congratulating the aged King of Hungary (who was also Emperor of Austria) on his eightieth birthday. As described by one of his friends and biographers, Géza Kende, Kohányi simply "knew no mercy and had no forgiveness for the Habsburgs."[9] His violent and often brutal anti-Habsburgism naturally made Kohányi into a less than objective observer of the Hungarian national scene. Occasionally it forced even the almost equally nationalistic and irreconcilable government of Hungary to bar his paper from its readers there.[10]

Kohányi began the publication of the *Szabadság* with the same intention that was also expressed by most of the prospective editors of Hungarian-American newspapers: namely that it should serve as a bond of unity among Hungarian-Americans. But as in most other instances, this goal also turned out to be an idle dream. In fact, only a few months after the birth of his paper Kohányi was already at war with the rival *Önállás* of Hazleton, Pennsylvania. And this was only the beginning. Within a few years half a dozen Hungarian-American newspapers were at each other's throats, often for no other reason than the fact that the founding editors disliked any kind of competition. A number of the ensuing "press wars" were solved only by the demise of one or another of the papers, while others ended when the better-heeled editors bought out their less viable rivals. A case in point is Kohányi's acquisition of the Cleveland-based *Magyar Napilap* (1902–1909), whose editor, Imre Fecsó, was perhaps his most vicious and vocal rival. This acquisition was a major turning point in the *Szabadság*'s struggle for existence, which ultimately assured its survival and its dominance over at least half of the Hungarian community in the United States. It had become a daily paper already three years before this momentous merger (1906), but not until the acquisition of the *Magyar Napilap* (1909) did the number of its subscribers increase radically, until finally by the 1930s it passed the 40,000 mark.[11] And there it remained throughout the 1930s and the 1940s. By the late 1940s and early 1950s, however, a gradual decline set in, which ultimately led to its return to semiweekly status in the 1960s and finally to a weekly in the 1970s. But this decline is connected to unforeseen developments following World War II that are to be chronicled in a later chapter of this work.

The *Amerikai Magyar Népszava:* The *Szabadság*'s Main Rival

If in the years before and after World War I the Cleveland-based *Szabadság* dominated half of Hungarian-America, then much of the other half was dominated by its younger rival, the *Amerikai Magyar Népszava* (American Hungarian people's voice) of New York City. The *Népszava*—as it was generally known—was founded in December 1899 as a weekly paper. Its founding editor, Géza D. Berkó

(1873–1927), had learned his trade as an associate of Gustav S. Erdélyi, the publisher-editor of the pioneer *Amerikai Nemzetőr*. As such Berkó knew from experience what a Hungarian-American newspaper ought to be in order to survive. He was also willing to learn from his future arch-rival, Kohányi. That Berkó turned out to be a "good student" is best indicated by the fact that by 1923 the *Népszava* surpassed the *Szabadság* in the number of its subscribers (36,214 to 35,563).[12] But this success was also due to a number of other factors. Chief among them was the fact that by the 1920s Berkó's paper was the only Hungarian-American daily that received direct subsidy from the Hungarian government so as to champion more effectively Hungary's national interests, and in particular the cause of revisionism (i.e., the revision of Hungary's post–World War I frontiers),[13] which naturally strengthened its already strong nationalist orientation. Some of the contributing causes of its success may have been its location in New York City (which had the largest number of Hungarians) and the early death of Tihamér Kohányi (1913), which deprived the *Szabadság* of its most effective editor and promoter.

Within less than three years after its foundation, the *Népszava* became a semiweekly (1902), and then in October 1904—two whole years before the *Szabadság*—Berkó turned it into a daily paper. By the latter part of that decade the *Népszava* and the *Szabadság* had swept most of their rivals off the national scene (those that remained were local or special-interest papers), and then dominated Hungarian-American journalism right up to the early 1950s, when new conditions in Hungarian-America made them increasingly obsolete. During the first half of our century, however—while coexisting with several dozen lesser papers—they had no real rivals in the United States. Their lesser rivals were forced to concentrate on certain localities or to cater to specific interest groups. In their main orientation, however, they were obliged to line up with one or another of these two dominant papers, as satellites of two "suns" in a single galaxy. The only exception to this rule were the "flagship" paper of the Hungarian-American socialists and communists (*Előre*, later *Új Előre*) and its own satellites, which, however, were largely outside the mainstream of Hungarian-American life. As such, they had relatively little influence outside the ranks of their immediate followers.

The Socialist-Communist Papers
of Hungarian-America

The first Hungarian-American newspaper with a socialist-internationalist orientation was the *Amerikai Népszava* (American people's voice), which was founded in Cleveland in 1895 but then moved to New York City in the very next year, where it soon expired. This ephemeral paper was followed in 1902 by the equally shortlived *Népakarat* (People's will) and then in 1905 by the rival *Előre* (Forward), which became the main forum of the American-Hungarian Socialist Workers' Federation. In 1911 the two papers merged under the title *Testvériség* (Brotherhood), but in 1912 they split again. In the same year the resurrected *Előre* became a daily with a circulation of nearly 10,000, and as such the third largest Hungarian-American paper in the United States. After World War I the *Előre* became associated with the newly formed crypto-communist American Labor Alliance (1921), and as such it soon folded under the powerful pressure of the strong anticommunist sentiments of the immediate postwar years. The defunct *Előre,* however, was almost immediately replaced by the newly founded *Új Előre* (New forward), which, like its predecessor, became the third-largest Hungarian-American daily and remained so for sixteen years (1921–1937). [14] According to some sources, by 1926 its circulation was over 30,000, which, if true, made it almost as popular as the two flagship papers of Hungarian-America. [15] The political philosophy of the *Új Előre,* however, went against the fundamental nationalism of most Hungarian-Americans, and this gradually undermined its popularity, which may have been fueled earlier by economic problems of the late 1920s and early 1930s. In 1937 the paper went bankrupt and was replaced by the United Frontist *Amerikai Magyar Világ* (American Hungarian world), and then in 1938 also by the crypto-communist *Amerikai Magyar Jövő* (American Hungarian future). None of these papers, however, was able to duplicate the success of the *Új Előre.* Neither the war years nor the post–World War II period was favorable for the dissemination of socialist, and particularly communist, ideas in the United States. By 1952 the *Magyar Jövő* also ceased to be published, giving its place over to the *Amerikai Magyar Szó* (American Hungarian word), which caters to a small and ever-decreasing audience. [16]

Basic Characteristics of
Hungarian-American Journalism

According to one source, by 1913 there were as many as forty-five Hungarian newspapers in the United States, and by 1922 their number increased to sixty-eight. Moreover, in the previous three decades at least half as many others were also founded, although unable to survive. This rapid rise and fall of papers was a permanent feature of Hungarian-American journalism, and it is with us even today. Even so, their numbers grew even beyond the above figure, particularly during the 1950s and early 1960s, when the influx of more literate and more politically active groups of immigrants pushed the number of concurrently published Hungarian-American papers well beyond the 100, and perhaps even the 150 mark.[17] This does not necessarily mean that the size of the reading public had increased (for it did not), but it does point to the increasing polarization of the Hungarian-American community into many scores of political and cultural interest groups.

The impermanency of Hungarian-American newspapers was never as great as during the 1950s and 1960s, but it was a constant feature of Hungarian-American journalism also before and after World War I. Virtually every year saw the rise and fall of one or more papers. Thus, with the exception of the major "national" papers, and perhaps a few larger local, religious, or fraternity publications, Hungarian-American newspapers came and went with customary regularity. This rapid turnover was partially the result of the diversity, and partially of the geographical dispersal, of the Hungarian-American community. The need for these papers was there, but the immigrants demanded much variety from the press, without guaranteeing the survival of any of these papers.

Although written in Magyar and espousing Hungarian national causes, Hungarian-American papers could hardly be compared to their contemporary counterparts in Hungary. Their content was geared to local needs, their literary standards were usually low, and their professionalism left much to be desired. Moreover, their existence and well-being were basically determined by the well-being and goodwill of their readers and advertisers, whose stranglehold was naturally reflected in the papers' columns and editorials. Moreover, because most of these papers were in the hands of individuals (or small groups) with specific personal, organizational, and religious biases, their editors generally refused to follow the policy of "fair play" that characterized most American and Hungarian papers of that period. The editors spent much of their time and effort in pursuing personal squabbles and vendettas, and in fighting "bloody" battles with various rival editors.[18]

In addition to fighting their personal battles, the editors of the two flagship papers—the *Szabadság* and the *Népszava*—also represented the rivalry and fought for the cause of the two largest Hungarian-American communities: Cleveland and New York. Thus, if one of these papers espoused a cause, the other either opposed it or came up with an alternative solution. And this was true about all aspects of Hungarian-American life, institutions, and their relationship to the mother country.[19]

If rivalry was an ever-present component of Hungarian-American journalism, so was the monopoly that many of the papers exercised in a particular locality or within a specific organization and its membership. This monopoly became even more pronounced during the late 1930s and the 1940s, when several Hungarian-American newspaper chains came into being. One of these was the chain established in 1934 by Márton Himler, the publisher-editor of the *Detroiti Magyarság* (Detroit Hungarians), who then controlled seven weeklies in Ohio. This monopoly became even more pervasive between 1939 and 1949, when both of the major daily papers (*Szabadság* and *Népszava*) fell under the control of Zoltán Gombos of Cleveland. Only the coming of the new wave of immigrants during the 1950s put an end to this monopoly, but at the expense of polarizing even further the whole Hungarian-American community.

The rivalry that characterized the Hungarian-American press because of the personal competition among the editors and publishers was further enhanced by the generally accepted custom among Hungarian-American associations and fraternities of selecting so-called "official papers." Because being selected always implied a virtual obligatory subscription by the membership of that organization, Hungarian-American papers often waged intensive and emotional campaigns for such endorsements. It meant a certain degree of financial security, but at the same time it also implied an obligatory catering to the membership, and in particular to the leadership of that organization. This in turn meant the subjecting of the paper's integrity and independence to the often parochial needs and tastes of the sponsoring organization, and consequently the even further lowering of professional standards.

Calendar-Almanacs

Side by side with its peculiar type of journalism, Hungarian-American society also produced various other types of popular publications. Besides works of belles-lettres, with their unique Hungarian-American themes and flavor, these publications included the promotional pamphlets of the local and national fraternities, the pious devotional tracts of the various religious organizations, the annual or occasional calendar-almanacs of the national and regional newspapers, naturalization aids for prospective citizens, textbooks for Hungarian-American schools, anniversary (jubilee) albums of societies and periodical publications, memoirs of some of the early (Kossuthist) immigrants, anti-Trianon political tracts that presented the Hungarian point of view concerning Historic Hungary's dismemberment, as well as an increasing number of so-called "scholarly" (really popular or semischolarly) works dealing with the Hungarian-American past and with United States–Hungarian relations.

Discounting the belles lettres and works on Hungarian-American history—which will be treated briefly later—the most interesting and revealing of these publications are the calendar-almanacs and the anniversary albums. They tell us a great deal about the lives, tastes, political preferences, cultural activities, and aspirations of this pioneer generation of Hungarian-Americans, while at the same time also summarizing their history as seen and assessed by themselves.

Almanaclike "calendars" have been part of the literary scene in Hungary ever since 1626, when the first Hungarian predecessor of the American *Old Farmer's Almanac* appeared in the city of Lőcse (Leutsche, Levoča). Entitled *Lőcsei Kalendárium,* this almanac and its many successors contained much useful information for everyday life, while also giving increasing space to literary pieces. These calendar-almanacs became so popular in Hungary that until the second half of the nineteenth century (and at times even beyond) they constituted almost the sole reading for most of the villagers. (The other popular reading, of course, was the Bible.) This attachment to the "calendar" among rural Hungarians apparently remained unchanged even after their immigration to America. Hungarian-American newpaper editors were well aware of this, and therefore they began to publish their own calendar-almanacs as soon as they were able to do so financially. Here again the two dominant dailies—the *Szabadság* and the *Népszava*—became the leaders. The *Népszava* published its first calendar-almanac in 1904 (for the year 1905) when it was transformed into a daily paper. The *Szabadság* followed suit almost immediately, and ever since that time they continued to publish their calendars year after year right into the post–World War II period.

The example of the two major dailies was soon followed by a number of weekly and regional papers. Thus by the interwar period such almanaclike calendars were being published by the *Katolikus Magyarok Vasárnapja* (Catholic Hungarians' Sunday), the *Bérmunkás* (Wage worker), *Új Előre* (New forward), *Lorain és Vidéke* (Lorain and its vicinity), *A Szív* (The heart), and many other papers; as well as by the Bethlen Home (the Hungarian Reformed Church's Home for the Orphaned and the Aged) in Ligonier, Pennsylvania. The latter, entitled *Ligonieri Bethlen Otthon Naptára* (The almanac of the Bethlen Home of Ligonier)—later simply *Bethlen Naptár* (Bethlen almanac)—was devoted largely to the affairs of the Hungarian Reformed (Calvinist) Church; while the *Históriás Kalendárium* (Historical almanac) of the *Katolikus Magyarok Vasárnapja* mostly to Catholic affairs, although with a much more extensive coverage of Hungarian historical, cultural, and literary topics.[20] Both of these calendar-almanacs are still being published today, although now they reach a much smaller audience and have much less influence on Hungarian-American developments than during the first half of this century.

A good example of the Hungarian-American calendar-almanac during the heyday of old-time Hungarian-American journalism is the *Szabadság Naptára* (*Szabadság*'s almanac) for the year 1931, which is also an excellent image of contemporary Hungarian-American society. Of its 194 pages only about 29 are devoted to the calendar proper and to such useful information as weather projections and popular historical dates. Of the remaining 165 pages, 33 are advertisements and 132 are devoted to essays, short stories, and poems. Of the twenty-five essays eight deal with topics of general information (including the discovery of the television), four with historical questions, and thirteen with various aspects of Hungarian-American life. Naturally, it is the latter that are most revealing about contemporary Hungarian-Americans, including their strange and painful existence between the "Old World," for which they long, and the "New World," which has given them so much, except the feeling of love and the feeling of security. Their eternal longing for the never-never land of the Mother Country that continues to live and to grow in their imagination is an ever-present and ever-recurring theme of these essays. And this also holds true for most of the short stories and poems authored by their own kind in America.[21]

Almost as revealing about Hungarian-American life of the inter-war period are the 106 advertisements in this calendar. The advertisers include many diverse institutions and individuals, from major American and Hungarian banks and corporations to Hungarian-American shop owners and professionals. From these advertisements it is amply clear that by 1930 Hungarian-Americans had risen far above the simple beginnings of the turn of the century. The ranks of the advertising professionals include physicians, dentists, lawyers, pharmacists, and various managers of financial institutions. The even greater number of small businessmen include dozens of trades, from butchers and innkeepers to barbers, undertakers, and travel agents. Moreover, the list of advertisers also includes a Hungarian-owned mortgage bank (Fekete & Sons of Chicago) and several other financial institutions with Hungarian managers and other financial experts. Equally interesting is the advertisement of the notary public Lajos Gartner of New York, who offers to legalize the stay of illegal immigrants, who apparently came in defiance of the quota system introduced in the 1920s.[22]

The calendar-almanacs of the various Hungarian-American newspapers do vary somewhat, but they all display the same characteristics as described above in conjunction with the *Szabadság Naptára*. The only real exception is the already-mentioned *Bethlen Naptár* of the Hungarian Reformed Church, which devotes itself year after year to the description of various congregations in the growing, but increasingly factionalized, Church. Although somewhat drab and uninspiring, these annual surveys are of considerable significance in portraying the status, failures, and achievements of the Hungarian Calvinists in the United States and Canada.

This also holds true for the anually updated list of Roman Catholic and Greek or Byzantine Catholic priests in North America found in the Catholic *Históriás Kalendárium*. Unlike the *Bethlen Naptár*,

however, the *Históriás Kalendárium* is more of a historical-literary
almanac than a narrow church register. As such it is much more
inspiring, but considerably less useful as a historical source for
Hungarian Catholicism in America.[23]

Anniversary or Jubilee Albums

Closely related to the calendar-almanacs were the anniversary or
jubilee albums of the Hungarian newspapers, fraternities, churches,
and other organizations. The number of these albums is vast, and
their sizes stretch from insignificant-looking pamphlets to folio-
sized, heavily illustrated, and highly decorated volumes. Such
albums were issued not only on the occasion of the numerous anniversary celebrations of the hundreds of Hungarian-American
churches, newspapers, and organizations, but also on such other
occasions as the visit to America of a prominent Hungarian personality, the dedication of Hungarian memorials in America, or the
celebration of an important event connected with Hungarian or
Hungarian-American history. Most of these albums—whether small
pamphlets or folio-sized volumes—are filled with photographs, lists
of personal names and biographies, and a profusion of unbecoming
and often offensive advertisements. But being listed in such an
album was of such significance to the average Hungarian-American
that he was willing to pay large sums to be included. Being left
out, on the other hand, was tantamount to a major personal insult
that usually resulted in long and lasting personal animosities, and
at times even in withdrawal from the membership of the offending
organization or the readership of the erring newspaper.[24]

While the small, pamphletlike "albums" give us very little information beyond a few factual details about an event or an organization, this does not hold true for the large anniversary albums
of the major newspapers and national fraternities. These larger
works—although naive and philiopietistic—still contain much useful and usable information about Hungarian-Americans and their
life in America. This is particularly true for the anniversary albums
of the *Szabadság* and the *Amerikai Magyar Népszava,* whose editors
always included articles and surveys that—however amateurish—
tried to show the overall achievements of the immigrants in their
adopted country. But these achievements are also reflected in the
included biographies, institutional histories, and perhaps even more,
in the enclosed advertisements.

One of the earliest and most impressive of such major anniversary publications is the decennial album of the *Amerikai Magyar Népszava*, published and edited by the *Népszava*'s successful editor, Géza D. Berkó, in 1910. Entitled *Az Amerikai Magyar Népszava Jubileumi Díszalbum, 1899–1909* (The jubilee album of the American Hungarian people's voice, 1899–1909), this work of over 400 pages reads like a capsulized version of the Hungarian-American past and life during the period of the great economic immigration.[25] After the customary introduction by the editor and the likewise ever-present messages from prominent Hungarian statesmen and politicians, we are presented with a number of popular essays on various aspects of the Hungarian-American past. These include essays on the *Népszava* itself, on Hungarian-American history, on the history of the Hungarian Catholic, Calvinist, and Greek (Byzantine) Catholic churches in America, as well as another two-dozen contributions (essays, short stories, reminiscences, and poems) on Hungarian experiences and achievements in the New World. The last seventy-odd pages of the album are taken up by advertisements and the brief biographical sketches of the most important advertisers. It is most interesting that of the 119 advertisers 36 call themselves "bankers" or "directors of banking houses," even though the great majority of them were simply owners of small travel agencies that arranged the tickets for immigrants, repatriates, and their families, and at the same time also exchanged Hungarian *korona*s for dollars, and vice versa.[26] This phenomenon, by the way (where small money exchange shops are called "banks" and small machine or repair shops "factories"), was a common feature of contemporary immigrant life. It was the direct result of the tendency among the immigrants to magnify their real or alleged successes in America in the eyes of their relatives, friends, and compatriots in the Old Country.

The above jubilee album of the *Népszava* was only the first of such grandiose undertakings by Hungarian-American newspapers and fraternities. It was followed by many others, including the *Golden Jubilee Album* (1950) of the same newspapers, whose bilingual title already foreshadows the partial switch to the English language. Similar to its predecessor, this work of over 300 pages also contains the usual assortment of greetings, advertisements, and informative essays on Hungarian-American life and experiences.[27] These include a short history of Hungarians in America by the Rev. Edmund Vasváry, the "dean" of old-time historians of the Hungarian-American past, a similar essay on the *Népszava,* and a number of short essays on such institutions and organizations as the Hungarian Committee, the Hungarian Section of the Voice of America, the American Hungarian Federation, the Hungarian-American press, the Hungarian National Sport Federation in Exile, the American Hungarian Relief Action, the American Hungarian Reformed Federation, the Bethlen Home for Orphans and the Aged, Hungarian-American college and university professors, and Hungarian-American artists and musicians.[28] All in all, although displaying the usual degree of amateurism, this semicentennial album of the *Népszava* is a mine of information both for the facts and the psychology of Hungarian-American life.

Although outwardly perhaps even more imposing, the nearly 400-page golden-jubilee album of the Cleveland-based *Szabadság,* entitled *Hungarians in America* (1941), is actually less useful as a source book of the Hungarian-American past. Edited by John Kőrösfőy, this work is conspicuous among such major memorial albums of the first half of this century in that it is completely in English.[29] This can only be explained by the fact that it appeared during the dark days of World War II, when Hungarian-Americans—like all other immigrants and their descendants from the enemy states—had to be extra careful to prove their loyalty to the United States. Its content consists of two brief essays, "Hungarians in America" and the *"Szabadság,* 1891–1941,"[30] and hundreds of brief biographical sketches of Hungarian-Americans. These sketches are organized under the headings of various Hungarian-American settlements throughout the United States, each group being preceded by a short note on each of these settlements. In examining the content of this volume, one has the suspicion that inclusion in this work depended more on one's ability to pay than on one's achievements in Hungarian-American life.

This also holds true for many of the other similar publications, including the two-volume memorial album entitled *Magyar-Amerika irásban és képekben* (Hungarian-America in words and pictures), put out by the editor-publisher of the weekly *St. Louis és Vidéke* (St. Louis and vicinity) in 1937–1939,[31] and the numerous silver- and golden-anniversary albums of the major fraternal organizations, such as the Verhovay Association (1936), the Rákóczi Aid Association (1913, 1938), the American Hungarian Reformed Federation (1921, 1940), and the American Sick-Aid and Life Insurance Association

(1942), generally known as the "Bridgeport Federation." Although differing in size, approach, coverage, and the quality of their content, these memorial albums display some or most of the features described above. Next to them, the average working-class Hungarian-American household may only have had a Bible and perhaps a few examples of contemporary Hungarian-American literature (mostly poetry and short stories) whose themes and quality conformed to the oft-mentioned cultural level of the immigrants and their offspring.

All in all, Hungarian-American newspapers, almanacs, and yearbooks fulfilled a most useful function during the heyday of the great economic immigration. Like the churches and the fraternities, these publications carried the message of hope and the feeling of belonging to the forlorn immigrants scattered throughout the northeastern United States. They kept their language and culture going, they served as bonds of unity among them, as well as between them and their homeland, and thus made their lives more bearable and livable. A similar role was also played by Hungarian-American literature, which—perhaps precisely because it was simple and naive—was able to express the feelings and satisfy the needs of those hardy immigrants who, in spite of their successes, remained suspended between two worlds and were torn between their love for their new and their old homelands.

Chapter Seven

From World War I
to World War II:
Becoming Americans

The immigrants' continued attachment to Hungary was rather natural, particularly in light of the tendency until the interwar period to regard their stay in America as temporary. But this natural attachment was also fostered by the Hungarian government, which tried to keep their desire to return home alive and also wished to use the immigrants for its own national-political goals. The government realized that it was really beyond its power to stem the tide of emigration, even though it was increasingly viewed by some as a national castastrophe.

Attempts to control emigration from Hungary reach back to the early 1880s, when the Hungarian Parliament—giving in to the demands of the large landowners who were losing their workers—passed the country's first emigration law (1881). While neither this nor the subsequent emigration laws (1903, 1909) went so far as to deny the right of free emigration, they increasingly reflected the government's desire to control this exodus and to exercise some degree of influence over the nature and composition of the emigrants.

By the early 1900s another factor was added: considerations of national welfare as reflected in the ethnic-national composition of those departing. While the great majority of the early economic emigrants were non-Magyars (Germans, Slovaks, Ruthenians, etc.), and as such many Hungarian leaders regarded their exodus as desirable, this was no longer true after the turn of the century. By the early 1900s the Magyars made up the largest single bloc of the emigrants. The loss of their own kind in such great numbers in a situation where they hardly constituted half of the country's population made the Hungarian political and national leaders virtually frantic. Some of them began to speak of emigration as the death march of the Magyars toward self-extinction. These ideas then were picked up and spread all over by poets, writers, and journalists, who made the phenomenon of mass emigration into an issue of life or death for their nation.

While these frantic clarion calls were based more on fear than on the realistic assessment of the situation (for the losses by the Magyars were far less than presumed and popularized), they did affect the thinking of most Hungarians of whatever ideological or political persuasion. The complacency and boastful pride that had characterized the decade of Hungary's millennial celebrations (i.e., the Hungarian conquest of A.D. 896) were now replaced by a feeling of fear and desperation. And this despair was all the greater as the government knew fully well that—given the freedom of movement across state lines that characterized the age of economic liberalism—it was really beyond its powers to stem this exodus. Thus it had to come up with an alternative program that, while accepting emigration as inevitable, would try to keep the notion of repatriation alive among the emigrants. It was thus that the semiofficial "American Action" came into being. Initiated in 1904, it was only the first of several such efforts by successive Hungarian governments to make the best of an unavoidable situation.

The "American Action"

The American Action was developed in a secret program plan in 1903 and then implemented with very little success between 1904 and 1914. It had three main goals: (1) to retain the fidelity of the immigrants with the ultimate goal of repatriation; (2) to neutralize the anti-Hungarian agitation of the non-Magyar immigrants from Hungary; and (3) to tone down the Hungarian immigrants' strong anti-Habsburg agitation.[1] The latter goal was deemed essential by many Hungarian national leaders because by the early 1900s the majority of them viewed the somewhat fragile dualistic arrangements between Austria and Hungary as the sole guarantee for historic Hungary's territorial integrity. Without Austro-Hungarian dualism—so they believed—independent Hungary could hardly retain its fringe territories, inhabited mostly by non-Magyar nationalities.

The American Action's goals were to be achieved by extending the Hungarian government's influence (if not control) over Hungarian-American churches, ethnic organizations, and the press, largely through a system of subsidies. The Action was particularly geared to the parishes and congregations of the established churches, which were correctly deemed to be the most widespread of the immigrants' institutions. Moreover, it was hoped that their control could be undertaken through the mediation of their respective mother churches in Hungary. While this goal proved to be basically insurmountable in the case of the Catholics (because of the international organization of the Catholic Church), it was much more successful in the case of the Protestants and the Greek Catholics. Both of these were "national" churches and both had close ties to Hungary and the Hungarian hierarchy, although the situation in the latter case was complicated by the fact that the great majority of the Greek Catholics were not Magyars but Ruthenians.

Insofar as the American Action had any success at all, it proved to be most successful with the Calvinists. They were all Magyar-Hungarians, they had close and deep ties to Hungary and Hungarian history, and, what is at least as important, the welfare and livelihood of their pastors depended solely on the financial well-being and generosity of the individual congregations. The latter consideration made the pastors of the Calvinists congregations the most willing listeners to offers of financial subsidy from the Hungarian government, particularly when this subsidy concerned not only the mortgages of their church buildings but also their own salaries. Conditions of such support, however, included the acceptance of the Hungarian Mother Church, resisting Americanization espoused by the rival Reformed and Presbyterian churches of the United States, and keeping the flames of repatriation alive among the immigrants. Many pastors accepted this offer, partially because the goals were in line with their own hopes and aspirations. Yet, as already discussed above, these same conditions also became seeds of contention and dissension among Hungarian-Americans. Moreover, once leaked to the public, they also aroused the wrath of the United States government.

The Problem of Loyalty during World War I

After the outbreak of World War I Hungarian-Americans found themselves in an increasingly difficult situation. Unable to understand the real cause of that world conflict, they viewed their mother country's participation in it as a struggle of righteousness. They were tied to Hungary emotionally and ideologically, and the real causes and issues in the war had no meaning for them. Thus, although realizing that American sympathies lay with the Entente Powers, the Hungarian-American community went into action almost to a man to aid the mother country. Many young men volunteered to return home to serve in the Hungarian armed forces. (The sea blockade by the Entente prevented most of them from doing so.) Others, including the large fraternities and other associations, initiated campaigns to collect funds for Hungary. Still others purchased Hungarian war bonds. In a similar vein, Hungarian-American newspapers discussed Hungary's involvement in the war in great detail and expressed the hope that the mother country would emerge victorious. At the same time, Hungarian-American churches routinely held special prayer services for Hungary's victory. In doing all this, the Hungarian-American community was basically one with its German counterpart, whose activities and efforts were likewise directed toward justifying the righteousness of the German involvement in the war.[2]

These efforts, however, were met by the increasing disapproval of the largely Anglophile American society as well as by the anti-Hungarian and anti-German agitation of the non-Hungarian and non-German immigrants from the Austro-Hungarian Empire. As the war progressed, so did the visible Anglophile tendency of the American public. It was accompanied by the growth of the so-called "Americanization Movement," which manifested itself partially in the growing suspicion of the loyalty of the immigrants from the states of the Central Powers, and partially in the rising demands for their quick assimilation.

The situation became much graver during late 1916 and early 1917, when America's involvement in the war on the Entente side was all but declared. Then, following the United States declaration of war on April 6, 1917, it became critical, for the growing war hysteria manifested itself in hate campaigns against immigrants from the enemy states.

The sympathies of Hungarian-Americans remained unchanged throughout the war. In light of the above developments, however, the expression of these sympathies did change, which is also reflected in their press. During the early phase of the war, Hungarian-American editors openly espoused the alleged justice and righteousness of their mother country's cause. By 1916, however, they became increasingly cautious. Then, after the United States entry into the war, they ceased all pro-Hungarian agitation. They did this, however, not out of conviction but out of fear. It was the fear of reprisals that made them caution their readers to keep their views to themselves and hope for the best. By late 1916 and early 1917, the pressure against Hungarian-American newspapers and organizations became so great that they found themselves compelled to formulate various declarations of loyalty to the United States and the Entente cause. To give some visible manifestation of this "loyalty," Hungarian-Americans undertook to organize loyalty parades. They also began to celebrate American national holidays. This phenomenon was new to them, for up to then they would celebrate only Hungarian national holidays. Further to demonstrate their "loyalty," Hungarian-American associations and fraternities also began to buy American Liberty Bonds. By 1918 some Hungarian-American leaders established an "American Hungarian Loyalty League." In addition to proving the alleged—but hardly real—loyalty of Hungarian-Americans to the Entente cause, this League was also intended to serve as an instrument for "saving Hungary" after the war, which was not going well for the mother country. Whether organized of their own free will, or "at the direct request of the U.S. Government"—as claimed by some[3]—the Loyalty League proved to be far from popular among Hungarian-Americans. In fact, when the leaders of the various local organizations voted to join the League, many of their members openly rebelled against this decision.

Only the socialists and communists among Hungarian-Americans refused to support the war effort, both the Hungarian effort at the beginning and the United States effort toward the end of the war. But as they represented only a relatively isolated portion of the Hungarian-American public, their voice and influence were also limited. Moreover, their antiwar propaganda did not endear them to the strongly pro-Entente American public. In fact, in the increasingly anticommunist atmosphere of the postwar years (i.e., the "Red Scare"), these socialist-communist groups fared even worse than did those who—overtly or covertly—continued to sympathize with the mother country.

However one tries to re-create the painful spiritual-emotional struggle that filled the minds and lives of Hungarian-Americans during the fateful years of the war, it is really impossible to do so. Their primary emotional ties were with the country of their birth. Yet, many of them had also developed attachments to America.

And this holds true even for those who still hoped to return to Hungary. For others—who constituted a small but ever-increasing percentage of the immigrants—the United States was their permanent new homeland. It was here where their children were born, and it was here where they too wished to spend the remaining years of their lives. To see their two countries on the opposite side of a large world conflict put them into a vile and impossible situation. To quote a contemporary observer:

The fact that fate had endowed . . . [us] with two homelands now fell upon us like a lash that tore into our very souls. Not only were we forced to cease our noble efforts to aid our brethren, but we were also compelled . . . to purchase American War Bonds, to work in factories manufacturing war materials . . . and to shed our blood [fighting against our brethren]. . . . On top of this all, Hungarian ethnic islands found themselves in an alien world that surrounded them with a fermenting stream of suspicion and hate. . . . If there ever was a period of trials for our souls, nerves, hearts . . . and minds, and for our loyalties to our new country, and unshakable love for the land of our birth . . . , then those were the times.[4]

And what was worse about all this was that these trials and tribulations did not cease with the end of the war. The war was followed by a series of punitive treaties that, in Hungary's case, ended in the country's dismemberment, including the loss of large Magyar-inhabited territories, which also affected the lives and fates of many Hungarian-Americans.

The Impact of Trianon: The Decision to Stay Permanently

The treaty that was signed in the Petite Trianon Palace of Versailles on June 4, 1920, was the harshest among the treaties that followed World War I. On the basis of this treaty (known as the Treaty of Trianon) historic Hungary lost 71.4 percent of her territory and 63.6 percent of her population, and of the four beneficiary states Rumania alone received a larger share (39,000 square miles) of the country's former territory than was left to Hungary (35,900 square miles). While some of these losses could be justified on the basis of ethnic-linguistic considerations, this was not true for a sizable portion of the lost territories, which also involved the transfer of about 3.5 million Magyar-speaking Hungarians to the new "succession states," the majority of whom lived directly adjacent to the new frontiers.

The impact of these losses upon the contemporary Hungarian mind was devastating, and this was equally true for Hungarian-Americans. The latter experienced this shock effect while still under the impact of the emotionally exacting experiences of the war years.[5] On top of this all came the unpleasant news that the immediate homelands of a great many of them were placed under foreign rule. This phenomenon was the direct result of the fact that the largest percentage of the immigrants came from the country's ethnically mixed outlying areas. Although the end of the war reopened the possibility of repatriation, many of them had no more homeland to return to. Their villages and towns were now part of new states, with strange names, dominated by nationalities who for centuries had been minorities in the Kingdom of Hungary.

This factor alone would have changed most of the immigrants' basic desire to repatriate after the war. But this was not the only reason for their ultimate decision to remain, however difficult it was for them to acknowledge this fact even to themselves. At least as important were various economic and social considerations, whose significance would have been more pronounced had the immigrants' decision to stay not been naturally attributed to the first of these causes.

The fact of the matter was that, by the early 1920s, the majority of the originally "temporary immigrants" had second thoughts about repatriating permanently. During their stay in the United States they had become used to the amenities of a rapidly advancing industrial society. Thus, notwithstanding all the accompanying drawbacks and vexations, America still appeared to offer more to them than did the land of their birth. Hungary in those days was still primarily an agricultural country with an exclusive social structure, which still lay heavily on the lower social classes. Many of the immigrants have also established permanent roots in America, and did so without being conscious of it until having to face the decision to repatriate or not. They had acquired homes, established families, had children born to them in the United States, and a number of them had also become owners of automobiles. Moreover—and this is equally significant—they have tasted the benefits of a democratically oriented society where, notwithstanding their differences with

Anglo-Saxon Americans, they felt much more at ease than in the still class-conscious world of their homeland. A good number of them did not even appreciate the extent of their own transformation until returning to Hungary. Only back home did they realize the depth of their attachment to the American way of life, and then returned once more to stay permanently. But many of them returned also much poorer, having lost their accumulated capital in Hungary's postwar inflation. These had to start over again.

Another factor that may have kept many of the immigrants from repatriating after the war was the growing effort of the American industrial establishment to keep their workers. This became particularly evident toward the end of the war, and continued for a few years thereafter, with the aim of keeping industrial wages on a low level. This effort manifested itself also in advertisements in immigrant papers promising toleration, good treatment, and at times even free lots for their homes and garden plots.

Notwithstanding the problems they faced in Europe and the efforts to keep them in America, the immediate postwar years (up to 1924) still saw the repatriation of perhaps 32,000 Hungarian immigrants, three-fourths of whom were men. But this repatriation was largely offset by the renewed immigration trend of the same years. Available statistics on these immigrants are confusing and often contradictory, yet we can safely assume that the same years witnessed the immigration of almost as many Hungarians as the number of those returning. (There were between 28,000 and 29,000 immigrants up to 1928, with perhaps another 15,000 up to the United States entrance into World War II.) The situation is complicated by the fact that many of the Hungarians now came from the neighboring new states, that many of those who came from Hungary were not classified as Hungarians (e.g., Magyar Jews), and by the sizable illegal immigration after the exclusionary immigration laws. Of those coming before the Immigration Restriction Act of 1924, which limited the number of annual immigrants from Hungary to 473, many were returning repatriates. But as over half of these immigrants were women, it is evident that a good number of the repatriates still chose to stay in Hungary in spite of the many problems they encountered in the physically truncated, economically dislocated, intellectually and spiritually dazed, and politically and socially backward-looking country of their birth. But the repatriates—whether staying or returning once more—constituted only a small fraction of the total number of immigrants and their descendants in the United States.[6] A large majority of the Hungarian-Americans had decided to stay in America without the experience of repatriation. And this decision to remain permanently was unavoidably accompanied by a psychological reorientation that ultimately turned the temporary immigrants into permanent settlers. In coming to this decision, however, the immigrants also had to alter their way of life. Instead of pursuing a policy of self-isolation, they now had to strive to become part of the mainstream of American life. In other words, however they may have disliked this idea or feared the results, they now were compelled to seek the path toward becoming full-fledged Americans—at least within the limits permitted by their attachment to the past.

Americanization and Adjustment to Permanent Settlement

In line with the immigrants' original resolve to return to Hungary, before World War I only about 15 percent of the Hungarians became United States citizens. By 1920 this percentage rose to 28.4 percent, and then by 1930 it reached 55.7 percent.[7] Admittedly a sizable percentage of this growth can be attributed to the increase in the size of the native-born generation and to the slow thinning out of the ranks of the earliest immigrants. But another significant factor in this increase was the success of the so-called Americanization movement, which began during the latter phase of the war and picked up speed during the 1920s.

The main exponent of this move toward naturalization was Mór Cukor (1869–1957), a noted Hungarian-American lawyer and community leader in New York, who organized the Hungarian American Citizenship League in December of 1917. He urged his compatriots to take out their American citizenship papers, pointing out that "our patriotic spirit and feelings will in no way diminish if we adjust to the country on whose soil we have found our happiness."[8] As Cukor's clarion call coincided with increased pressures for Americanization from the society of the host country, the revived American Hungarian Federation (founded in 1906) also became involved in this movement. In 1918 it organized a "Congress on Americanization" (September 18), inviting the director of the United States Office of Education to be its main speaker, who then gave "many useful ideas for implementation" to the attending delegates.[9] Following the Federation's leadership, soon many other local and regional organizations took up the cause of citizenship. Thus, by the 1920s, the seeking or acceptance of United States citizenship became a rather common phenomenon among the immigrants, impeded at times only by their linguistic shortcomings, which prevented many of them from passing the required examination. This change of heart by Hungarian-Americans reflected their new resolve to stay in America, as well as their desire to begin participating in American political life. For the first time in their immigrant history Hungarian-Americans began to vote in great numbers, although this voting was still done largely through the typical bloc-vote system that characterized the immigrant communities in those days even more than now.

Accepting the idea of settling permanently in the United States also altered the thinking and way of life of Hungarian-Americans. These changes included decisions concerning their work, their place of residence, and their attitude toward the maintenance of Hungarian-American organizations and the community in general. Prior to this conscious decision to make their stay permanent the primary consideration of the immigrants was to earn and to save as much as possible, even if this meant working under the most unsafe and grueling conditions and living in dilapidated boarding houses amidst the already described circumstances. They were willing to delay the rewards of their labor, in return for the promise of a better and brighter future at home. But now, as that projected "future" evaporated, their attitude toward their work and immediate surroundings changed. They now wished to work and to live only under much-improved conditions, even if this meant giving up their jobs for less well paying ones, and spending a considerably larger portion of their earnings for their livelihoods. This resulted in a gradual internal migration among Hungarian-Americans. They began to leave their jobs in the mines, moving into the nearby larger towns and cities, where they accepted jobs in factories, shops, and service establishments. Many of them also bought their own homes and established their own shops in the increasingly larger Hungarian quarters of these settlements. As a result of this migration, the Hungarian quarters in some of the larger northeastern cities grew into the well-known "Little Hungaries" of the interwar period, with their multitude of shops, businesses, financial establishments, churches and synagogues, business and social clubs, political and cultural organizations, theaters and bars, editorial offices and printing presses, and occasionally even some college or university programs in Hungarian studies.

Perhaps the most important of these changes was in the living habits of Hungarian-Americans. Whereas prior to World War I the typical Hungarian immigrant lived in a boarding house, renting a bed or the right to sleep in a bed for a certain period of the day, in the early 1920s he bought or built his own family home and was hoping to establish his own business. Although most Hungarian-Americans eventually ended up in large cities, they seldom settled for long in large apartment complexes—except perhaps in certain sections of New York City. Most of them being of rural background, they naturally disliked the confinement of a typical urban apartment house. Moreover, they had a powerful urge to own their own homes, along with a small plot of land where they could practice their almost innate inclination to cultivate the land. The result was the birth of a whole series of villagelike towns on the peripheries or in specific selected areas of large cities such as New York, Cleveland, Pittsburgh, Detroit, Chicago, Passaic, Trenton, New Brunswick, Youngstown, Toledo, and others.

One of the most typical and best known of such Hungarian urban settlements was the Upper Buckeye Road Hungarian Community of Cleveland. In its heyday during the interwar and immediate post–World War II periods, this community was a world in itself. The side streets of the Upper Buckeye Road, stretching through thirty city blocks and at least ten to fifteen blocks on either side, were filled with many thousands of comfortable one-family homes with structural patterns and decorations (e.g., the front porches and arcades) that distinctively reflected the cultural heritage of their builders. Although now mostly in disrepair and largely taken over by the rapidly expanding local black community, these Upper Buckeye Road homes are mute witnesses to the work and willpower of those many tens of thousands of Hungarians who have opted to make America their permanent new homeland, and who have raised at least two generations of native-born Hungarian-Americans in these formerly beautiful homes of a bygone age.[10]

If their beautifully built and neatly kept family homes have lifted the Hungarian immigrants out of their lowly position as "boarding house dwellers," so did their new dress and new social and cultural habits. Hoping to live down the derogatory "Hunky" image (which, probably, lay more heavily on the Slovaks, Croats, Ruthenians, and other less-literate nationalities of the former Austro-Hungarian state), the permanently settled and naturalized Hungarian-Americans also made a conscious effort at least to look and act like native-born Anglo-Saxon Americans, if they were unable to speak English as well as the latter. Their new dress and new social and cultural habits were meant to serve precisely this goal, although many of their related activities were still done almost exclusively in Hungarian clubs, organizations, and churches. Their native-born children, however, went further in this assimilation process. Their speech patterns did not distinguish them from other urban working-class Americans, and as such they were able to join organizations outside the immediate Hungarian-American circles.

Social Polarization in Hungarian-American Society

This Americanization-assimilation process, which finally rooted the immigrants firmly in American soil, was accompanied by an increasing social polarization of the Hungarian-American community. Before World War I, social differences—with the exception of the very small number of intelligentsia, such as clergymen, teachers, journalists, writers, and artists—were either nonexistent or hardly perceptible. This was the result of the relatively homogeneous social-economic background of the immigrants and of the fact that, irrespective of their background (peasant, unskilled worker, skilled worker, etc.), in America they were all forced to join the same unskilled or semiskilled industrial labor force. These conditions then soon molded them into a single underprivileged "ethno-class," bound together by its common roots, common language, and the common misery of its members.[11]

After transplanting themselves from the mining places and boarding houses to the cities and privately owned homes, however, the immigrants found themselves face to face with new opportunities for economic and social advancement. Many of them were able to take advantage of these opportunities either by opening up their own shops, businesses, or manufacturing establishments and making it financially or by furthering their education and moving up into the white-collar category. Given these opportunities for advancement and the unavoidable success of many who took advantage of them, it was inevitable that the formerly homogenous Hungarian-American immigrant working class would break up into several subclasses, based on newly acquired economic status or intellectual-educational position.

This process of polarization was further enhanced by the coming of the much more highly educated immigrants of the interwar period. Although fewer in number, they included many highly skilled professionals, most of whom could never have fitted into the narrow confines of the low-statused Hungarian-American community.

Discounting the returnees of the early 1920s, the interwar intellectual-professional immigrants came in a number of separate waves and included several different types. The most significant groups among them were (1) the left-leaning, mostly noncommunist, intellectuals who were involved in the revolutions of 1918–1919, and who for this reason were compelled to leave the country and find a haven in the United States; (2) the unemployed professionals (engineers, physicians, scientists, lawyers, teachers, economists, journalists, etc.) who were unable to find employment commensurate with their education in the economically crippled and dislocated Hungary of the 1920s and 1930s; and (3) the highly skilled and internationally acclaimed scientists, social scientists, artists, writers, mathematicians, and composers—many of them of Jewish origin or outspoken critics of Nazi Germany—who left Hungary during the 1930s because it was falling progressively under German influence. It was the latter group that brought the greatest amount of talent in the shortest possible time to the United States, on the basis of which later authors felt compelled to speculate about the "mystery of the Hungarian talent."[12]

While enriching American society, the coming of the interwar immigrants also increased social and cultural polarization among Hungarian-Americans. The newcomers' education and cultural and social background made it impossible for them—even if they would have wanted to—to fit into the relatively simple world of the Hungarian-American community. In fact, for this very reason they wanted to seek their fortunes in native American society. And if they were unable to do so, it was regarded as a sign of their "defeat." Whether among the successful or the "defeated" ones, they generally looked down on the old-timers and criticized their naive and "lowly" social and cultural manifestations—often with malicious irony. Given this attitude, a real mixing between the old-timers and the newcomers seldom took place, even when the latter were compelled to make their living in and off the established Hungarian communities of North America (e.g., some of the less successful physicians, artists, journalists, or lawyers turned into notary publics, travel agents, and money-sending agents). Even the latter would only establish closer contacts with the few intellectuals of the old community (e.g. clergymen, journalists), and perhaps with the financially successful and socially rising members of the second generation. But whatever their position within the community, the latter were still highly disillusioned and disappointed both with the "dumb laborers" of their own nationality and with American society, which—so they believed—prevented them from "competing with American professional men in American neighborhoods."[13]

Those with international fame and high social standing in Europe before their immigration made no contacts, unless by chance, with the Hungarian-American communities. They would simply merge into American society and their professional class. This was naturally easier for those in the natural and physical sciences and the technical fields than for those in the social sciences, the humanities, or law— the latter of which was totally untransferable to American society. But as American society in those days was still less appreciative of the intellectuals than contemporary European society, not even those in the latter groups were fully satisfied. They missed the European intellectual world and the way of life that went along with it. Their disappointment, however, could in no way be compared to that of the "defeated" intellectual whose world was perforce limited to the ethnic community. The latter felt very bitter and tried to compensate themselves by emphasizing their real or allegedly exalted social origins. The most common approach was to claim membership in the nobility—a "solution" that was practiced even by some of the most successful intellectuals who later made it in American society. Being a member of the nobility still carried some weight with Americans, who were fascinated by it. Thus at times some of these intellectual immigrants tried to pass themselves off as barons or counts. In general, however, most of them were satisfied with simply adding the prefix of nobility to their names. Thus, once across the Atlantic, many common Hungarian names blossomed forth with *de*'s (Latin and French) and *von*'s (German).[14] (This practice, by the way, was also pursued by many of the post–World War II immigrants and 56-ers for the same self-compensatory psychological reasons.)

The numerically small but intellectually significant Hungarian intellectual immigration of the 1930s brought almost inestimable gains to America in such diverse fields as classical music, psychology, social theory, physics, biology, and atomic theory. These gains, however, added little to the everyday life in the "Little Hungaries" of America's great northeastern cities. There life continued in its simplest form. It consisted mostly of hard work, punctuated by numerous cultural events reminiscent of village life in Hungary, and of a struggle for economic well-being, social acceptance, and Americanization without at the same time total de-Hungarianization of the second generation. All this was accompanied by a struggle for Hungary, or rather by what the actively involved Hungarian-Americans believed to be Hungary's national interests. And here the most important single unifying factor was the injustice of the Treaty of Trianon, about which all Hungarians were of one mind. This included everyone from Europe to America, from the top intellectuals to the simplest workers, from Catholics and Protestants to Jews and atheists, and from those farthest to the left on the political spectrum to those farthest right.

Political Struggles for Hungary

Although the latter part of World War I and the immediate postwar years saw a rapid rise in the trend to acquire American citizenship, Hungarian-Americans were still far from the point where they would have wished or dared to venture into the field of American domestic politics. While an increasing number of them voted—and did so mostly for the Democratic party—their political energies throughout the interwar period were really channeled into purely Hungarian causes. Next to making a decent living, helping the mother country was still their number-one goal. They were absolutely shocked by what befell Hungary after the war, and undoing the Treaty of Trianon was of primary consideration to them. In this goal they worked hand in hand with the representatives of the Hungarian government, even though Hungary's conservative social and political system was far from appealing to them. They likewise marshaled their resources and enthusiasm to aid their brethren in Hungary in every possible way. They organized drives to send packages to Hungary, dug into their pockets to send financial help to their relatives and friends, made efforts to try to undo Hungary's economic isolation via the United States government, and, above all, cooperated with various Hungarian revisionist organizations to get a hearing for the Hungarian complaints concerning the terms imposed upon them after the war.

In these efforts they were strongly encouraged both by the Hungarian government as well as by various social and political organizations and other power groups in Hungary, who suddenly "discovered" the Hungarian-Americans as a possible source of help to their country. In doing so, however, they generally far overestimated the real economic weight and actual political significance of the Hungarian-Americans, who hitherto were not very highly regarded by them. Having the total number of immigrants from Hungary in mind, these organizations and their spokesmen generally spoke of a million and a half or two million Hungarians in America, and did so at the time when the United States census of 1920 showed that the Magyar-speaking immigrants and their native-born (but still also Magyar-speaking) children totaled less than half a million (495,845). [15]

The Hungarian government also made the mistake of overestimating the significance of the immigrants. It sent delegation after delegation, headed by some of Hungary's most prominent personalities, including the representatives of the three most powerful religious groups. These included the Catholics, who were represented by the noted Jesuit orator and publicist Pater Béla Bangha; the Calvinists, who dispatched their most influential churchman, Bishop Dezső Balthazár of Debrecen; and the Jews, whose emissary was Ferenc Székely, a relative of the prominent Hungarian-American journalist and editor Izsó Székely of the *Amerikai Magyar Népszava.*

Efforts were also made to put political pressure on the United States government via the Hungarian-American community, even though the community's weight was still most minimal. As a result of this effort, in 1919 the revived American Hungarian Federation presented a memorandum to the United States Senate that contained Hungary's position on the territorial conflict with its new neighbors. The document was drafted by the historian Eugene Pivány, who, after his repatriation in 1915, returned once more to the United States in 1919, specifically for the purpose of leading the Hungarian-Americans' anti-Trianon crusade. [16] This was followed by a major demonstration in Washington, D.C. (March 29, 1920), organized by Géza Berkó, the editor of the *Amerikai Magyar Népszava,* demanding the application of the Wilsonian principle of national self-determination to all of the arbitrarily detached Hungarian territories; by efforts to pull all related Hungarian activities under the umbrella of a yet to be organized "World Federation of Hungarians"; by numerous other demonstrations, petitions, and organizational attempts throughout the early 1920s; and then—after realizing the futility of their endeavors—by a gradual decline of Hungarian-American activism.[17]

Besides a lack of visible results for their efforts, this decline in the mid-1920s was also the result of two other factors: first, the growing number of rivalries that channeled an increasing amount of Hungarian-American energies into personal and group conflicts; and second, the increasing realization by the whole community that their actions were aiding a political regime in Hungary that was far removed from the ideals of democracy and personal freedom that they cherished so much. In this realization they were also influenced by the reports of the political immigrants of the revolutions of 1918–1919, who described their experiences rather subjectively soon after their arrival in the United States in the early 1920s. Particularly damaging were the reports about the so-called "White Terror" that followed the overthrow of Béla Kún's communist regime (March-August 1919). Because of the very heavy participation of Jewish intellectuals in that regime, its overthrow was accompanied by anti-Semitic outbursts throughout Hungary.

Not even after the decline of postwar political activism did the Trianon question cease to be the number-one political issue among Hungarian-Americans. It remained a front-page issue in most of their newspapers and in much of contemporary Hungarian-American literature. But, seeing the futility of their efforts, by the mid-1920s Hungarian-Americans began to channel an increasing portion of their energies into the problem of survival as a national minority in the United States. This remained true for all of the late 1920s and 1930s, and it was also one of the two dominant themes both at the much-heralded Hungarian National Congress of Buffalo (May 1929) and at the two Hungarian World Congresses organized in Budapest by the World Federation of Hungarians in 1929 (August 22–24) and 1938 (August 16–19), respectively. Thus, while at these congresses every representative denounced Trianon, and although lip service was also paid to such more traditional problems as the question of repatriation and the ways and means to utilize Hungarian-American economic and political resources for the enhancement of Hungarian national goals, most of the efforts at these meetings were devoted to such more mundane problems as the question of the survival of the Magyar language in America, the preservation of Hungarian or at least bilingual schools, the availability of good textbooks for native-born Hungarian-American children, the survival of the Hungarian-American press and Hungarian-American culture in general, and the ways and means to strengthen the emotional ties of the Americanized second generation to the mother country. These questions, by the way, have remained constantly recurring problems for the Hungarian-American community ever since, in spite of the infusion of new blood into the community in the decades following World War II. [18]

Attempts to Raise Ethnic Consciousness

The struggle for the retention of Hungarian identity and Hungarian affiliation of the native-born second generation became particularly critical during the 1930s, when the latter began to outnumber their immigrant elders. Whereas in 1930 the two groups constituted basically the same percentage of the Hungarian-American community (274,400 immigrants versus 271,840 native born), by 1940 the latter had a distinct numerical superiority over the former (437,080 versus 299,228). Moreover, by this time a sizable percentage of the immigrants were retired and aging, and as such of secondary importance for the future of the community. [19]

The issue became critical much beyond the significance of the normal gap between the immigrant and native-born generations because of the inferiority complex experienced by Hungarian-Americans, and in particular by their native-born children in American society. This feeling of inferiority—which naturally did not apply to those highly trained scientists and other intellectuals who immediately acquired prestigious and well-paying positions—was a natural by-product of the fact that the majority of the immigrants were people of humble origin. They had left Hungary with the values of a rural society and came into a highly industrialized society, where they were forced to occupy the lowest rungs on the social ladder. The natural feeling of fear and inferiority stemming from

this rural background was augmented by the "rejection" they suffered at the hands of native Americans, by the latter's total lack of
knowledge about Hungary and the Hungarians, and by their tendency to generalize about the immigrants on the basis of their
experiences with some of the early hapless newcomers. Nor did it
help the situation that the Hungarian immigrants were part of the
so-called "new immigration" of the late nineteenth and early twentieth century, which brought many millions to the United States
who were judged to be "undesirable" by the Anglo-Saxon "nativ-
ists." The exclusionary immigration laws of the early 1920s were
also directed against these "undesirable" new immigrants, and thus
added to their feeling of being stamped as lower-class human beings.

Being so categorized was painful to the Hungarian immigrants,
but it did not affect them as much as it did their native-born sons
and daughters. The latter did not wish to segregate themselves into
the separate and distinct immigrant world of their elders. Thus,
when they reached their teens, they began to reject the life, ways,
and even the language of their forebears. While obliged to speak
Hungarian with their parents—many of whom never learned English beyond the bare essentials—they refused to use other than
English in public. They also rejected their parents' social and cultural
values.

This growing chasm between themselves and their children was
naturally very painful to the immigrants. It increased their own
feelings of inferiority and confused them with respect to their own
goals and desires. On the one hand they wished their children to
make it in American society. On the other hand they dreaded losing
their children to an alien world. In other words, they wanted their
children and grandchildren to remain Hungarian, to appreciate the
values and traditions they themselves held in high regard, but at
the same time they also wished to see them successful and satisfied
with life.

As evident from the pages of contemporary Hungarian-American
newspapers and from the proceedings of Hungarian-American organizations, the immigrants became particularly desperate in their
search for solutions during the 1930s. The picture that emerges
from these debates consists basically of the recognition that their
Hungarian traditions had little meaning to their children; that in
order to retain their sons and daughters for themselves and for their
institutions, it was they who would have to adjust their Hungarian

identities to American realities; and that the most they could hope to achieve in this matter was to retain in their children at least some interest for matters concerning Hungary and the Hungarians by proving to them that "the Hungarians are not a lowly nation."[20] They hoped to do this by bringing them into contact with "real Hungarian culture and spirituality." Thus the conclusion of this debate was that the Americanization of their children was inevitable. Yet it was still possible to retain them up to a certain point, but only by demonstrating to them that they had no reason to be ashamed of their Hungarian background. The result was a renewed effort to reconquer some of the interest and affection of the second generation, but with methods totally different from those used in the early phase of this struggle.

In the early days of mass immigration the newcomers tried to compensate for their feelings of inferiority by stressing both to themselves and to their children, beyond any sense of realism, the alleged superiority of the "Magyar race" and the supposedly unusually "glorious and heroic" nature of Hungarian history. Now efforts were made to bring the younger generation into contact with the truly valuable aspects of Hungarian culture, and to do so in the spirit of realism. For this reason renewed attempts were also made to secure the help and cooperation of the mother country. Books were sought—and some received—that summarized the achievements of Hungarian history and civilization. These were still far from the detached presentations found in scholarly volumes, but at least they did try to supply more credible psychological props for the members of the younger generation in search of some meaning for their "Hungarianness." Attempts were also made to bring the second generation into closer contact with the "living" Hungarian culture in Hungary via improved bilingual schools, better Hungarian book collections in local public libraries, and various theater groups. Some of the latter consisted of touring ensembles from Hungary. Others, however, were locally organized and consisted both of professional actors as well as amateurs, including at times also many of the young people whom they were meant to retain or to recapture for Hungarian culture. The 1930s also witnessed the rise of bilingual and English-language publications and periodicals geared to the native-born generation whose command of English was already on a higher level than their command of Hungarian. These included the *Young Magyar American,* a periodical edited by

Béla Báchkai representing the American Hungarian Federation, an almanac entitled *Second Generation* put out by the Cleveland-based daily the *Szabadság,* as well as a series of translations of some of the jewels of Hungarian literature. In 1941 there also appeared a scholarly summary of Hungarian history by Dominic G. Kosáry, which is still being used today even by some nonspecialist scholars.[21] All of these were published by the Cleveland-based Benjamin Franklin Bibliophile Society, Inc., which was likewise headed by Báchkai.

These renewed efforts of Hungarian-Americans for the allegiance of their offspring also included attempts to send some of their children to Hungary to attend special university-level programs on Hungarian culture. The most successful and significant of these programs was the Summer School at the University of Debrecen, where many young Hungarian-Americans have learned to reassess their formerly low opinions about Hungary, the Hungarians, and about themselves. Participation in these programs did not alter their basic self-identification as Americans, but it made them more aware of the true nature of Hungarian culture and learning, and also strengthened their relationship with the Hungarian-American community.

Occasionally this search for recognition prompted Hungarian-Americans to support unusual undertakings, which they looked upon as spectacular manifestations of Hungarian know-how, willpower, and determination. The best known of these affairs was the trans-Atlantic flight of two young Hungarians—Sándor Magyar and György Endresz—on July 15–16, 1931, in a one-engine airplane named *Justice for Hungary.*[22] This flight duplicated Lindbergh's earlier feat with the *Spirit of St. Louis* and carried the two daring young men from New York to Budapest in twenty-five hours and forty minutes. Appropriately enough, it was financed by a Hungarian-American businessman from Michigan (Emil Szalay), who was also in search of recognition. The two goals of this undertaking were to call attention to Hungary's grievances and to throw the spotlight on Hungarian-Americans. It was successful in the sense of securing international publicity and in raising the ethnic pride of Hungarian-Americans, although it did not alter Hungary's international position. For Hungarian-Americans, however, it was still a consciousness-raising event, as were such other events as the erection of the Kossuth statue in New York (March 15, 1928), with the participation of over five hundred Hungarians from the Old Country.

As expected, it was also accompanied by various demonstrations in favor of revising Hungary's new borders.

The search for recognition was paralleled by the desire to demonstrate Hungarian-American contributions to American history and civilization. Lacking professional historians and the means to attract them to this field, they were obliged to entrust this task to their clergymen and journalists. Many of the latter went to work to collect information concerning Hungarian contacts with America. Most of the information they found consisted of small details of dubious significance for American history (e.g., the deeds of some early travelers, the lives of noted personalities, identification of towns and counties named after Hungarians, details about Kossuth's trip to America and the brief Kossuth craze that accompanied it, Hungarian participation in the Civil War, as well as information about contemporary or near-contemporary Hungarians who have made it in American society in the field of science, music, sports, journalism, business, scholarship, or movie-making), but such details were important for the Hungarian-American psyche.

The most successful of these collectors of Hungarian-American memorabilia were the already-mentioned Eugene [Jenő] Pivány, who continued his work after his permanent repatriation to Hungary in 1920, and Edmund [Ödön] Vasváry, a Reformed clergyman, whose hundreds of related articles appeared for well over half a century on the pages of the major Hungarian-American newspapers, such as the *Amerikai Magyar Népszava* and the *Szabadság*. Vasváry's best-known work is his book *Lincoln's Hungarian Heroes* (1939), which was a direct by-product of the Hungarian Reformed Federation's effort to participate in the consciousness-raising movement of the 1930s. With this work Vasváry succeeded in carving out a place—however small—for the Hungarians in that momentous event of American history.[23]

In addition to emotional-national considerations, the older generation's desire to raise the Hungarian consciousness of the second generation was also prompted by the recognition that without such renewed consciousness the great Hungarian-American organizations (including the largest fraternities) would rapidly fade away, leaving the older members without financial support in their old age. The seriousness of the situation was amply demonstrated by a researcher in 1940, who showed that by that time over 60 percent of the members of the great majority (83 percent) of the Hungarian-American associations consisted of American-born individuals. His final conclusion was that, given the continuation of this trend, "the Hungarian character of the insurance associations will disappear," or they would simply go out of existence.[24] This recognition, which simply proved the existence of a generally known trend, was of primary importance in prompting these associations to establish English-speaking branches, to increase their English-language publications, and in general to try to cater to the native-born generation. But this effort never reached the point where the older members would have been willing to relinquish control over their fraternities to their offspring.

Whatever their shortcomings, these efforts of the 1930s did have some success. This was all the more so as the supposedly "assimilated" native born proved to be less than fully assimilated. They did not feel at home in the world of their fathers, but neither did they feel completely at ease among Anglo-Saxon Americans. They were basically fence-sitters or "marginal men," unable to purge themselves of feelings of inferiority, and thus they tried to cover up their background as much as possible. At the same time, however, they were unable to tear themselves completely away from the bonds of their heritage. Nor were they able to discard their inferiority complexes until well into the post–World War II period (the late 1960s and 1970s), when the real beneficiaries of this changing attitude were their own children and grandchildren.

Assimilation and social mobility among second-generation Hungarian-Americans have not been studied adequately. What has been written may only have local significance. One of the most quoted of the existing works is E. D. Beynon's study of the mid-1930s, which is shockingly revealing to the modern reader. It presents a far from ideal picture of the social differences, class antagonisms, and the frantic search for social mobility and social acceptance by a wide variety of Hungarian-American types.[25] Julianna Puskás's recent summary of this question is much kinder, reflecting her own somewhat overidealized view of the Magyar peasant. According to Puskás, the social mobility and process of assimilation of the second generation during the interwar period was characterized by the following factors: (1) The children of peasant immigrants generally became workers, mostly of the semiskilled type; (2) the children of skilled workers generally became technicians, some earning college degrees or at least remaining on the level of skilled workers;

(3) members of the second generation displayed much geographical mobility, which indicates their desire to break away from the confinements of the ethnic ghetto; (4) biological assimilation, i.e., intermarriage with other ethnic groups, was also rapid among the second generation, although this intermarriage took place almost exclusively with other nationalities from the former Austro-Hungarian Empire (Slovaks, Croats, Serbs, Ruthenians, Poles, etc.), followed by the Italians and the Irish; (5) their desire to break away from their undesirable roots often led them to reject not only their nationality but at times even their parents, which caused much pain and suffering to the latter on top of their own experiences of rejection; (6) the ranks of the second generation, however, also included those whose reaction to the lack of acceptance by American society took the form of "inward turning."[26] These usually became more consciously "Hungarian" than was expected, and they were also vocal in advertising their "proud heritage." But this type was still more the exception that the rule. The goal of the average second-generation Hungarian-American was to be accepted as an American while also being permitted to retain some link to his own heritage.

The Trials of World War II

In addition to renewed efforts to "save" the second generation from complete assimilation, while at the same time seeking greater acceptance in American society, the 1930s also witnessed the brewing of new pressures and emotions in Hungarian-American society. The news from the homeland was disquieting. Hungary was falling increasingly under the influence of Mussolini's Italy and Hitler's Germany. While this association did bring some long-sought gains for the country in the form of the partial revision of her new frontiers, it also carried the country irrevocably into the arms of those dictators. Moreover, the rise of the radical right in Hungary resulted in a number of laws (e.g., the anti-Semitic laws of 1939 and 1941) that brought universal condemnation to the country. This fact, however, did not prevent Hungarian-Americans from being overjoyed at these territorial gains, as acknowledged by a secret OSS report dated July 13, 1943, which also pointed out that once the United States entered the conflict, Hungarian-Americans all "proved to be loyal to America."[27] They still had much affection for Hungary, but on this occasion their loyalties to their new country proved to be much stronger than during the First World War. In 1917 and 1918 they purchased United States war bonds only out of fear; during World War II they did so out of conviction.

By the 1940s most Hungarian-Americans regarded the United States as their true homeland, but they did not wish to abandon Hungary, either. Thus, while convinced that the Axis had to be defeated, and contributing much to this cause (over 50,000 of them served in the United States armed forces), they did try to explain Hungary's role on the side of the enemy as that of an "unwilling satellite." This was basically the attitude of most Hungarian-American community leaders, and this view was also reflected in the majority of the Hungarian-American newspapers and the various memoranda prepared by the American Hungarian Federation (AHF) and submitted to the United States government.

The role of the AHF by the time of the war had become most important. It had been reorganized once more at its Pittsburgh convention in 1939. Then, assured of financial support by the major fraternities and churches, it was relocated in Washington, D.C., to be near the center of power. Moreover, to make certain that Hungarian interests would be adequately represented, the Federation's directors appointed Professor Tibor Kerekes of Georgetown University to be its national secretary. Kerekes performed the duties of this office ably and with vigor for nearly a decade (1939–1948), always stressing the point that the government of Hungary was not its own master, and that one is obliged to distinguish between the government and the people of any country.[28]

One of the most interesting offshoots of this effort was the AHF's link to the so-called "Free Hungary Movement," headed by the self-exiled Hungarian politician Tibor Eckhardt. Before his sudden emigration and arrival in the United States (August 1941) Eckhardt had been the leader of the Independent Smallholders' party in Hungary. But following Hitler's attack against Yugoslavia and the suicide of Hungary's Prime Minister Paul Teleki, Eckhart left Hungary (allegedly with Regent Horthy's approval) to become the spokesman of the nation that was unable to speak for itself anymore. His Free Hungary Movement was manned by various anti-Nazi ex-diplomats and supported by the American Hungarian Federation as well as by most of the major newspapers and national fraternities. As demonstrated by its first proclamation, dated September 27, 1941, the movement was strongly anti-Nazi, but it was equally anti-Soviet and anticommunist and refused to denounce Hungary's recent territorial gains. For this reason it immediately became the target both of the other "Free Movements," headed by rival Czech, Yugoslav and Rumanian exiles, and of various leftist movements holding different views concerning the Soviet Union. These attacks eventually led to the suspension of Eckhardt's movement less than a year after its launching, and to Eckhardt's own retirement from political activities until after the war. The same political orientation continued to be represented by the American Hungarian Federation—although with relatively few tangible results.[29]

During the war there also arose several rival Hungarian political movements, headed by left-leaning intellectuals, who for a while enjoyed the trust and support of various American political circles. These included the Movement for a New Democratic Hungary, the Federation of Democratic Hungarians, the Hungarian-American Council for Democracy, as well as a rival Free Hungary Movement centered in London and headed by the radical Count Michael Károly of 1918–1919 fame. All of these, however, were the brainchildren of recently arrived intellectuals who had no real connections with the Hungarian-American community, and whose views—however commendable in many instances—were so far removed from those of the Hungarian-American majority that they had no hope for any sort of mass support from among the latter's ranks. Moreover, Károly's London-based movement was so procommunist and pro-Soviet that it was even rejected by his longtime friend and political ally, the noted progressive liberal sociologist and ex-politician Oscar Jászi. Thus, although led by widely known personalities (the legal scholar Rusztem Vámbéry, the actor Béla Lugosi, Oscar Jászi, etc.) and in most instances representing progressive idealism and democracy, none of these movements had any hope of capturing the attention and support of the average Hungarian-American. They were thus "heads without bodies" that "functioned on the peripheries of the Hungarian-American community."[30] The majority of Hungarian-Americans were still believers and supporters of the down-to-earth Kossuthist nationalism of their immigrant forefathers and believed that Hungary's demand for territorial revisionism was simply an attempt to implement the Wilsonian principle of national self-determination. Thus they were not about to accept the leadership of persons and organizations that failed to stand up for these principles. It was for this very reason that, notwithstanding its many shortcomings, it was still the American Hungarian Federation and the movements connected with it that best represented the wishes and views of most Hungarian-Americans. These pro-Hungary views also found expression in the American Hungarian Relief Committee, which the AHF and its supporters organized at the end of the war.

Chapter Eight
Since World War II: The Great Political Immigration
Efforts to Help the Refugees

Of the nearly half a dozen organizations, councils, and committees that tried to pass themselves off as the true representatives of the Hungarian-American community and of Hungary's national interests only the American Hungarian Federation survived the war. The others failed to survive because they had very few followers among Hungarian-Americans. For all practical purposes, their generally well-meaning and idealist organizers only represented themselves and a few of their dedicated followers among the political immigrants from Hitler's Central Europe. As such, they were bound to run out of steam once the crisis of war ended.

In addition to failing to rally mass support to their respective causes, these various "summit" organizations also failed to live up to the needs of the immediate postwar years. Thus while their leaders were playing with ideas and planning grandiose schemes for the physical reorganization and spiritual restructuring of East Central Europe and Hungary, the people of that war-torn region were homeless, naked, hungry, and sick, and in need of shelter, clothing, food, and medicine. And, interestingly enough, only the traditional Hungarian-American organizations, the AHF and the major fraternities, responded properly to these needs. These were the same organizations that were routinely and regularly labeled "simple," "backward," "nationalistic," and even "reactionary" by the various intellectual spokesmen of the rival organizations.

The most visible manifestation of this "proper response" to the actual needs of postwar Hungary and the Hungarians was the establishment of the American Hungarian Relief Committee (AHRC) in September 1944.[1] Its founders were all prominent members of the "old elite," i.e., the leaders of the major national fraternities and the spokesmen of the largest Hungarian-American communities. The national fraternities, such as the Verhovay, the Rákóczi, the Reformed, and the "Bridgeport" associations, were also the Relief Fund's most important regular contributors, although the collection drives were conducted throughout Hungarian-America. Also important was the participation of a number of prominent and wealthy Americans such as Countess L. Széchenyi (née Gladys Vanderbilt), who had already played a major role in the establishment of the Relief Committee for Hungarian Sufferers after World War I.[2]

The declared goal of the AHRC was to aid the Hungarian victims of the war both in Hungary and in other parts of Europe. In the course of the half a decade of its existence, it sent about $3 million in food, medicine, clothing, and even agricultural machinery to Europe. Initially most of this went to Hungary, but later—particularly after 1947 and the intensification of the Cold War—to various émigré camps in Germany and Austria.

The passage of the two Displaced Persons acts of 1948 and 1950, respectively, opened up the hitherto closed doors of the United States to many tens of thousands of refugees from among over a dozen or more formerly allied or enemy nationalities.[3] This added new dimensions to the work of the AHRC. In addition to continuing to aid the refugees, it now also became involved in helping them emigrate to the United States, in receiving them upon arrival, in finding them housing and jobs, and in starting them off in their new surroundings. This work required the dedication of many hundreds of individuals, most of whom contributed their time without any compensation.

Throughout much of this period the primary sponsor of the AHRC was the American Hungarian Federation, which, under the effective leadership of Professor Tibor Kerekes, continued to fight for a more lenient view and better treatment of Hungary and Hungarians throughout the world. During the war the Federation had bombarded the presidential office and the United States Congress with petitions asserting Hungary's basic inculpability, while after the war it tried to arouse sympathy for the nation and prevent the reimposition of the same harsh territorial settlements that it was forced to suffer after World War I.[4] Because of much more significant considerations of international politics, neither the AHF nor anyone else was able to prevent the imposition of even harsher terms (i.e., the loss of additional territories to Czechoslovakia), but the Federation did gain the sympathy of a number of United States law-makers and may have had a role in the gradual softening of American views toward Hungarian refugees. It would, however, be too much to claim that its influence was decisive. Much more important was the worsening of United States–Soviet relations and the resulting change of attitude toward the strongly anticommunist refugees from Hungary.

Postwar Immigrants: The Three Waves of Refugees

With the cessation of hostilities in the spring of 1945, war-wrecked Germany and Austria were awash with millions of refugees. They included everyone from former concentration-camp inmates, persecuted racial and religious minorities, and dissident intellectuals and political leaders who managed to survive the Nazi holocaust and the destructions of the war to the personnel of the defeated armies, representatives of the upper- and middle-level social and political elites of Germany's former allied and victim states, and hundreds of thousands of others of the lower classes who were simply driven there by the currents of war. They included even deserters from the Soviet army (mostly non-Russians) who took this chance to escape from the land made inhospitable by Stalin's terrors. While many of the upper- and middle-level social, political, and military elites of the states surrounding Germany were Hitler's victims, many others had been sympathizers of Germany who fled before the advancing Soviet armies in hope of finding better treatment at the hands of the Western Allies. Only a small percentage of these were actual Nazis, but a sizable segment—including many of Hitler's victims—were people of strong nationalist and anticommunist convictions.

For the next five to six years after the war, Germany and Austria housed millions of these refugees in many scores of makeshift camps. True, in a year or two following the cessation of hostilities, a great many of them were repatriated to their respective homelands, but almost as many continued to remain in Germany and Austria, hoping that conditions in their countries would soon change to a point where they too would be able to return. But the hoped-for change never came. Between 1947 and 1949—after a period of coalition governments—the states of East Central Europe all fell under the monolithic control of their respective communist parties and became satellites of the Soviet Union. At the same time, the postwar disaffection between the Soviet Union and its former Western Allies intensified into a full-fledged Cold War, and for the next decade or so the countries of East Central Europe were all closed in behind what Churchill had aptly called an "Iron Curtain."

The drawing of the Iron Curtain also altered the lives of the refugees. On the one hand they now realized that the chances they were hoping for would not come in the visible future, and on the other hand they were also given to understand that the only alternative for most of them was overseas emigration.

In 1945 the millions of refugees in Central Europe also included about half a million Hungarians, many of them, such as former concentration-camp inmates and the members of the retreating Hungarian army, being "involuntary refugees." Most of these were repatriated to Hungary within two years after the war, along with many civilians (mostly of the lower social ranks) who had little to fear and who felt that the postwar coalition governments afforded them enough assurance of fair treatment that they could take their chances. Those who chose to remain (perhaps 120,000 strong, to be joined between 1946 and 1950 by another 40,000)[5] were either former members of the upper- and middle-level social and political elite, members of the professional officer corps of the Royal Hungarian Army, members of the Hungarian gendarmerie, or former members of various rightist political parties. These groups chose not to repatriate either out of fear or because they were convinced that soon they would be able to return victoriously after Hungary's inevitable and impending liberation by the Western Powers. But this wait turned out to be longer than expected, for the hoped-for "liberation" never came. Thus in the period between 1949 and 1951 the majority of them opted to emigrate to various North and South American countries and Australia. A number of others stayed in Germany or Austria or emigrated to such nearby lands as France and a few other European countries. Those who came to the United States numbered about 16,000. These so-called 45-ers constituted the core of the postwar immigrants, generally called Displaced Persons or DPs. They represented the society, ideology, and worldview of an age that came to an end in 1945.

The 45-ers or DPs were preceded, joined, and followed in this trans-Atlantic migration by the so-called 47-ers, most of whom really fled Hungary between 1947 and 1949. The elite among them were those political emigrants who had participated in the various postwar coalition governments of Hungary, but then were gradually pushed out of power by their erstwhile partners, the communists. These included leaders and members of the Smallholders party, the National Peasant party, the Social Democratic party, and a few other smaller leftist groups. As opposed to the 45-ers, these 47-ers represented various shades of liberalism and socialism. They were known both for their opposition to the defunct conservative and rightist regimes of pre-1945 Hungary as well as for their displeasure with communism and with the Soviet control of Hungary. Being unable or unwilling to toe the Soviet line, between 1947 and 1949 they were all pushed out of power and forced to emigrate. Thus they suddenly found themselves in the company of their former opponents, the 45-ers. These two émigré groups were divided from each other only by a few years in terms of the date of their emigration, but they represented two totally different worlds. As such, they could hardly be expected to get along with each other, and this was proven conclusively during the next few years.

Because of their connection with defeated Germany, the 45-ers carried little weight with the Western Powers. This was not true for the 47-ers, who were generally known as liberals and as advocates of a Western type of democracy for Hungary. The latter were thus well received in the West, and for the next few years enjoyed the political and financial support of the Western governments, including that of the United States. In fact, most of them emigrated to the United States, where they were treated as the true representatives of the people of Hungary, and through much of the 1950s were also accepted as the most prominent spokesmen of the Hungarian-American community, although their relationship to that community was very minimal.

The political elite among the 47-ers was followed by thousands of politically less exposed people who have left Hungary between 1947 and the mid-1950s largely because of their growing disenchantment with the increasingly repressive political regime that had imposed itself upon their country under Mátyás Rákosi's Stalinist dictatorship. The majority of these eventually also settled in the United States, adding another 10,000 or so to the 45-ers, but not necessarily mixing with them, at least not on the upper social-political levels. These two rather distinct groups—for the lack of a better term called "Postwar Immigrants"—made up most of the 26,532 Hungarian refugees who entered the United States between 1945 and 1956, that is, between World War II and the Hungarian Revolution of 1956.[6]

Another 47,643 came between 1956 and 1960 in consequence of the Revolution of 1956, of whom 38,045 came immediately after the revolution. They again represented a totally different world from those of the 45-ers and 47-ers. Whereas the majority of the former two groups were middle-aged people, many with their families and with considerable achievements behind them, the 56-ers were generally young and single, either still studying or at the outset of their careers. Most of them were in their late teens, twenties, or early thirties, and over two-thirds of them were males. Moreover, although a number of them (really a very small percentage of them) did participate in the actual fighting, most of them were really apolitical and left Hungary simply because the borders were suddenly thrown open. They also represented a different social stratum than did the earlier postwar immigrants. The newcomers were already the products of the powerful social transformation that had taken place in Hungary before the revolution. Thus, irrespective of their parents' former status, they were part of the relatively homogeneous new class of young and prospective technocrats who were meant to serve as the "second fighting generation" of the new communist system in Hungary. For this reason their education and training had been anticlassical and practical, antitraditional and progressive, antinationalist and prointernationalist, and even anti-Hungarian (i.e., disparaging of Hungarian historical traditions) and pro-Soviet. Their practical training and education—whether completed or not—opened up good prospects for them in American industrial establishments or in one of the technical colleges or universities. At the same time, their lack of strong national sentiments made them good prospects for quick Americanization and assimilation. Thus, outside of a relatively small core of political activists and a sizable segment of the less educated or less daring among them who settled in established Hungarian-American communities, the majority of the 56-ers simply melted into American society. They took advantage of the wide variety of new opportunities that were opened up for them. They were also the first among the postwar immigrants to marry non-Hungarians in overwhelming numbers, and consciously to cut themselves off from Hungarian-American communities, organizations, and most aspects of Hungarian-American life. A number of the latter became successful both professionally and financially, producing, along with a segment of the second-generation offspring of the 45-ers and the 47-ers, the most valuable and influential group among Hungarian-Americans today.[7]

For a while it seemed that the majority of the 56-ers were permanently lost to the Hungarian cause. The 1970s and early 1980s, however, saw a sudden reappearance of many of them in Hungarian circles. Apparently, after fifteen, twenty, or twenty-five years of having cut themselves off from their own kind, the memories of the past began to haunt them, followed by an ever-increasing craving to establish contacts with their brethren and share in some of the cultural aspects of Hungarian and Hungarian-American life. But this reawakening was far from painless, for it was usually accompanied by a sudden realization that the language, culture, and history of their forefathers had no meaning for the members of their own families and that there was very little they could do about it.

The Adjustment of the Postwar Immigrants

Upon arrival in the United States, the refugees (whether 45-ers or 47-ers) found a functioning Hungarian-American community that had done much to aid them in their plight after the war. The latter also signed many so-called "assurances," which permitted a sizable portion of the DPs to enter the country. Moreover, the newcomers were aided during and after their arrival, most of them being settled in the existing Hungarian-American communities in the midst of the old-timers. Yet the relationship between the latter and the newcomers turned sour almost from the start. The friendship and cooperation expected by the old immigrants never materialized. Very few of the new immigrants joined existing Hungarian-American organizations for any length of time (with the exception of the churches), and the wall of social and cultural distinction that became apparent immediately only grew higher and wider with the passing of years. Ultimately there was very little anyone could do about it. The world of the old economic immigrants—be they members of the first, second, or third generations—was so vastly different from the world of the new political immigrants that the two groups could never meet on a common platform. To start with, the very cause of their respective departures from Hungary was different. But much more significant were the social-educational-cultural differences that divided them, especially in light of the strong class consciousness that had characterized interwar Hungary, and to a lesser degree even the political leadership of the immediate postwar years. The majority of the 45-ers and 47-ers—although strongly disagreeing among themselves concerning their political views—still represented the social and political elite of their respective historical periods. Both of these groups also contained a sizable percentage of petty-bourgeois elements, which, although not part of the ruling class, were intensely political and generally very nationalistic. Most of these elements came from those "middle levels" of Hungarian society (about 28 to 38 percent of the population), which—according to a recent researcher[8]—have always constituted the so-called "masses" in all of twentieth-century Hungary's mass movements. They were the ones who within a period of three decades supported Károlyi's socialism (1918), Béla Kún's communism (1919), Horthy's counter-revolutionary nationalism (1920s and 1930s), Szállasi's right radicalism (early 1940s), and Rákosi's Soviet communism (late 1940s and early 1950s).

While representing several classes and a number of subgroups within these classes, all of these postwar political immigrants were bound together by their strong anticommunism and their desire to return to Hungary after the country's hoped-for liberation from Soviet control. Beyond these factors, however, they were divided by their specific political goals concerning Hungary's future.

As an example, the 45-ers all stood for some sort of conservative or rightist nationalist solution. The socially more exclusive conservative nationalists included among their ranks the so-called "legitimists," who would have preferred the restoration of the Habsburg dynasty in the person of Otto von Habsburg; the "free electionists," who were similarly monarchists, but wished to see a "true Hungarian" on the throne of Hungary; the supporters of interwar Hungary's regent, Admiral Nicholas Horthy (who meanwhile had himself become a "legitimist" in 1946); the advocates of various other "regencies"; the champions of "directed democracies" under the leadership of one or another of their favorite "leaders"; as well as the supporters of a Western type of democratic system, although preferably without giving too much weight to the views of the uninitiated public. Many of the upper layers of these immigrants were of the gentry class, claiming membership in one or another rank of the Hungarian nobility. A goodly portion of them, however, were really relatively recently assimilated Germans or Slavs (including a sizable segment of the professional military officers and the bureaucrats). Yet they still liked to trace their ancestry to the conquering Magyars of the ninth century. Aside from those who were members of the petty bourgeoisie, the basic training of this group was unmarketable in America. It consisted of diplomas from military academies and doctorates from one of Hungary's several law schools— the latter being the most easily attainable university degree in interwar Hungary, virtually mandatory for all upper- and middle-level state or county bureaucrats. (Most law-school graduates did not become practicing attorneys, which required a period of apprenticeship and the taking of a rigorous state examination.) The skills offered by these two degrees, however, were not transferable to the United States. Thus their holders—most of them in mid-career and unable to speak English—found themselves in the unenviable position of being forced to accept the most menial jobs in shops, factories, and other establishments of physical labor. In fact, even their social and intellectual inferiors within their own group, the artisans and the shopkeepers, fared much better. Possessing more marketable skills, the latter usually became skilled workers or shopkeepers. In contrast, very few of the former social, political, and military elite were able to rise above the rank of unskilled workers. (In Cleveland during the 1950s, for example, three Hungarian ex-generals and many more former top government officials were working as common laborers.)[9]

Much better was the lot of the 47-ers, and in particular of the politically prominent personalities among them. Being relatively highly regarded in the West, they were held up as representatives of the Western type of democracy in Hungary. Upon arrival they were given relatively important positions in one of America's Cold War institutions (e.g., the Free Europe Committee and one of its subsidiaries, such as Radio Free Europe, the various National Committees), with appropriate financial remuneration. Even the least prominent among the politically active among them fared better than the most prominent members of the 45-ers. First, they were not tainted by the charge of having been pro-German or Nazi collaborators. Second, proportionately many more of them brought marketable skills and occupations than did the 45-ers. Their relationship to the old immigrants, however, was equally bad. They too were divided from the latter by a whole intellectual and cultural world, stemming from their education, experiences, and political-ideological outlook.

Being unable to fit into either American or the existing Hungarian-American society, and being forced to make their living in a manner that befitted neither their social background and education nor their past careers and experiences, the only way the 45-ers were able to keep their sanity was to regard their stay in the United States simply as a temporary solution. They would remain here—so they believed or forced themselves to believe—only until the inevitable liberation of their country. This view was strengthened by the "liberation of Captive Nations" policy, which was popular in certain American political circles in those days. Meanwhile they went to work to build a separate world for themselves into which they could withdraw after the obligatory trials "imposed" upon them by American society, which was "unable" to value their talents. The result was the establishment of many scores and even hundreds of social and political organizations whose purpose was partially to advance the cause of "liberation" and partially to ensure that for the interim their founders would feel at home in a world that was basically hostile to them, unappreciative of their education and know-how, critical of their social and cultural traditions, and only partially supportive of a narrow aspect of their political views, namely their strong anticommunism. In fact, it was only their anticommunism and anti-Sovietism that found favor with America's ruling political circles during the 1950s. Otherwise their conservative-nationalist and rightist views were rejected, and they themselves were regarded as a liability to America's image as the home of liberalism and democracy. For this very reason, very few of the 45-ers made it into those organizations of the political immigrants that received any meaningful recognition and financial help from the United States government. Such recognition and financial subsidies were reserved for the 47-ers and for those few earlier immigrants who left Hungary during the war to protest the country's official pro-German stand.

Early Organizations of the 45-ers

The roots of the most widespread organizations of the 45-ers reach back to the late 1940s. They were founded by various prominent personalities or power groups in one of Germany's many refugee camps, at the time when they still thought that their return to Hungary was imminent. These mostly ephemeral organizations represented all shades of the deposed elite, from the monarchist aristocrats and conservative nationalist gentry groups to specifically military associations and far-rightist neo-Nazi groups. The most important link between them was their anticommunism and anti-Soviet stand. They all wanted to liberate Hungary, and they all were drawing up grandiose if totally unrealistic plans for the reorganization of Hungarian society after their hoped-for return.

Of the many, at times tragicomical, efforts at organizing the supporters of the old regime (among them the holding of a Parliament-in-Exile and the electing of a new "Regent" in 1947 in the German town of Altötting),[10] the most successful were those aimed at establishing major associations for certain specific power groups among the refugees. One of the most successful of these organizations was the *Magyar Harcosok Bajtársi Közössége* (Fraternal association of Hungarian veterans), commonly known as the MHBK. Founded in 1947 under the leadership of General András Zákó, the MHBK was intended primarily to be the central association of the Hungarian professional military officers. Once emigration spread it to other continents, however, it increasingly became a social organization as well. Its 15,000 to 20,000 members (who with their families accounted for 60,000 to 80,000 of some of the most influential refugees in several dozen countries) were organized into hundreds of local branches, which then increasingly became centers for the perpetuation of old ways and for the inculcation of the youth with the views of their parents. But they also became temporary havens for many of the déclassé members of the old elite.

For a while the MHBK was rivaled by the *Magyar Szabadság-mozgalom* (Hungarian movement for freedom), founded in 1946 by General Ferenc Kisbarnaki-Farkas, the same military officer who in 1947 was elected Hungary's new "Regent" by the Parliament-in-Exile at Altötting. (The former regent, Horthy, fell into disfavor with Kisbarnaki-Farkas and many of the professional army officers because of his decision to throw his support behind Otto von Habsburg, and his subsequent effort to play the MHBK into Archduke Otto's hands.) According to the leaders of this movement, by 1953 the *Szabadságmozgalom* had 21,268 members organized in 108 local chapters in 32 countries. If this claim is correct, then this movement may have been as widespread as the MHBK. But, for whatever reasons, its influence waned, leaving the MHBK as the primary representative of the ruling military elite and its supporters among the immigrants. The only other military-based organizations with relatively wide appeal were the *Magyar Királyi Csendőr Bajtársi Közösség* (Royal Hungarian gendarmerie benevolent association) or MKCSBK, and its Cleveland-based affiliate, the *Magyar Csendőrök Családi Közössége* (Familial association of Hungarian gendarmerie) or MCsCsK. The MKCSBK's and MCsCsK's influence, however, never rivalled that of the MHBK, because of their smaller size, and the fact that most of their members also held memberships in the MHBK. Both the MHBK and the MKCSBK initiated regular periodical publications soon after their foundation (in 1947 and 1949, respectively), in which they advocated their views concerning Hungary's past and perceived future. They also published news about their members, as well as about some of their military feats during World War II. Here again the MHBK's *Hadak Utján* (On warpath) was more influential and had a wider appeal than the MKCSBK's *Bajtársi Levél* (Comradely newsletter).

Although the central leadership of the MHBK remained in Germany even after the mass emigration of the late 1940s and early 1950s, much of its weight and financial base was shifted to the United States, with the American branch playing an increasingly preeminent role. Notwithstanding its broad base and popular appeal, however, the MHBK never received the "official" recognition of the United States government that the latter bestowed on the less broadly based, but favored, political organizations of the 47-ers.[11]

In addition to the above widespread and largely military-controlled organizations, the 45-ers also established a host of other associations, few of which were free from unrealistic and basically unattainable political goals. These include the *Magyar Vitézi Rend* (Hungarian order of knights), whose main goal is to perpetuate notions of medieval chivalry and to continue to "knight" the offspring of the original members; the Cleveland-based *Felszabadító Bizottság* (Committee for liberation), founded by General Gyula Kovács, the erstwhile chief of staff of the Second Hungarian Army, which perished in the Soviet Union in the winter of 1942–1943; the similarly Cleveland-based, but more culturally and socially oriented, *Magyar Társaság* (Hungarian association), established by

John Nádas, a publicist and a former secretary general of the government-sponsored Party of Hungarian Life, aided by Professor Ferenc Somogyi, formerly of the University of Pécs; as well as by several revisionist organizations that focus their attention on former Hungarian territories in Rumania, Czechoslovakia, Yugoslavia, and the Soviet Union (e.g., American Transylvanian Federation, Committee for Transylvania, National Committee of Hungarians in Czechoslovakia, Committee for the Liberation of Southern Hungary, Federation of Hungarians of Sub-Carpathia). Founded during the mid-1950s, initially most of the activities of these organizations consisted of spreading traditional Hungarian revisionism among Hungarians in the Western countries. During the late 1960s and 1970s, however, they all became more sophisticated, began to propagate their views in English and in the other Western languages, and readjusted the thrust of their propaganda from unqualified revisionism to the protection of Hungarian minorities in these surrounding states, in line with the newly popular concept of "human rights." In this work they were soon joined by a host of other, newly established organizations that pursued this same policy with a greater degree of efficiency and professionalism than did their predecessors. [12]

Although founded primarily with political goals in mind, all of these organizations also catered to the social and cultural needs of the 45-ers and to those among the later immigrants who were able to accept the views and cultural ways of the founders. With their increased attention to social and cultural functions, these associations thrived, but with their success they undercut the organizations of the old-time immigrants. The latter were forced to rely increasingly on the support of the bilingual or largely English-speaking members of the second and third generations, who were totally divorced from the world and thinking of the newcomers. This segregation between the two groups had the dual effect of speeding up the Americanization of the traditional organizations and their members and of hindering the assimilation of the new immigrants and their children.

Organizations of the Extreme Right

While the majority of the organizations of the 45-ers represented various shades of conservative nationalism, there was also a sizable group of extreme right wingers among them who carried on the cult of the executed Arrow Cross (Hungarian Nazi) leader Ferenc

Szállasi. The latter, generally coming from the ranks of the petty bourgeoisie, were attracted to rightist extremism because it combined strong nationalism with promises of radical social reform. Like their conservative compatriots, they also founded their own organizations in Germany from 1946 to 1948. But as most of them failed to gain admission to the United States, the center of their activities shifted to South America (mostly to Argentina) and to Australia.

Both before and after emigration, they coalesced into various so-called "Hungarist" movements, under such leaders as the poet-politician Géza Alföldi and General Árpád Henney, the latter being one of Szállasi's ministers who managed to avoid extradition and possible execution in postwar Hungary. The "Hungarists" were equally opposed to the conservative nationalists (whether monarchists or supporters of one or another form of "regencies") and to the leftists, including everyone from moderate liberals and socialists to outright communists.

Initially the most important organ of the extreme right was the *Hidverők* (Bridge builders), published and edited between 1948 and 1954 by Alföldi in Munich, Germany. Later, however, after Alföldi was found to be less of a "Hungarist" than an "opportunist," most of the "true Hungarists" switched their allegiance to the rival publication *Út és Cél* (Path and goal), which, with various changes in its title and place of publication, continued to appear into the early 1980s. Those under the leadership of General Henney established in 1951 an organization called *Magyar Országos Bizottság* (Hungarian national council). But as the movement was linked to ideas and events that were universally rejected both by the Eastern and the Western powers, it could not gain even the degree of acceptance and respectability that was enjoyed by such more conservative nationalist organizations as the MHBK and its sister associations.[13] Thus, although the ranks of the 45-ers (and even some of their successors) included a certain number of those who were advocates of one or another form of "Hungarism," their center of activity never shifted to the United States. Nor were they able to gain more than a peripheral role in Hungarian-American society and politics even among the newcomers. Yet the traditions of this movement were picked up by a fringe group among the 56-ers as well. But this more recent version of "Hungarism"—represented, among others, by the group around the newspaper *Szittyakürt* (Scythian horn)—

has been increasingly linked in recent years with the propagation of far-fetched views concerning the origins of the Hungarians (e.g., their alleged Sumerian origins) as well as with certain quixotic efforts to reshape Hungarian nationalism into a special "Hungarian religion."[14]

Organizations of the 47-ers

While the major social and political organizations of the 45-ers received no official recognition from the United States government, they did enjoy the support of the great majority of the postwar immigrants. As a matter of fact, even many of the aspiring members of the old-timers, in search of social recognition, joined these new organizations, which were much more prestigious socially than those founded by themselves.

The situation was just the opposite with organizations founded and controlled by the 47-ers. Although they had only minimal support among the immigrants, they were still regarded by the United States government as the official voice of the Hungarian-American community. The reason was that their organizations were typically Cold War institutions established with the approval of the United States government. They had to be manned by politically "acceptable" ex-politicians, and were to be used specifically to aid United States foreign-policy goals concerning Hungary and Eastern Europe. The most significant and best supported of these organizations was the Hungarian National Committee *(Magyar Nemzeti Bizottmány)*, established in 1948 in New York, which for a while was regarded as a virtual government-in-exile.[15]

Founded as a subsidiary of the National Committee for Free Europe (later renamed Free Europe Committee), the alleged goal of the HNC was "to represent the nation muted [by Soviet occupation], as well as to care for and to supply spiritual and political guidance to the dispersed Hungarians."[16] By 1954 the HNC had seventy-six members, including virtually all of the prominent and less-than-prominent politicians who had left Hungary after 1947. The actual leadership of the group was in the hands of the Executive Committee, presided over by Msgr. Béla Varga, the former speaker of the Hungarian Parliament (until May 31, 1947). The Committee's members included the most prominent personalities among the political immigrants, among them two former prime ministers, several former ministers, and the former leaders of all of the political parties purged between 1947 and 1949. In effect, the Executive Committee of the Hungarian National Committee was an undeclared government-in-exile, with its president being the "Prime Minister," and the heads of its various subcommittees serving as members of his cabinet.

Almost immediately after its establishment, the HNC became the center of political controversy among Hungarian-Americans. Whether representatives of the conservative nationalists, the right radicals, or of the radical left, they all accused the HNC of evil intent. To the conservatives and the right radicals they were pseudocommunists and perhaps even built-in agents of the Soviet system in Hungary; to the extreme left, on the other hand, they were traitors and "agents of United States imperialism." They were attacked for their political views, for their "collaboration" with the communists, but perhaps most of all for their lack of mandate from the Hungarian-American community. The spokesmen of most Hungarian-American organizations viewed them simply as appointed agents of certain American political interest groups who fulfilled their obligations in return for prestigious positions and regular monthly subsidies that saved them from having to work for a living. Undoubtedly there was also an element of envy in these accusations. But the plain truth was that the only basis of the HNC's power and prestige was the recognition by the United States government, in return for which they represented the interests of United States foreign policy vis-à-vis Hungary and the world. It is true that American policy in those days coincided, at least in part, with many of the wishes and desires of the immigrant community (including the members of the HNC), but this incidental overlapping of aims did not alter the HNC's tenuous position in Hungarian-American society.

In addition to representing United States governmental policy on Eastern Europe and Hungary, much of the HNC's efforts were directed toward defending itself against attacks from the outside. Many of its members also had to fend off internal intrigues and rivalries so as to prevent their demotion or even ejection from the Committee (e.g., the case of Tibor Eckhardt, who was demoted from membership in the Executive Committee for joining the MHBK).

Organizations of the 56-ers

In light of its lack of support by any sizable segment of the Hungarian-American community, and in view of the gradual decline of its usefulness to the United States government, by the mid-1950s the HNC was gradually losing its *raison d'être*. The Revolution of 1956 reinvigorated it for a while, but only temporarily. The 40,000 or so "freedom fighters" had only a few active politicians of some note. Yet, instead of joining the HNC, as had their predecessors, they opted to establish their own organizations. They did this with the approval of the United States government, which also favored the creation of a so-called Revolutionary Council *(Forradalmi Tanács),* which was to include all of the prominent leaders of the revolution. Ultimately, however, after the establishment of several rival organizations by such personalities as General Béla K. Király, the Commander of the Hungarian National Guard, Anna Kéthly, a leader of the Social Democrats, József Kővágó, a former mayor of Budapest, and others, the HNC was dissolved, and then reestablished, with the inclusion of several 56-ers, as the Hungarian Committee (HC) *(Magyar Bizottság).* The new HC had only sixteen members, including nine 47-ers and seven 56-ers, who represented the Smallholders' party (9), the Democratic People's party (2), and the National Peasant party (2), with three unaffiliated 56-ers. But this new HC had already lost the semblance of a pseudogovernment.[17] With the failure of the Revolution of 1956, the United States policy of the "liberation of captive nations" suffered a permanent defeat. As a result, there was no more need for a pseudo-government-in-exile, and the HC gradually lost its significance among the United States policymakers.

During the 1960s the role of the HC was increasingly assumed by the American Hungarian Federation, which, had been taken over from the early immigrants by the politically active members of the 45-ers and 56-ers. As compared to the HC, the AHF was much more outspoken in its anticommunism and its nationalism. It was also more to the right on the political spectrum. For these reasons it was less acceptable to the United States government, but much more representative of the views of the postwar immigrants in general. Thus with the rise of the new "ethnic politics" in America during the 1960s and 1970s, the voice of the AHF was increasingly listened to by the vote-conscious politicians in the United States Congress and the government in general.

In addition to the AHF, the increasingly politically active Hungarian-American community in the postrevolutionary decades was represented by half a dozen other organizations, many of them with branches throughout the world. But in a number of these organizations the several waves of postwar immigrants were merged into one interest group.

The most successful of the associations of the 56-ers was the Hungarian Freedom Fighters' Federation (HFFF), which grew out of a similar association organized by General Király in 1957.[18] But as General Király became disenchanted with the personal rivalries in his organization and with immigrant politics in general, he withdrew from the movement in 1964. Thereafter it broke up into several factions, with the HFFF representing the mainline, and the Hungarian Freedom Fighters' Movement (HFFM) one of the several splinter groups. But these splinter groups represent only a small fringe in the Hungarian-American community. This also holds true for the various socialist organizations.[19] They have a much stronger base in Europe, for the more conservative Hungarian-Americans generally view them as cryptocommunists "who have no place in Hungarian-American life."[20]

This is in stark contrast to the role of some of the more nationalist, revisionist, or human-rights organizations, many of them founded or restructured in the 1970s when the oppression of the Hungarian minorities in the surrounding states became more pronounced. The most influential among these are the Committee for Human Rights in Rumania, the Transylvanian World Federation, and the Transylvanian Committee, all of which have contributed to raising the consciousness and reshaping the thinking of most Hungarian-Americans.

The Three Segments of Hungarian-American Society

The period since World War II has witnessed the coming of several waves of Hungarian immigrants who have settled on top of several earlier waves. After initially each going its own way, in the course of the last ten to fifteen years they became distilled into three separate and distinct groups. The first of these consists of the old-timers and their second-, third-, and fourth-generation descendants, who live a life of their own. Those of the old immigrants who survived into the 1960s and 1970s continued to live in their ethnic neighborhoods (i.e., the "Little Hungaries"), while their native-born descendants gradually moved into the surburbs, giving their place over to other minorities. They gradually merged into the native American working class and to a lesser degree into the professional classes. The second group consists of the postwar immigrants who now are an amalgam of the bulk of the surviving 45-ers, some of the 47-ers, and a sizable segment of the 56-ers, who are bound together by their common way of life and common political beliefs. They live in close proximity with many of the old-timers, but they have very little to do with one another and with each other's institutions. The third group is made up of the majority of the 56-ers and that portion of the offspring of the 45-ers who have successfully integrated into American society. The latter received all or most of their education in the United States and then moved out of the ethnic neighborhoods and established themselves in American society either as high-ranking professionals or at least as persons of some success in trade, industry, and the lesser professions. Today it is the amalgam of these two subgroups—the successful members of the 56-ers and of the second-generation 45-ers—that constitutes the most valuable, productive, and influential segment of the Hungarian population in the United States. And this holds true even though the members of this group have little to do with the everyday goings-on in Hungarian-American communities or with their so-called "ethnic politics." They simply do not live in or near these communities, nor do they generally agree with the dominant ideological orientations of their organizations. The members of this group are usually much more flexible ideologically and considerably more liberal politically than their elders, who still carry the scars of their disestablishment and political persecution.[21]

Although both successful, the paths to success of the two subgroups within this "successful" segment of Hungarian-Americans was far from identical. The 56-ers were received and treated as "heroes, as freedom fighters . . . and as the ideological kin to Americans."[22] Thus they were given opportunities that were unavailable to any of their predecessors or successors. They were also free from the psychological and cultural burdens of a world that had disappeared in 1945. Not so the offspring of the 45-ers. They have grown up within the limits imposed upon them by the spiritual-cultural-ideological world of their formerly influential, but now déclassé, parents. They have encountered American society only belatedly, often ten to fifteen years after being born or after coming to the United States. Then they were often forced to break the bonds of their upbringing, reshape their thinking, and at times even suffer "excommunication" at the hands of their elders or friends for adjusting to a world that was totally different from that of their upbringing.

Although this last group, this amalgam of 56-ers and second-generation 45-ers, is the most successful and in a way the most valuable segment of Hungarian-American society, it is not they but the "postwar immigrants" who were and still are at the center of Hungarian-American life. For this very reason, if one wishes to look into the inner workings of Hungarian-American society in the course of the three decades since the early 1950s, it is primarily the activities, hopes, and aspirations of these postwar political immigrants that have to be examined.

Chapter Nine
Society, Culture, and Inner Life of the Hungarian-American Community

If there is one thing that characterized and still characterizes all of the "postwar immigrants"—as defined above—then it is their strong nationalism, which is also one of the most important components of their anticommunism. For this reason, the generally accepted tenet concerning earlier immigrants to the effect that their "nationalistic feeling [is the] . . . result of nostalgia and of various forms of rejections they experienced in American society,"[1] does not hold true for the political immigrants of the immediate postwar period. For one thing, the majority of these immigrants were political refugees who were forced to emigrate only because of circumstances beyond their control. They had no intention of staying permanently, and thus no desire to integrate into American society. And they were already committed nationalists before their coming and consequently did not have to suffer the "rejection" of American society—whose "acceptance" they did not seek in the first place—to make them nationalistic. Third, as a sizable percentage of these immigrants came from interwar or immediately postwar Hungary's social and political elite and the relatively well-to-do middle classes, they had no reasons to experience feelings of inferiority when confronted with American society—as did their more humble predecessors. In fact, because of their learning and past social status, the majority of them felt superior to the relatively "uncultured" average American they encountered in their new places of employment. And this misconception was perpetuated among them for quite a while, all the more so as they made the mistake of generalizing about American society as a whole on the basis of their immediate experiences. This in turn further impeded their future success in America, for they saw no need to learn anything from those whom they regarded as being considerably below their own cultural and intellectual level. The fact that the society they came into contact with was not really representative of American society and culture in general did not even occur to them. They had no chance to meet the "other America," consisting of highly educated and even internationally known scholars, scientists, artists, writers, and others of great achievement, or any of the Americans of exclusive tastes and discriminating culture. Moreover, even if they would have been given the chance for such a meeting, the encounter would have been most awkward, for relatively few of these formerly highly placed persons took the effort to learn English on a level adequate for the understanding and appreciation of the finer aspects of American culture and learning.

In this way the new immigrants deceived and shortchanged themselves, and did so without ever really realizing it—at least not until they were able to take a small glimpse at that "other America" through the mediation of their "successful" sons and daughters. But it was precisely this conscious or unconscious self-deception that made it possible for them to survive under conditions that normally would have driven them to desperation. As such, this self-deception did serve a useful purpose, without much harm to the immigrants themselves. Most of them were middle-aged or above and lacked the transferable skills that would have made it possible for them to make it in American society on a level suitable to their education and experiences. But it did hurt and hinder many of their children, who for a while also suffered from the delusions of their parents and thus were impeded in their struggle to rise above the latter's current social status. Moreover, once they did rise (i.e., those who did) they were also obliged to point out to their elders the nature and extent of this self-deception—even at the expense of intra- and interfamily conflicts and the threat of being excommunicated by the self-righteous community.

Perpetuation of Culture: Its Positive and Negative Aspects

While the separate world built by the postwar immigrants for themselves and their children had undoubtedly hindered the members of the second generation (and perhaps also the younger members of the immigrant generation) from achieving their goals in life as fully and as quickly as possible, it also had certain positive aspects.

The most evident of these positive features was the fact that it saved the sanity of those who fell from high positions into the world of urban America's unskilled and semiskilled workers. From the vantage point of the future of Hungarian culture in the United States, however, it was equally important that they were able to pass on much of their culture, learning, and way of life to their children— a culture and way of life that had virtually been exterminated in Hungary of the post–World War II years.

In addition to the closely knit and largely authoritarian family structure, with its traditional social and ethical value system, the instruments of this perpetuation of interwar Hungarian culture were the postwar immigrants' social and cultural institutions. Some of these have already been identified among organizations founded specifically with certain political goals in mind, such as the MHBK, the MCsCsK, and the *Vitézi Rend,* all of which eventually established local chapters in all of the larger centers of Hungarian life in America. To these were added later a host of local organizations, including so-called "self-culture societies," academic circles, women's guilds, sport clubs, and in particular the Hungarian Scouts in Exile.

In shaping the minds of young Hungarian-Americans regarding their heritage, the latter organization may have been the most important. During the heyday of its existence—from the early 1950s to the mid-1970s—it stretched like a web all over the Western world from the Americas to Europe and even Australia. Although somewhat more flexible and progressive in its outlook than the organizations of the déclassé upper and middle classes, this youth organization was also basically the product of the same world and therefore—to a degree—the perpetuator of the same positive and less-than-positive ideas.

Founded in 1945 in Germany by the energetic Gábor Bodnár, a noted scout leader in Hungary, the early scout troops functioned in the various refugee camps of Central Europe.[2] With the onset of emigration around 1950, the center of the Hungarian Scouts in Exile was transferred to Garfield, New Jersey, where it remains to this day, still under the leadership of its founder. By 1980, when the movement celebrated its thirty-fifth anniversary, its membership included about 6,000 scouts, organized into seventy-nine troops, in a dozen countries, scattered over five continents.[3] About one-third of these scouts and troops functioned in the United States. At the same time, the organization also supported dozens of Hungarian

night and weekend schools, which—in their American context—
have largely replaced the earlier church schools of the old-time
immigrants. Although still going strong, in recent years the Hungarian Scouts also began to feel that "aging" and "dying out" process
that has taken hold of most of the Hungarian-American communities
and organizations in the United States.

The spirit that has dominated the Hungarian Scout Movement
in Exile during the nearly four decades of its existence was the same
spirit it had inherited from its predecessor in interwar Hungary. In
addition to the teachings of its Founding Father, Lord Baden Powell,
concerning the love and preservation of nature, its guiding principles
were embodied in the motto: "For God, Country, Family and Honor."
It was also guided by the traditional moral and ethical values that
go along with this motto. Thus, similarly to the other organizations
of the postwar immigrants, the Hungarian Scouts were, and still
are, exponents of a strong Hungarian nationalism, coupled with a
belief in the injustices of the Treaty of Trianon. In teaching Hungarian history and geography, for example, they still operate on the
basis of "Greater Hungary," up to the point where many of their
young charges are hardly familiar with Hungary's current borders.
While in a sense this is understandable—particularly in light of
the other extremes practiced by schools in Hungary, at least until
recent years—this tendency was and is simply another aspect of the
same self-deception pursued by the postwar immigrants vis-à-vis
American society. Being told very little about the realities of Hungary since Trianon (not to speak of today's Hungary, which still
seems to be an anathema in most immigrant circles), whole generations of young Hungarians have grown up in the distinct misbelief
that Hungary's Trianon frontiers are really only temporary, and that
today's "communist Hungary" is also only a temporary phenomenon
of little consequence that will go away like a bad dream. But in
the meantime over six decades have passed since Trianon, and the
allegedly "temporary" communist Hungary had lasted considerably
longer than the idealized world of their own parents during the
interwar years.

And this last point is of at least equal significance. For concom-
itantly with the misinformation about the real nature of Trianon
and about the realities of today's Hungary (which is still being
portrayed as if nothing had changed since the Stalinist system of
the early 1950s), the youngsters associated with the schools and

cultural associations run by postwar immigrants are given a grossly overidealized view of interwar Hungary. Thus they are being subjected to generalizations about the world of their elders on the basis of the latter's privileged social position in that world. At the same time, they are being told virtually nothing about those social, economic, and cultural inequalities and injustices that made interwar Hungary into one of the most archaic class societies in contemporary Europe.

While obviously appealing and comforting to the older immigrants, this practice carries with it the danger of backfiring, for many of these students are bound to learn the truth sooner or later. And the possibility of such revelation increases in direct ratio to their degree of success and assimilation into the upper middle classes of American society, where reliable information about interwar Hungary's social and political system is easily available, as is information concerning today's Hungary. In the latter case, information derived from scholarly sources can even be supplemented by direct exposures based on personal visits. Given these realities, the fiction of a "wonderful past" versus a "terrible present" is ever more difficult to perpetuate among members of the younger generation.

While their practice of perpetuating self-deceptions has to be judged negatively, the social and cultural organizations of the postwar immigrants also had much good to offer to those who grew up under their guidance. These included the instilling of high moral values (including those of the Judeo-Christian heritage and of civic patriotism), the perpetuation of refined social graces and behavioral patterns that are both charming and increasingly rare in our mass society of today, and the similar perpetuation of bilingualism and biculturalism on a level that at times surpasses the quality level of current American and Hungarian societies together. And the reference here is to people of a social standing comparable to the former status of the postwar immigrants. Moreover, the inculcation of this bilingualism and biculturalism was so successful—particularly during the 1950s and 1960s—that in some instances even the grandchildren of the immigrants are being brought up with the same standards as were their parents. This generally has a positive impact on their future. For, contrary to the situation of the early economic immigrants, this high-level bilingualism actually helps them to excel far beyond the possibilities of an average monolingual person. These third-generation descendants of the political immigrants easily become multilingual and also possess the discipline to undertake long and arduous studies in one of the highly respected professional fields.[4]

A Typical and Influential Organization of the Postwar Immigrants: The Hungarian Society of Cleveland

Given the many centers of Hungarian-American life in the United States, and the many hundreds of organizations Hungarian-Americans have founded for the purposes of perpetuating their own way of life both for themselves (as a refuge from the world) as well as for their children and grandchildren (as a way to prove their alleged superiority to the strange world around them), it would be impossible to discuss the inner life of many, or even a few, of these organizations. All we can do is discuss the development of only one of these, namely the Hungarian Association of Cleveland. This selection is all the more appropriate as the Hungarian Association is one of the largest and most influential, yet at the same time most typical, of the organizations of the postwar immigrants. Moreover, it was born and has functioned ever since in the city that—discounting Greater New York, with its much dispersed and very fragmented Hungarian community—holds the largest and most compact Hungarian-American community in North America.[5]

Like many of the postwar immigrant organizations, the roots of the Hungarian Association also reach back to Europe. In this instance it was first established in the summer of 1948 in Innsbruck, Austria, at the initiative of Dr. John Nádas, a conservative publicist and an aspiring politician in interwar Hungary. After the emigration of its founder, it was replanted and refounded in Cleveland, where it was registered in accordance with the laws of the State of Ohio in the fall of 1952. Since then it has functioned there and has grown into a complex organization with many subsidiary associations, still under the leadership of its founding president.

As described in the Association's recently published official history, its "primary goal has always been the preservation of our Hungarian heritage. . . . [It] has kept alive the proud consciousness of the Hungarians among its members and their families, and it has cultivated carefully the language and the national heritage of the Magyars. [To this end] it has celebrated every Hungarian national holiday, and through the instrumentality of its lecture series, literary and cultural evenings, afternoon teas, and grand balls it has made a conscious effort to demonstrate to the outside world that it wishes to remain faithful to the millennial homeland of the Hungarians in the spirit of their national traditions; and that it is willing to do everything within its power to advance the cause of liberation of Hungary in the shortest possible time."[6]

Whatever their tangible results, these goals were very much in line with the spirit and aspirations of the majority of the postwar immigrants. To see them realized, the Cleveland Hungarian Association did in fact initiate and implement a whole series of plans and activities. These included (1) the establishment of regular annual lecture series (called "Open University") to keep the spirit of its members alive and the public informed; (2) the organization of public demonstrations against the Soviet occupation of Hungary; (3) the sponsoring of weekend schools and university-level Hungarian cultural and language programs; (4) the foundation of "research institutes" and the initiation of publications series so as to advocate the Association's views concerning Hungary and East Central Europe; (5) the holding of annual contests on a wide variety of topics for the purposes of cultivating, preserving, and advancing Hungarian culture and learning both among Hungarians and Americans; and (6) the preservation of Hungarian communal life as known to the Association's members and their social class in Hungary, through Sunday-afternoon social gatherings, which have also served as psychological props for its members.

The Revolution of 1956 and the coming of thousands of new refugees to Cleveland gave new impetus to local Hungarian social, cultural, and political life. (Proportionately many more 56-ers came and remained in Cleveland than is generally presumed in works dealing with the assimilation of the "freedom fighters.") In addition to renewed hopes, the Hungarian Association also gained many new members from among those of the 56-ers who were really representatives of interwar Hungary's social and intellectual world. Partially as a result of this infusion of "new blood," and partially because of the relative economic comfort achieved by the postwar immigrants by the late 1950s, grandiose plans were drawn up for the expansion of the Association's scope and influence. It was with this backdrop of developments that on November 24–25, 1961, the first "Hungarian Conference"—soon to be renamed "Hungarian Congress"—

was held under the sponsorship of the Hungarian Association. And this was only the beginning, for ever since that time the convening of such congresses became an annual affair, with the increased participation of delegates not only from the United States but from Canada, South America, Europe, and even Australia. They are drawn together by their commonly shared traditional social and political philosophy, by their strong nationalism and outspoken anticommunism, and by the opportunity to exchange views with others of similar convictions. The proceedings of each congress are published in annual volumes under the title *Krónika*.[7] The content of these volumes reflect very little political realism, but a great deal of enthusiasm and an unusual attachment to Hungary and Hungarian culture as they were before the total collapse of their world in 1945.

The convening of these Hungarian congresses in the years following 1961 was only the first of several such new initiatives by the Hungarian Association of Cleveland. In 1965 it was followed by the establishment of the "Árpád Academy," which—named after the late-ninth-century ruler of the conquering Hungarians—was meant to be an institution to recognize the scientific, scholarly, literary, and artistic achievements of Hungarians all over the world. In practice, however, the criteria of selection were and are strongly influenced by the political convictions of the candidate. (Some of its most prominent members included Joseph Cardinal Mindszenty, the Primate of Hungary, and C. A. Macartney, a well-known Oxford historian of Hungary and the Danube Basin. Both men were known for their conservative convictions.)

The foundation of the Árpád Academy was followed five years later (1970) by the establishment of the "Árpád Federation" to recognize individuals who have achieved distinction in social and political leadership positions, and then in the mid-1970s by the foundation of a series of international professional associations (for physicians, engineers, educators, etc.), as well as the already-mentioned "Transylvanian World Federation" *(Erdélyi Világszövetség)*. All of these organizations and associations function under the authority of the Cleveland Hungarian Association, all of them hold their conventions in conjunction with the annual "Hungarian Congress" in Cleveland, and all of their members—at least their most active members and spokesmen—are advocates of a strongly nationalistic and anticommunist conservative social and political order.

The organizer, leader, and moving spirit of all of these activities has been and still is the now octogenarian John Nádas, who, in the course of the last twenty or so years, has also been one of the noted spokesmen of the conservative-nationalist line within the American Hungarian Federation. The Association's scholarly institutions and activities are guided and coordinated by Professor Ferenc Somogyi, a noted legal expert and constitutional historian, formerly of the University of Pécs. Although not necessarily of one mind in all matters, these two men are bound together by their traditionalism and their emotional and intellectual attachment to the world that came to a crushing end in World War II. But among upholders of such traditionalism they represent a middle-of-the-road moderate line—rejecting both left and right radicalism as well as the far-fetched dreams of the "apostles" of various "Hungarian religions" and their search for the alleged "Sumerian," "Egyptian," and "Meso-American" roots of the Magyars.

Although somewhat removed from the realities of modern American society and politics, the Hungarian Association of Cleveland has been an interesting part of the Hungarian-American world ever since the early 1950s. During this period it has fulfilled the most useful functions of giving intellectual shelter to those whose whole world collapsed in 1945 and perpetuating not only the outdated but also some of the worthy ethical, moral, and cultural values of that world. The Association and its leaders have not been able to adjust themselves to the world of today—be it today's Hungary or today's United States. But that is something few could expect from men who, for whatever reasons, were unable to find a spot in American society that would have been commensurate with their education and former social standing, and who have been denied even the right to defend their deeds—achievements and mistakes—by the hardly faultless remakers of modern Hungary in the years following World War II.

Organizations of the Old-Timers

While the Hungarian Association of Cleveland is undoubtedly one of the most typical and most influential organizations of the postwar political immigrants, it has very little to do with the world of the pre–World War II immigrants and their descendants. True, a number of the more aspiring members of the earlier immigrants do attend some of the Hungarian Association's functions (usually those of the native-born second generation who have risen to professional status and have a leadership position in the community), but they have very little role in running it and in influencing its direction. The majority of the old-timers and their offspring, therefore, function in their own societies and organizations. And the situation is very similar in all of the major centers of Hungarian life in the United States.

The most typical surviving associations of the old-timers are the so-called "Hungarian Homes" (*Magyar Házak*) (e.g., McKeesport, Hazelwood, Pa.), urban sectional and business clubs (e.g., Cleveland Hungarian Businessmen's Association, North Side Hungarian Society of Pittsburgh), associations based on one's regional origin in Hungary (e.g., Gömör County Club, Szatmár County Association, both of Cleveland), and various so-called "Grand Committees" born during the interwar period to coordinate the political actions of the many diverse Hungarian-American organizations in a particular locality (e.g., United Societies = *Egyesült Egyletek* of Cleveland, Grand Committee = *Nagybizottság* of Pittsburgh). Most of these associations—outside of the Grand Committees—were and are typical working-class clubs where members relax among their own social peers, converse, drink, play cards and billiards, hold dances and commemorative events, and engage in other diversions. Major Hungarian national holidays are usually celebrated jointly by many of these organizations, usually under the sponsorship of the "Grand Committee," or more recently also by one or another of the major organizations of the postwar immigrants.

Because the social life and atmosphere in these old-timers' clubs are somewhat akin to those of a Hungarian village inn or one of the workmen's associations in Hungary, many of the working-class members of the postwar immigrants also joined them. This was all the more so as they were accepted only reluctantly by the still class-conscious upper layers of their own immigrant groups, and as such they did not feel at home in the latter's organizations. Those who joined the old-timers' associations gradually assimilated to them, accepting their customs, ways, and speech habits to a point where by the early 1980s it was difficult to distinguish between the two groups. The language they use at these organizations is usually a mixture of working-class English and working-class Hungarian, which a recent social anthropologist has correctly identified as "Hunglish."[8] There are two versions of it: Hungarian with the heavy admixture of Americanisms, and English with a heavy admixture of Magyarisms.

Those local organizations of the old-timers that survived into the early 1980s (and many of them did not) did so by adjusting to the needs of the native-born generations of working-class Hungarian-Americans. The fraternities, even the major national ones, fared much worse in the decades since World War II. The small ones disappeared either before or immediately after the war. But during the 1950s two of the four largest fraternities also went out of existence. These were the Rákóczi Association and the "Bridgeport Association," both of which were merged into the more successful Verhovay Association, which then assumed the name of William Penn. The Reformed Federation and the Catholic Society did survive to our own days, but only with growing financial difficulties and amidst continued talk of inevitable merger with the William Penn.

The transformation of the Verhovay into the William Penn Association of Pittsburgh was the result of two factors: relatively few of the postwar immigrants opted to join it or any other fraternity, but went instead with one of the major American insurance associations; and the increased Americanization of the native-born generations, many of whom also selected regular American companies. It was precisely the desire to forestall this exodus and to compete in the truly American market that prompted the Verhovay Association to move in the direction of Americanization—at least in its name.

This drive toward Americanization, however, proved to be much less successful than expected. By the late 1960s and early 1970s it was patently evident that the William Penn, even in its new enlarged form, was not in a position to compete with the multi-billion-dollar giants of the American insurance industry, and that its only hope for survival was to return to its Hungarian roots. Thus, under the leadership of its recently retired (1983) president, Elmer Charles [Károly], it started a re-Hungarianization drive. This process was also fueled by two other factors: the impact of the new "ethnic revolution" upon the consciousness of the third- and fourth-generation Hungarian-Americans and the renewal of contacts with the "New Hungary" that had emerged under Kádár's policy of liberalization.

Establishment of contacts with the mother country was all the easier for the prewar immigrants and their descendants, as they had no political axes to grind and no memories of political persecutions. Moreover, being largely of rural and working-class background, they liked many of the social changes they witnessed during their visits to Hungary. What particularly appealed to them was the eradication of the old class structures and much of the class consciousness that used to characterize interwar and pre–World War I Hungary, and that had also been brought over to the United States by the postwar immigrants. When the Hungarian authorities became aware of these favorable impressions, they and their cultural institutions made a special effort to reach out to the old-timers, their leaders, and their most influential institutions. One of the high points of this improved relationship came in 1978, when President Elmer Charles of the William Penn Association was appointed an official member of the United States delegation that accompanied the return of St. Stephen's Crown ("Holy Crown") to Hungary.[9]

Today the William Penn Association is still dedicated to its new policy of concentrating on Americans of Hungarian extraction and effecting a merger among all of the remaining Hungarian-American fraternities. It does so with the hope that it will survive to carry on the traditions and goals laid down by the founders nearly a century ago.

Political Activism

One of the interesting peculiarities of Hungarian-American life is that until recently Hungarian-Americans have not been able to make a significant showing in the area of American domestic politics. And even some of the recent gains are minimal when compared to those of some of the other nationalities from eastern and southeastern Europe. In fact, Hungarians may be alone among nationalities of comparable size and time spent in the United States who can show hardly any representation in the United States Congress, and are similarly underrepresented in city and state politics. Of the past and current United States congressmen with Hungarian roots (Berger, Weiss, Lantos) none of them was involved in Hungarian-American life, none of them was elected by constituencies of their own nationality, and none represented Hungarian-American communities or interests while in office. The only exception may turn out to be Thomas Lantos of California, a 56-er, who since his election (1980) has shown some interest in matters concerning Hungary and the Hungarians (among them the Hungarian minorities in Transylvania-Rumania), but not in line with the views and expectations of the outspokenly anticommunist, conservative-nationalist or rightist-nationalist leaders of the postwar immigrants.

Some of the reasons for this political underrepresentation may be the following: (1) most of the old-timers did not become United States citizens until the 1920s and 1930s, and even then few of them became sufficiently fluent in English and daring enough to run for an office; (2) the native-born second generation was largely unqualified and unavailable for political office until after World War II, when their ethnic organizations were pushed into the background by those of the postwar immigrants, who again were unqualified for linguistic and political (lack of citizenship) reasons; (3) Hungarian-Americans were crippled politically by Hungary's poor image from its association with Germany in two world wars; (4) the uniqueness of the Magyar-Hungarians, i.e., the fact that they have no ethnic and linguistic relatives among the immigrants such as the Slavs, several of whom can combine to elect one or another of their spokesmen to a public office.

These and perhaps other factors limited much of Hungarian-American politics even in the decades following World War II to a kind of "ethnic politics" that manifested itself in the presentation of petitions to various United States governmental agencies and in attempts to put group pressures on some of these agencies and individual politicians via their Hungarian-American ethnic organizations. Until relatively recently, these efforts brought few results beyond such nominal "gains" as form letters from the president, members of the United States Congress, and from one or another of the approached agencies. The situation began to change only in the late 1960s, largely as a result of new initiatives by a few of the most widespread and representative Hungarian-American organizations, such as the American Hungarian Federation, the Hungarian Freedom Fighters' Federation, and some of the organizations established for the protection of the Hungarian minorities in the surrounding states.

The most significant of these efforts was the drive to acquire United States citizenship for all Hungarians and then to exercise their power of the vote. They were all told to join the ranks of one of the two major parties. In practice, however, the old-timers and most of their working-class descendants continued to vote for the Democratic party, while the majority of the postwar immigrants moved into the ranks of the Republican party. The latter did so because of their belief that the Democrats "are soft on communism," while many of the 56-ers and the "successful" offspring of the 45-ers and 47-ers did so because of their established middle-class status—unless coming from a traditionally liberal family. It is to be added that these affiliations are difficult to substantiate statistically. But they are generally known in the Hungarian-American communities, and can also be substantiated up to a point by the political preferences of the various types of Hungarian-American newspapers. Thus, while before World War II basically the whole spectrum of the Hungarian-American press (outside the few communist papers) were in the Democratic camp, in the period since the early 1950s the situation has altered radically. Whether newly founded or simply taken over from the old-timers, the overwhelming majority of the postwar immigrants' papers support Republican candidates at all levels of government.

The most visible achievement of this new policy of "moving into party ranks" was the appointment of László Pásztor, a 56-er, as director of the Nationalities Division of the Republican National Committee in 1969. While in this office (1969–1973) Pásztor enlisted the support of a significant portion of the formerly Democratic ethnic vote. Simultaneously he also coordinated the East European segment of this group to direct the Republican party's attention once more to the policy of "the liberation of captive nations," which used to be popular in the early 1950s. But the growing detente between the two superpowers made this effort less than successful. This was all the more so as, contrary to the strongly anticommunist members of the postwar political immigrants, an increasing number of the younger generations were more interested in opportunities for social and economic advancements than in the Cold War mentality and political goals of their elders. Moreover, in this American-born or at least American-raised and educated second generation there also arose the desire to establish contacts with the land of their ancestors. This was usually followed by visits, which inevitably altered their views concerning today's Hungary and the whole question of East-West relations.

Main Political Issues since 1950

In the course of the last three or so decades since the arrival of the postwar immigrants, the Hungarian-American community had been mobilized by a number of issues, all of which—true to the Hungary-centered nature of Hungarian ethnic politics—concerned either the immigrants' former homeland or the Hungarian-American community. (The best proof for this one-directional orientation of the political immigrants is to be found in the *Proceedings* of the twenty-odd Hungarian Congresses in Cleveland, all of which deal only with Hungarian or Hungarian-American questions, with no attention whatsoever to those aspects of American domestic politics that have no bearing on Hungary or the Hungarians. [10])

During the early 1950s Hungarian-Americans expected and demanded the implementation of the "policy of liberation." In 1956 they mobilized to aid the revolution and then, after its collapse, to help the tens of thousands of "freedom fighters." In the late 1950s and early 1960s the thrust of their political activities was to demand the implementation of United Nations resolutions concerning Hungary, including the withdrawal of Soviet troops, the holding of U.N.-supervised free elections, and the ending of reprisals against imprisoned revolutionaries.

After the "Hungarian Question" was removed from the U.N. agenda, Hungarian-Americans once more returned to the policy of liberation, which they pushed throughout the late 1960s and early 1970s. At the same time, however, their attention was also caught by Hungary's efforts to normalize its relationship with the West, as well as with its former citizens abroad. This was extremely unwelcome to the leaders of the postwar political immigrants, all the more so as it coincided with Cardinal Mindszenty's coming to the West (after fifteen years of seclusion at the American Embassy in Budapest) and the consequent effort of these leaders to revitalize their anticommunist crusade. They feared that this normalization would take the wind out of their sails. To prevent this, they launched their own counterattack. Among other things they pointed to the Hungarian government's consistently pro-Soviet foreign policy, comparing it unfavorably to that of maverick Rumania; they criticized its lack of sufficient attention to the disastrous demographic problems in Hungary (i.e., low birth rate, extremely liberal abortion policy, etc.), interpreting them as a conscious effort to eradicate the non-Slavic Hungarians from the Carpathian Basin; denounced its seeming lack of effort to speak up forcefully for the increasingly oppressed Hungarian minorities in the neighboring socialist states, which by the 1970s had become the single most painful problem for all Hungarians everywhere; and interpreted its undeniable effort to gain sympathizers among Hungarian-Americans for the "New Hungary" that had emerged during the 1960s and 1970s as simply another form of "communist penetration" into the fabric of American society. They were particularly incensed at Hungary's success in having been able to carry through its policy of normalization, which was sealed in 1978 by the United States decision to return the Crown of St. Stephen, while almost simultaneously granting "Most Favored Nation" status to Hungary. They interpreted these measures as basically "immoral acts" that "legitimized an illegitimate regime."

By the late 1970s and early 1980s, however, the voice of the Hungarian-Americans was far from uniform. For several reasons the normalization of United States–Hungarian relations also found support among an increasing number of them. And what is of special significance is that this support came largely from the ranks of the younger and more successful professional groups, who knew quite well that the Hungary of the late 1970s was not identical with that of the early 1950s, and whose weight and influence in American society were by now considerably greater than those of the traditional political immigrants.

A number of the latter even became involved in the so-called "Mother Tongue Movement," which, launched in 1970, was one of Hungary's efforts to reach out to the Hungarian communities abroad and, in the spirit of the new ethnic revival, help them in their efforts to preserve their linguistic and cultural heritage. While the Mother Tongue Movement undoubtedly has its own political opportunists—a charge made by the political immigrants—the majority of its activists and supporters, both here and abroad, are educators, scholars, scientists, administrators, and community leaders whose primary goal is the preservation and perpetuation of the cultural heritage of their ancestors.

The success of the Mother Tongue Movement also prompted the Hungarian World Federation—the institution in charge of these activities—to organize similar get-togethers for economists, physicians, scientists, historians, etc., in the hope of improving its relations with Hungarians abroad through the mediation of these professionals, who are more interested in scientific and cultural matters than in Cold War politics. Hungarian-Americans have played a significant role in all of these conferences and exchanges because of their significance and their numbers among Hungarians abroad.

The many controversies stemming from the Hungarian government's effort and success in normalizing its relations with the United States and in demonstrating to an ever-increasing number of Hungarian-Americans that today's Hungary is not identical with that which they or their parents left behind have divided Hungarian-Americans to a point far beyond what they have ever experienced before. One's attitude toward the mother country became the touchstone of one's relationship to and acceptance by the traditional Hungarian-American society. For a while the supporters of the policy of reassessment were subjected to social ostracism and even personal attacks in the Hungarian-American press. While this had very little impact on those professionals whose contacts with the community were minimal, but it did prevent many others from openly expressing their views on this matter.

Yet, none of these developments was able to prevent the process of self-examination by an increasing number of Hungarian-Americans or the ever more popular tendency among them to disregard the directives of the various immigrant "summit" organizations and the proclamations of their "world congresses," and simply carry through their own "normalization" with the mother country. Most of them did this by returning for personal visits, and even by sending their American-born children to Hungary to take a look at the land and culture of their forefathers.

This trend toward normalization has been supported by such professional associations as the American Association for the Study of Hungarian History (1970) and the American Hungarian Educators' Association (1975). During the 1970s and the early 1980s it was also aided by the increased scholarly exchanges between Hungary and those American institutions of higher learning that have some offerings in Hungarian studies (e.g., Indiana, Columbia, Rutgers, Duquesne), as well as by the lecture and performance tours of various Hungarian intellectuals and artists sponsored by the New York publisher Sándor Püski. This normalization was likewise favored by an organization of the "successful" Hungarian-American intellectuals known as the *Itt-Ott* (Here and there), which holds annual congresses and publishes a periodical under the same title

(Itt-Ott). Of perhaps equal importance is the fact that in recent years this trend toward "realism" has also been felt within the ranks of some of the major Hungarian-American organizations that have traditionally been staunch opponents of communist Hungary and powerful critics of the policy of normalization. The best example of this is the American Hungarian Federation, an organization that in the course of the past two or three years has witnessed the growing influence of the supporters of normalization. This in turn has led to growing factionalism and bitter infighting, resulting in a still-unresolved split that has put the very existence of the Federation in jeopardy. As a matter of fact, in July 1984, one of the two main factions (headed by László Pásztor and John Nádas) split from the AHF and founded the rival American Hungarian National Federation (*Amerikai Magyarok Országos Szövetsége*). The much fragmented AHF is now headed by Tibor Dömötör, the recently consecrated bishop of the newly established Independent Hungarian Reformed Church in America (1983), who only a few years earlier also founded a new Hungarian Reformed Home for the Aged (The Lorántffy Home) as well as a Hungarian Reformed Seminary (The Gáspár Karoli Seminary), both in Akron, Ohio.

Chapter Ten

Journalism, Publishing, Literature, Learning, and Scholarship Since World War II

The Restructuring of Hungarian-American Journalism

The coming of the postwar immigrants in 1950 found the Hungarian-American community with at least forty-five newspapers. According to one contemporary survey, there were two dailies (the *Szabadság* and the *Amerikai Magyar Népszava*), twenty-nine weeklies, five papers with religious affiliations, three fraternal publications (one each for the Verhovay, the Rákóczi, and the Bridgeport associations), four unclassifiable papers (including the monarchist *Krónika* and the humorous weekly *Dongó* [Bumblebee]), and finally two unnamed communist papers, which, according to this survey, "cannot be counted among publications that represent the Hungarian spirit."[1]

While this list is undoubtedly incomplete, it does indicate that old-time Hungarian-American journalism was still flourishing at the time when the new wave of immigration began. Yet, by the late 1950s and early 1960s the situation had changed drastically. Many of the papers on this list either folded, were in the process of going under, or have been taken over by the newcomers. In the latter case, their language and content changed radically, as did their political orientation.

In the course of the same brief decade a series of new papers were also started by the postwar immigrants, which represented a wide variety of political orientations yet were within the spectrum of conservative nationalism to right-radical nationalism. Most of these papers proved to be ephemeral. Others, however, managed to stay alive by increasing the number of their readers, but by doing so they undermined most of the old-time newspapers and then pushed them off the market completely. But whether ephemeral or of long duration, the overwhelming majority of these papers were emphatically political, strongly nationalisitic and anticommunist, and prone to representing certain well-defined groups or ideologies within the above-described political spectrum. They were also characterized by a propensity to engage in intense ideological debates, personal quarrels, and mutual recriminations with those with whom they disagreed.

Of all the journalistic projects of the postwar years the most ambitious was the effort by the Catholic priest József Galambos to establish a dominant daily that would represent the views of the postwar immigrants. Galambos was a powerful nationalist of strong political convictions who took strong exception to the content, tone, and political orientation of the old-time dailies. In his view the editors of the *Szabadság* and the *Amerikai Magyar Népszava* knew little about the great issues concerning Hungary, nor did they really care. Thus, like a twentieth-century Savonarola, Galambos went about proselytizing for his cause. He also agitated in a small monthly entitled *Végvár* (Frontier fortress, 1953–1956), which he wrote and edited himself. The result of his efforts was the birth in 1956 of the *Szabad Magyarság* (Free Hungarians). Galambos himself never saw the birth of his paper, for he died of physical exhaustion a year before its launching.

Contrary to Galambos's dream, the *Szabad Magyarság* never became a daily paper. It was published for six years in New York (1956–1962) by a group of his ideological supporters and then went under in a slander suit initiated (and won) by Zoltán Klár, the editor of the old-time socialist paper *Az Ember* (Human being). Apparently, in their effort to push their radical nationalist ideology, the editors of the *Szabad Magyarság* went so far in their personal attacks that it became unacceptable even to the generally very tolerant American press laws.[2]

Having been destroyed financially by the award to their adversary, the editors tried to resurrect their paper under the title *Magyar Szabadság* (Hungarian freedom). But by that time they had also been undermined by the internal rivalries that had plagued them from the very start, and which now found their way onto the front page of their paper, as well as into various circulars and countercirculars to their readers. It was in the midst of these circumstances that the *Magyar Szabadság* went under after only two years (1963–1965).

The demise of the *Magyar Szabadság* still left numerous significant weeklies in the hands of the postwar immigrants. Of those that survived into the early 1980s, the most widely read include the conservative nationalist *New Yorki Magyar Élet* (New York Hungarian life), which is published in Toronto; the *Katolikus Magyarok Vasárnapja* (Catholic Hungarians' Sunday) (Cleveland-Youngstown), which, after being taken over by the new immigrants, had been reshaped by its editor, the novelist István Eszterhás, into a nationalist political paper; the *Amerikai Magyar Élet* (American Hungarian life) (Chicago), which, like the *New Yorki Magyar Élet*, caters to the interwar middle classes; the *Az Ujság* (News)—between 1975 and 1981; *Magyar Ujság* (Hungarian news)—which was transformed by its editor, Father Zoltán Kótai, from a socialist into a middle-of-the-road nationalist paper, representing primarily the postwar immigrant community of Cleveland; the *Magyarság* (Hungarians) of Pittsburgh, which, under Jenő Szebedinszky's editorship, was reshaped from an old-time newspaper into a voice of rightist nationalism; and the more substantial but equally right nationalist *Kanadai Magyarság* (Canadian Hungarians), which, while published in Toronto, is really a North American paper, geared equally to the United States and the Canadian market. Of special significance are the monthlies, the *Nemzetőr* (National Guardian) of Munich, Germany, which, under the editorship of the poet Tibor Tollas, claims to represent the ideals of the Revolution of 1956, and which has a very wide readership in the United States; and the Cleveland-based *Szittyakürt* (Scythian horn), edited by Tibor Major, which is probably the most widely read paper of the far right published in the United States. It combines a form of rightist nationalism with the advocacy of the alleged Near Eastern roots of the Hungarians (Sumerians, Medians, etc.).

It should be mentioned here that the members of the Hungarian-American community read and are influenced by a great number of émigré papers published in Europe. In addition to the *Nemzetőr*, some of the more widely read papers include the *Hadak Útján* (On warpath), published by the old military establishment; the *Irodalmi Ujság* (Literary gazette) of Paris, which is the paper of the left-leaning liberal intelligentsia; the *Új Látóhatár* (New horizon) of Munich, which carries on the traditions of the so-called Populist

Movement in Hungary; the *Katolikus Szemle* (Catholic review) of Rome, the periodical of the progressive Catholic intelligentsia; and the *Új Európa* (New Europe), which until its recent demise (1983) liked to appear cosmopolitan but was really a thinly veiled monarchist paper supporting Otto von Habsburg.

And the papers of the old-timers? Most of the regional and local papers that have not been taken over by the newcomers ceased publication during the 1950s and 1960s. Of the two major dailies, the New York–based *Amerikai Magyar Népszava* and the Cleveland–based *Szabadság*—with much-reduced circulation (ca. 10,000) and with virtually identical content—continued to cater to an ever-shrinking audience consisting largely of the remaining old immigrants and those of their children who still read Hungarian. By the early 1970s both of these papers ceased to be dailies and now are published twice weekly by the same owner-editor, Zoltán Gombos of Cleveland.

The 1970s witnessed a rapid decline in the status of the Hungarian-American press. There are still many dozens of papers, and others were still being founded as late as the early 1980s (e.g., *Cleveland Híradó* [Cleveland chronicler] and *Új Idő* [New time], also of Cleveland), but most of them cater only to small audiences, and few have the chance to survive beyond a year or two. In the course of the last decade or so the readership of all papers has been steadily declining. There are no more dailies, and the frequency of publication of most papers has also decreased, the dailies becoming biweeklies, the weeklies becoming two-weeklies or monthlies, and the monthlies becoming two-monthlies or quarterlies.

The reasons for this phenomenon include the dying off of the old generations of both the pre- and postwar immigrants, the lack of interest and linguistic competence of the younger generations, and the radical increase in the influx of good quality publications from Hungary, which in many areas have much more to offer than their émigré counterparts. As such, the future of Hungarian-American journalism is far from bright. Unless some unexpected event will alter the situation, dozens of papers will fold during the 1980s, leaving only those that are able to adjust to the new realities and can offer something that neither the Hungarian press nor the American press can offer.[3]

During its heyday in the period between 1950 and 1975, Hungarian-American journalism was characterized by radical politicization, powerful nationalism, and strong anticommunism, but also by factionalism, personal and group rivalries, lack of self-criticism, and by an equal lack of literary-aesthetic criticism of works that were politically acceptable. In spite of these shortcomings, however, this press played an important part in keeping the Hungarian spirit and Hungarian way of life going under conditions that were far from ideal. With sufficient resilience, some of the more worthy papers may yet survive into the twenty-first century.

Publishing and Publishers

One of the hard realities of Hungarian-American journalism was and is that—outside of the major dailies and a few large weeklies—most papers have been one-man operations. Their publishing, editing, much of their writing, and at times—particularly in the early days—even their printing was done by one and the same individual. This still holds true today for many small papers, and it also applies to book publishing. This means that the majority of the books put out by and for Hungarian-Americans are being published by their authors themselves at their own expense. And this is often true even when the published work carries the name of a publisher. Many times these are fictional "publishers" that do not really exist; or if they do, in all probability they have published the work with the author's own subsidy. There are some exceptions to this rule, but they are few and far between.

This does not mean that Hungarian-American authors were and are totally without publishers. In the interwar years these publishers were usually identical with the printing presses of the larger Hungarian-American papers, such as the *Szabadság* of Cleveland, the *Amerikai Magyar Népszava* of New York, and the *Magyarság* of Pittsburgh (Pannonia Press). Most of the Protestant publications, on the other hand, were printed at the Bethlen Press of the Hungarian Reformed Church in Ligonier, Pennsylvania. But, unless of specific interest to these newspapers and institutions, all of the works published by these presses had to be subsidized by the authors. (Many of them did this by collecting subscribers for their as yet unpublished works.)

With the coming of the postwar immigrants the situation changed only in that the number of the published works increased dramatically. The new immigrants wished to propagate their views not only in newspapers and periodicals but also in books and pamphlets. Thus, almost immediately after their arrival, they established small part-time publishers that operated through the financial contributions and physical labors of some of the immigrants.

Two of the earliest of such publishers were the "Amerikai-Magyar Kiadó" (American Hungarian publisher) of Munich and Cleveland, and the "Kossuth Kiadó" (Kossuth publisher) of Cleveland. The first of these published usually political works, while the latter specialized in textbooks for the immigrants' children. These were followed in the late 1950s and the early 1960s by such publishers as the Occicental Press of Washington, D.C., operated by István Csicsery-Rónay, who concentrates on publishing high-quality literary works; and the "Árpád Könyvkiadó" (Árpád publisher) of Cleveland, which is the Hungarian Association's official publisher, putting out works connected with the activities of the Association. Also during the 1960s was launched the American Hungarian Literary Guild and its affiliate, the Danubian Press of Astor, Florida. Headed by the novelist Albert Wass, these presses publish both literary and political works—including Wass's own novels in both languages. A sizable portion of these publications are of a type that reflect the owner-publisher's conservative nationalist philosophy and his concern for the Hungarian minorities in Transylvania (Rumania), which is his own more immediate homeland.

While the Danubian Press is one of the more prolific Hungarian-American publishers, it is surpassed by far by the Cleveland-based Kárpát Publishing Co., operated until his recent death (1981) by the Catholic priest Father Zoltán Kótai. Kótai began his publishing activities in postwar Germany in 1946. After spending nearly a decade in Argentina, where he was involved in similar publishing ventures, in the late 1950s he transferred his seat of activities to Cleveland. There he bought the longtime socialist paper *Az Ujság* (later *Magyar Ujság*) and transformed it into a middle-of-the-road nationalist paper to fit needs of the postwar immigrants. He also edited a literary-cultural monthly, *A Kárpát* (Carpathian), and then went into book publishing. In the course of the next two decades the Kárpát Publishing Co. put out over three hundred separate titles (which is a prodigious number in Hungarian-American terms). Many of these were prayer books and other religious works, but an even larger share consisted of Hungarian classics that were placed into the hands of Hungarian-Americans before becoming readily available from Hungary. Father Kótai also published the works of many immigrant authors, whose honorarium was usually a few hundred copies of their own works. The rest were retained by the publisher and then offered for sale in the hope of being able to recoup his investment—which did not always occur.

In addition to these publishers, the press of the *Katolikus Magyarok Vasárnapja,* which has been reshaped into a political paper, has also published dozens of political works, as well as Hungarian classics unavailable in Hungary for political reasons. Occasionally several other Hungarian printing presses also became publishers. These included those operated in the 1970s by the Rev. Andrew Hamza and István Szatmári, both of New Jersey, who published works in Hungarian literature, history, politics, and art, often subsidizing some of these publications with their own labor. For a while in the early 1970s Rev. Hamza published and edited a high-quality literary journal entitled the *Ötágú Síp* (Five-branched blow-pipe).

In recent years these older publishers were joined by a few others, such as Püski Publishers of New York, operated by Sándor Püski, a noted interwar Hungarian publisher and since 1970 the owner-operator of the largest Hungarian bookstore in the United States, which specializes in modern Hungarian literature and sociography; Framo Publishers of Chicago, which publishes mostly avant-garde Hungarian poetry, including the work of the owner-operator, Ferenc Mózsi, who also edits the literary journal *Szivárvány* (Rainbow); and Classic Printing of Cleveland, which since the early 1960s has become the primary printer of Hungarian books throughout North America. Operated by László Berta, in the late 1970s Classic Printing also began to appear as a publisher, putting out such works on Hungarian history and culture that the owner saw fit to subsidize with his own labor.

Simultaneously with these mostly Magyar-language publishers, in the late 1960s and 1970s a number of Hungarian-American organizations also began to publish works in English. These include the American Hungarian Foundation of New Brunswick, New Jersey, which under the directorship of August J. Molnar publishes pamphlets and handbooks on Hungarian-American life and culture; and the Hungarian Cultural Foundation of Atlanta, which, founded and directed by J. M. Értavy-Baráth, specializes in publishing English translations of Hungarian poetry. During the 1960s the *Hungarian American Review* of St. Louis, edited by László (Leslie) Könnyü, also published some books on Hungarian literature and Hungarian-American history—the majority of them by the editor himself, who is also a poet and a writer.[4]

The existence of these few publishers does not alter the fact that in most instances Hungarian-American authors who write in Hungarian simply publish or at least subsidize their own works. And this is true even if some of these works are published in English without the backing of a university, college, or another scholarly institution. In most instances these authors are also their own distributors. Their outlets are the few Hungarian bookstores in the larger cities, some of their personal friends scattered throughout the Hungarian-American communities, and they themselves. Often they try to sell their works to audiences at public lectures or other performances, or send them out unsolicited to several hundred acquaintances, organizations, and other addresses in the hope of some remuneration, good reviews, or at least some "recognition." This situation is best described in a recent interview with the Swedish-Hungarian poet Géza Thinsz, which appeared in the pages of the *Élet és Irodalom* (Life and literature), the official Budapest paper of the Hungarian Writers' Union.[5] Being asked about the publisher of his works, he responded: "They are put out by a publisher that specializes on publishing Géza Thinsz's works." He then went on to explain that he usually publishes his own works in 1,000 copies, of which he sends out 800 as "complimentary copies" to his friends and acquaintances.

In light of the above, the life of a Hungarian author in America is far from enviable. Unless he breaks into the English-language market, he has no chance of making a living from his writings. But it is precisely this situation that permits people with little or no talent or scholarly background to publish their "literary" and "scholarly" works with impunity. And because this situation exists in conjunction with an atmosphere where honest literary or scholarly criticism is impossible without one's being accused of personal vendetta or, even worse, of being a "communist" or a "fascist," there are some persons totally devoid of any talent and learning who walk around freely in the Hungarian-American community demanding recognition as "poets," "novelists," or "historians."

Literature and Reading Habits

While the absence of honest criticism—bemoaned by many gifted Hungarian authors[6]—is not the only characteristic of Hungarian-

American literary life, it is certainly one of its main features. Its other characteristics, until the coming of the postwar political immigrants, included (1) the continuation of the populist and popular traditions of nineteenth-century Hungarian literature (e.g., Sándor Petőfi and János Arany); (2) the lack of intellectual polish in the works of the various Petőfi and Arany-epigons, partially because of their own shortcomings and partially because of the need to keep them on the level of their humble readers; (3) and their primary attention to such topics as alienation, loneliness and helplessness, the hardships of their daily toils, and most of all, their longing for their homeland, families, and friends.[7]

The best known among these pioneer writers, most of whom were poets, are Adam Abet (1867–1949), Gyula Rudnyánszky (1858–1913), László Pólya (1870–1950), György Kemény (1875–1952), György Szécskay (1880–1958), László Szabó (1880–1961), Árpád Tarnóczy (1884–1957), and József Reményi (1892–1956). With the exception of Abet, who was a socialist, they all followed the Kossuthist-nationalist traditions, they all disliked the Habsburgs, and they were all clamoring for total independence for Hungary. But once independence came in the form of the much-reduced "Trianon Hungary," they all reacted with horror and began to idealize even the immediate past. With very few exceptions, they and their kind all made their living by editing or writing for Hungarian newspapers, by becoming traveling salesmen for these newspapers, and by peddling their own works and a few other simple publications to their subscribers and prospective subscribers. The only exception to this rule among these better-known poets was József Reményi, who, unlike most Hungarian literati of those days, did make it in American society. After writing for American newspapers, he was appointed lecturer (1929) and then professor of comparative literature at Western Reserve University. For this very reason, Reményi was far removed from the hardships of Hungarian-American life, and he wrote more for sophisticated audiences in Hungary than for his companions in exile. He was also the first significant interpreter of Hungarian literature to American audiences.[8]

Mention should also be made of Pál Szarvas, a Pittsburgh newspaperman who wrote under the pseudonym of "Indian." He wrote simple weekly rhymes *(Heti Strófák)* about the tragedies and comedies of Hungarian-American life during the 1920s and 1930s.[9] While these verses can hardly be called poetry—nor did he claim so—their content and atmosphere are probably more telling about the lives, loves, and miseries of his fellow immigrants than even the best literary pieces of the above authors. Moreover, they were also more widely read by Hungarian-American workers.

The simplicity and earthly humbleness of Hungarian-American literature during the first half of this century were replaced after 1950 by a totally different kind of literature. The events leading up to World War II and the turmoil that followed drove many of Hungary's well-known authors into exile. These included the playwright Ferenc Molnár (1878–1952), the novelists Lajos Zilahy (1891–1978), Ferenc Körmendi (1900–1972), Sándor Márai (1900–), and Albert Wass (1908–), the poet György Faludy (1910–), the sociographers Imre Kovács (1911–1981) and Gyula Gombos (1913–), and dozens of others who ended up on one of the other continents. Not all of them were or are advocates of the same political philosophy, nor did they all leave Hungary at the same time and for the same reasons. What they all had in common was the status of recognized authors. Yet of these literary men only one, Ferenc Molnár, was able to attain recognition with the American public. Molnár even increased his fame, achieving international recognition and the status of becoming Hungary's best-known author abroad. This "recognition", by the way, has no relationship to his much more humble position in twentieth-century Hungarian literature. In all probability this was the result of the popularity of his literary genre, combined with a considerable amount of good fortune. As compared to Molnár, for example, the much greater composer Béla Bartók hardly received any recognition before his death. He died in 1945 in New York, a bitter and disappointed man.

While all of the authors enumerated above have settled in the United States (at least for a significant portion of their émigré lives), only a few of them became Hungarian-American writers in the traditional sense of that term. Most of them did not mix with the community, were not involved in Hungarian-American life, and wrote very little about Hungarian-American experiences. They were or are simply Hungarian novelists and poets in exile. (The only real exception is Wass, and to a lesser degree Faludy and the two sociographers Kovács and Gombos.)

Much different was the situation with those who after immigration made their homes in Hungarian-American communities, retained contacts with those communities, or became poets and novelists after their immigration. The intellectual and cultural world of these authors was increasingly determined by their experiences as "Hungarians in America" or as "Hungarian-Americans," and their audiences also came almost exclusively from the Hungarian-American community.

In the course of the past three decades the ranks of these poets, novelists, essayists, and others have grown into many hundreds. To keep track of them is almost impossible, for virtually every Hungarian-American community has its share of celebrated or recognized authors. Their ranks are also swollen by those "lonely souls" who live far away from these Hungarian centers, and it was precisely their "loneliness" in an "alien sea" that brought the poet out of them. Their "literary works," however, are seldom more than emotional personal confessions, written in a language that has not been able to keep up with the modern Hungarian literary language and has also been corrupted by the authors' alien cultural-linguistic surroundings.

Naturally, there are exceptions to these generalizations, and Hungarian-Americans do have their share of good to excellent poets and novelists, the best of them being undoubtedly Márai, Faludy, and Wass, all of whom had already been recognized authors in Hungary during the 1930s. The others include such more traditional poets as Tibor Flórián, Tamás Tűz, Ferenc Fáy, József Kossányi, Márton Kerecsendi-Kiss, Imre Sári-Gál, Iván Béky-Halász, Lajos Illés, László Könnyű, György Gyékenyesi, and others. In some instances this "traditionalism" implies only attachment to more traditional poetic forms; in other instances, however, it also means the advocacy of a more traditional worldview. There are also a number of noted modernist writers who in some instances represent the far-out avant-garde. They include the novelist and publicist Tamás Aczél and the poets József Bakucz, László Baránszky, Ádám Makkai, Elemér Horváth, Sándor András, György Vitéz, László Kemenes-Géfin, Ferenc Mózsi, and several others, whose works, naturally, have greater appeal to the literally inclined members of the younger generations than to their more conservative elders (It should be noted here that a few of these authors reside in Canada, but often it is very difficult to distinguish between "American" and "Canadian" authors, all the more so as they often move across the border.)

While Hungarian-American poetry does constitute a certain segment of the readings of Hungarian-Americans, it is really a rather small segment. Discounting the fact that most members of the younger generation are more at home in English than in Hungarian, poetry has much less of an appeal today than it did a generation or two ago, and considerably less than it still has in Hungary.

As to the members of the older generations? Being political immigrants in the fast-moving world of modern America, most of them want to read works that expose their political beliefs at considerable length, bring back memories about the world they have lost, or simply offer easily digestible diversions from their everyday toils and problems. Much of this is more easily done in prose than in poetry, let alone in the largely incomprehensible imagery of avant-garde poetry. It is for these reasons that the works that have enjoyed the greatest popularity in the course of the past three decades are in one of the following categories: (1) traditional nineteenth- or early twentieth-century literary classics that portray the "good" and "heroic" days of Hungarian history as these are understood by the immigrants; (2) light prose that offers simple diversion from the problems and hardships of everyday life; (3) unabashed political novels that praise the immigrants' own "virtues" and the "virtues" of their heroes, while at the same time depict the "evils" of their adversaries; (4) strictly political treatises that elaborate political ideologies resembling their own or denounce contrary ideologies; (5) and historical works or pseudohistorical studies that speak of the "greatness" of their ancestors or alleged ancestors, or of their own "heroism" in their struggle against Soviet communism. These preferences clearly explain the reasons for the tendency to reprint Hungarian classics before they were available from Hungary. They also explain the unusual popularity of such escape literature as the novels of Claire Kenneth (1921–) and of several less well known authors that are in the category of the "Harlequin" and the "Silhouette" romances; as well as the similar popularity of the less easily digestible political novels by such authors as Albert Wass, Lajos Fűry (1913–), and to a lesser degree István Eszterhás (1907–). These authors write what the older and largely middle-class political immigrants crave for: to escape to a "night in Cairo" (Kenneth), or to relive vicariously the "heroic days" of World War II (Wass, Füry), the trials, tribulations, and triumphs of their own immigrant life (Wass, Füry, Eszterhás), the great ages of Hungarian history (Wass, Füry, Eszterhás), or life in beautiful Transylvania of yore when it was still Hungarian (Wass). It is for the same reasons that the majority of the political immigrants (especially men) prefer outright political works to belles lettres—be these by Otto von Habsburg, by one of the several World War II generals, or by any one of Hungary's many ex-politicians. This also holds true for historical works, particularly those that deal with various aspects of the origins of the Hungarians, or with one of the great periods of Hungary's millennial history. [10]

Search for Past Greatness and for the "Unreal"

The popularity of works that explore various new theories concerning the origins of the Hungarians has reached proportions that can only be compared to a world-wide epidemic; and Hungarian-Americans are right in the middle of it. What is most interesting about this phenomenon is that most of the practitioners of this "search for our true heritage" are not professionally trained scholars; or if they are, their training was usually in fields other than archaeology, ancient history, linguistics, ancient classical languages, etc., that are needed for the legitimate study of this question. It is equally interesting that, once caught in the web of belief, the new converts themselves become "linguists," "historians," and "archaeologists," and soon add a series of new "discoveries" to the corpus of accumulated information—which they then regard as part of the "unimpeachable truth."

Briefly, the advocates of these new theories—although often clashing concerning details—reject the traditional view that the Hungarians are Finno-Ugric people and thus related to the Finns, Estonians, and several other much smaller ethnic groups in the Soviet Union. They hold that the Hungarians are the direct or indirect descendants of one or several of such once great peoples as the ancient Sumerians, Egyptians, Medes, Etruscans, or even the Mayans, pre-Vedic Indians, etc. Some of them go so far as to search for their roots on the mythical continents of Mu and Atlantis. Their arguments are based partially on linguistic comparisons between the "agglutinative" Magyar language and the similarly "agglutinative" languages of the Sumerians and perhaps some of the other mentioned peoples, and partially on new conclusions drawn from the reread and reinterpreted ancient classics, including cuneiform inscriptions, hieroglyphics, and the works of various Greek, Persian, Roman, Indian, Byzantine, Islamic, and other historians and travelers.

The originator of this movement in the United States was the historian Ida Bobula (1900–1981), who published a series of studies concerning Sumerian-Hungarian relations as early as the 1950s. She was followed by numerous others, each of whom added something to her theory, at times expanding it beyond recognition. These included Viktor Padányi, Imre Szelényi, Géza Kúr, Tibor Baráth, Mátyás Jenő Fehér, Sándor Nagy, Ferenc Badiny-Jós, and many dozens of others who came forth with increasingly visionary views concerning the Hungarian past. A number of these also republished the works of several of their predecessors in Hungary, whose works were handled by the uninitiated as though they were works of recent scholarship (József Cserép, Ede Somogyi, Jenő Csicsáky, József Aczél, János Galgóczy, Ferenc Zajti, Zsigmond Varga, etc.).[11]

The difference in the scholarly quality of these works is considerable, stretching from works that offer challenging theories that are reasonably well explained to amateurish pamphlets that are simply confessions of faith. Ultimately, however, it is not the scholarly quality that determines the "significance" of one of these works, but rather the increasingly popular belief in the Near Eastern and other "classical" roots of the Magyars. Belief in these views among certain immigrant circles is an article of faith, and adherence or nonadherence to it is really a "political" or "religious" decision.

This search for the unusual, extraordinary, and even the unreal can only be explained in light of the harsh realities of modern and recent Hungarian history. This is not the first time that we have witnessed the rise of such tendencies, but the popularity of this type of escapism into the past is usually connected with major crises and radical breaks in Hungary's historical evolution. Nor is this a phenomenon that is limited to Hungary and the Hungarians. The history of the national revival movements of East Central and Southeast Europe is filled with such searches for the unreal, i.e., for events and achievements that never really happened. And this is still easily demonstrable when one studies the officially proclaimed dogmas of the historiography of a number of neighboring peoples (Rumanians, Slovaks, etc.), which are propagated and defended with the fervor of religious fanaticism. And here we have come to another aspect of Hungarian émigré life: the birth of various so-called "Hungarian Religions."

In the course of the 1970s several of these "Hungarian Religions" were founded throughout the world—mostly in Argentina and Canada; but they also have considerable number of followers among Hungarian-Americans. In fact, as mentioned earlier, one of the champions of these "religions" is the Cleveland-based *Szittyakürt,* although abroad there are several papers that are dedicated exclusively or largely to the propagation of one or another of these faiths.

Perhaps the most colorful "prophet" of one of these religions is Ferenc Badiny-Jós, who has already been mentioned among the better-known advocates of the Sumerian roots of the Hungarians. In addition to authoring several widely read works on his historical theories, in 1973 he also published a "catechism" of his new religion entitled *Magyar Hit* (Hungarian faith). He further elaborated his theology in the journal *Ősi Gyökér* (Ancient roots), which he edits, and where he freely intermixes his religious and historical views, all coming together in the ancient Near East, and all somehow linked to the alleged ancestors of the Hungarians. While these views are generally disregarded by most serious scholars, they do have considerable influence upon the older generations of the political immigrants. They will probably be assessed by later generations as one of those strange manifestations that seem to be "normal" among émigrés who have lost everything and who tend to console themselves with a search for the "unreal."

Search for the Hungarian-American Past

Much more real and realistic is the increased tendency among Hungarian-Americans to research their own history and to establish college- and university-level Hungarian-studies programs for the teaching and the perpetuation of their language and culture. While this trend is not completely new, much of it is the by-product of the ethnic revival of the 1960s and the temporary popularity of East European studies during the late 1950s and the 1960s.

The pioneers of the study of the Hungarian-American past include such historians and publicists as Sándor Márki (1857–1925), Jenő (Eugene) Pivány (1873–1946), Károly (Charles) Feleky (1865–1930), Géza Kende (?–1927), Ödön (Edmund) Vasváry (1888–1977), and Emil Lengyel (1895–), all of whom contributed in one or another way to the development of this discipline. Their work was paralleled in Hungary by those who studied the various aspects of Hungarian emigration to the United States (Gusztáv Thirring, Andor Löherer, Loránt Hegedűs, Alajos Kovács, Géza Hoffmann, Iván Nagy, Imre Kovács, Dénes Jánossy, István Gall, etc.); and then continued in the United States by some of the postwar immigrants (John Kósa,

Leslie Könnyű, Joseph Széplaki, István Török, etc.). The quality of the works of these authors is rather mixed, stretching from excellent statistical analyses, through respectable historical summaries, to popular articles and brief chronological accounts. Yet virtually all of the works by the above authors are still superior in quality to most of the publications (i.e., pamphlets, commemorative brochures, etc.) put out by many of the Hungarian-American organizations to record events in their history and to perpetuate the consciousness of their members.

With a few rare exceptions, the situation in Hungarian-American historical research did not begin to change until the 1960s and the 1970s when several dozen prospective scholars wrote Ph.D. dissertations on topics dealing with the history, culture, language, institutions, noted personalities, and the assimilation of the immigrants. While very few of these dissertations have appeared in print, most of their authors have published and continue to publish some of the results of their research. As such, in combination with works by other scholars who have joined this effort in the midcourse of their careers, reliable and readily available information continues to increase year by year. And this holds true not only for the popular historical field (P. Bődy, N. F. Dreisziger, J. A. Fishman, M. L. Kovács, Z. Kramár, S. Papp-Zubrits, T. Szendrey, S. B. Vardy, B. Vassady, F. S. Wagner, etc.), but also for linguistics (E. Bakó, A. Kerek, W. Nemser, etc.), literature (L. Könnyű, A. H. Vardy, etc.), ethnography (L. Dégh, M. Hollós, M. Sozan, B. Maday, A. Vázsonyi, etc.), sociology (P. Benkart, A. S. Weinstock, etc.), education (K. Nagy, A. H. Vardy, S. B. Vardy, etc.), as well as archival studies and bibliography (A. Boros-Kazai, M. Boros-Kazai, R. Biro, I. Halász de Béky, L. L. Kovács, A. J. Molnar, F. Vitéz, etc.).

Similarly, efforts to look into the past of the Hungarian migration and the Hungarian-American past were also renewed in Hungary during the 1960s. The most valuable results of these efforts are the two recent major syntheses by István Rácz (1980) and Julianna Puskás (1982), both of which cover this question in much detail up to World War I, and to a lesser degree for the interwar period (Puskás); and the as yet unpublished work of Miklós Szántó, which is a detailed sociological analysis of the post–World War II immigrants' way of life throughout the world. Also significant are the shorter studies of such other scholars as G. Deák, L. Éva Gál, István

Gál, J. Gellén, B. Kálmán, I. Kovács, J. Kovács, C. Kretzoi, A. Lengyel, D. Nagy, I. Polányi, F. Szászi and P. Szente.

The flareup in Hungarian-American historical, linguistic, sociological, and other research was accompanied by a growing effort to collect the sources of their past, to establish Hungarian-American library and archival collections, as well as to record the activities of some of the larger communities.

There were already two major interwar collections (those of Pivány and Feleky), but neither of these survived the war. Thus following World War II new efforts had to be undertaken. The most successful of these was that of the American Hungarian Foundation of New Brunswick, New Jersey. Founded and directed by August J. Molnar (1955), the library and archives of the Foundation now house what is undoubtedly the largest collection of Hungarian-American materials outside that held by the National Széchényi Library of Budapest. Also significant are the archival collection of the Hungarian Reformed Federation in Ligonier, Pennsylvania, the Hungarian collection of the Immigration History Research Center of the University of Minnesota, and the smaller and more specialized collections of such organizations as the Hungarian Scouts in Exile of Garfield, New Jersey, the American Hungarian Library and Historical Association of New York City, and the Hungarian Cultural Foundation of Atlanta. No less significant, although naturally less accessible, are such major private collections as the Szathmáry Archives of Chicago, the Udvardy Library of New Brunswick, the Vardy Collection of Pittsburgh, the Szendrey Collection of Erie, Pennsylvania, the Könnyű Library of St. Louis, etc. Moreover, the major university or public libraries that hold significant Hungarian collections also contain some materials concerning Hungarian-Americans. By far the most significant of these is the Library of Congress, followed by the New York Public Library, the Cleveland Public Library, and the libraries of Columbia University, Harvard University, Indiana University, the University of Illinois, the University of California at Los Angeles and at Berkeley, and Stanford University. The Canadians have two major collections, including those of the University of Toronto and the Library of the Hungarian Cultural Center of the same city. The size of these collections, which range from 50,000 down to about 10,000, do not necessarily reflect their quality (the Cleveland Public Library's holdings, for example, contain primarily belles lettres, with very little scholarly material), or their significance for the study of the Hungarian-American past.[12]

University-Level Hungarian-Studies Programs

The study of the Hungarian-American past has been the subject of individuals who were usually not connected with programs of Hungarian studies at any one of America's major universities. As a matter of fact, comprehensive Hungarian-studies programs did not come into being until well after World War II, and then they were much more concerned with *Hungarian* than with *Hungarian-American* history, culture, and linguistics. And not even today did this emphasis change, with the exception of the activities of a few select scholars in linguistics, sociology, and culture anthropology who are connected with one or another of these programs.

The pioneer Hungarian-studies programs founded during the first half of this century (e.g., Bloomfield College, 1904; Franklin and Marshall College, 1922–1936; Elmhurst College, 1941–1959) were all connected with the Hungarian Reformed Church's effort to prepare pastors for its flock in America. They consisted of basic language courses and occasional courses on Hungarian history, literature, and culture—all taught by a single individual who was also a pastor of the Reformed Church. Even more limited was the scope of the occasional offerings at Columbia University, the University of Pittsburgh, Western Reserve University, etc., during the 1920s and 1930s. Moreover, the "Hungarian Lectureship" established at Columbia University in 1939 by the Hungarian government lasted only a little over two years.

The situation changed drastically after World War II because of the combination of several factors. These included (1) the Cold War and the consequent rise of East European Studies in the United States; (2) the rise of American structural linguistics and the subsequent growing interest in Uralic and Altaic Studies; (3) the passage of the National Defense Education Act in 1958, which resulted in the foundation of four Uralic and Altaic Centers (Columbia, Indiana, Berkeley, and Colorado) and in several dozen Russian and East European institutes; and finally (4) the rise of the new ethnic consciousness, which renewed the popular interest in the language, history, and culture of the hitherto not too highly regarded immigrants from eastern and southeastern Europe, including the Hungarians. All of these factors combined to produce two significant centers of Hungarian Studies (Columbia and Indiana), and off and on perhaps two-dozen other smaller programs consisting of language courses and a few occasional courses in the related fields. During the early 1970s many of these smaller programs disappeared and the Columbia University program was also cut down to a bare minimum. The only major program that survived was that of Indiana University (Bloomington), which—under the direction of Professor Denis Sinor since 1962—came to dominate the whole field. In 1979 this program was further strengthened by the establishment of an endowed "Chair of Hungarian Studies" based on the half a million dollars contributed jointly by the Hungarian Academy of Sciences and Indiana University. Built into the university's Department of Uralic and Altaic Studies (the only one of its kind in North America) and connected with its strong Russian and East European Institute, as well as several related departments, at this time this program has no rivals in the United States and Canada (although the University of Toronto also has had its own Hungarian Chair since 1978). But this program at Indiana University is still primarily centered in Hungary and Hungarian studies, and only very secondarily in Hungarian-American studies.

In addition to the Hungarian Studies Program at Indiana University, today there are several smaller programs that have existed for a decade or more and also have their significance. These include those at the University of California at Los Angeles (M. Birnbaum), Cleveland State University (R. Oszlányi, later T. Lant), University of Pittsburgh and Duquesne University (S. B. Vardy and A. H. Vardy), and the summer program at Ohio Northern University (A. Ludányi), sponsored jointly with Portland State University (L. J. Éltető). There are also a few others of more temporary duration. But whether long-standing or ephemeral, all of these programs (with the exception of the well-established program at Indiana University) are kept going by the perseverance of one or perhaps two individuals who dedicate their time and effort to the survival of Hungarian learning in the United States. [13]

Some Hungarian Contributions to American Civilization

All the difficulties and problems notwithstanding, Hungarian-Americans have come a long way since the beginnings of their mass immigration about a century ago. And although their initial contributions to the making of America consisted largely of sweat and blood, by the 1930s and early 1940s the equilibrium began to swing in the other direction.

Hungarian contributions to the great scientific breakthrough concerning the development of America's atomic power and the rocket age are fairly well known. In fact, as Laure Fermi, the wife of the noted scientist Enrico Fermi, observed, "the scientific brain power" for the so-called "Manhattan Project," wherein America's first atomic bomb was developed, "was furnished by three Hungarians and one Italian." The Italian was Enrico Fermi himself. The three Hungarians were the great physicists Leo Szilárd, Eugene Wigner, and Edward Teller. She also failed to mention two others of almost equal significance: the great mathematical genius John von Neumann and the equally great aerodynamicist Theodore von Kármán, who is known as the "father of the jet age." And they were only the top of the heap. There were scores of other Hungarians connected with this and other wartime projects, including an eighteen-year-old Hungarian, John George Kemény, who subsequently became one of the great mathematicians of this age, and for a while also the president of Dartmouth College. [14]

While the role of Hungarian brainpower in the development of America's atomic might is at least passingly known, this is much less true for its role in the development of Hollywood and the whole American film industry, with all its impact on our modern civilization. [15]

The two men who were primarily responsible for this were Adolph Zukor (1873–1976) and William Fox (1879–1952), both born in Hungary and both driven by the intellectually oriented Hungarian immigrants' desire to excel. Neither Zukor nor Fox knew anything about the fledgling industry they were about to make big when they started their careers as petty businessmen in the ethnic ghettos of New York City. But, coming into America's great Age of Enterprise, they both recognized that "what the masses needed was mass entertainment." [16] Initially they tried to achieve their goals in New York City, but the Motion Picture Patents Company's monopolistic hold on the infant industry eventually drove them out to the California desert, where they found the ideal setting for the make-believe world that soon became the "dream world" of many hundreds of millions throughout the world. The result was Hollywood and all that it implied. And it implied much, for "what

Hollywood represented as the American way of life became *the* American way of life in the eyes of hundreds of millions from Murmansk to Capetown"[17]—even though much of it was really the product of the fertile imagination of these two Hungarian immigrants and their many scores of compatriots, whether these were their co-workers or their competitors. And we might add that this image of the American way of life influenced everyone not only from Murmansk to Capetown, but also those who lived between Hollywood and New York.

Zukor, Fox, and some of the other Hungarian-born giants of the American film industry became "American institutions" without most Americans realizing that they were Americans only by choice. Yet, not even these "American institutions" who, in a sense, "created" the American way of life for many millions of upward-moving Americans were able to escape their past and the tremendous pull that the land of the Magyars exercises upon their wayward sons. Zukor, for example, would often visit the village of his birth (Ricse) and shower his childhood friends with everything that only an American multi-millionaire could offer.

Among the many major companies these two ex-Hungarians founded were the two giants of the film industry: Paramount Pictures and Twentieth Century–Fox. There scores and hundreds of their fellow countrymen would labor on the creation and the perfection of a new world of make-believe. In fact, at one time the role of the Hungarians in the making of Hollywood was so pervasive that allegedly some of the studios had signs saying: "In this studio it is not enough to be a Hungarian."[18] And their dominance was even greater among the scenario-writers, who at one time were apparently mostly Hungarians, all of them named "László" (e.g., László Fodor, László Vadnay, László Görög, László Bús-Fekete, and even Miklós László—in the last instance "László" being his family name). No wonder that the saying went around that if one wanted to become a successful scenario-writer "it was not enough to be a Hungarian . . . , one [also] had to be called László."[19]

And these are only two, although most important, examples of the Hungarian impact upon America and American civilization. In one instance it was their role in the introduction of the Atomic Age, and in the other their popularization and dissemination of the American way of life as conceived by them and the simultaneous inculcation of "forward-looking, progressive [and] bold ideas into mankin'd"[20] while at the same time also giving pleasure to untold millions. But the role of Hungarian scientists and intellectuals was and is also significant in many other areas of science, technology, social sciences, and the arts, which only the lack of space prevents us from discussing in greater detail. Let it suffice to say that in the 1950s and 1960s five Hungarian Nobel Prize winners were active at American universities (Albert Szent-Györgyi, George von Békésy, Eugene Wigner, George von Hevesi, Denis Gábor), with the second-generation Daniel C. Gajdusek joining them in the 1970s. At the same time several of America's great symphony orchestras were conducted by Hungarians (e.g., Eugene Ormandy, Philadelphia; George Széll, Cleveland; Fritz Reiner, Pittsburgh and Chicago; Sir Georg Solti, Chicago; Antal Doráti, Minneapolis). By the 1970s and early 1980s hundreds and thousands of Hungarians had inundated the scientific, scholarly, cultural, artistic, and business world of America. Their influence is growing and their numbers are so many that it is virtually impossible to move in the middle and upper layers of these circles without encountering Hungarians—be they immigrants or native born.

Despite the difficult years of the late nineteenth and early twentieth century, America was basically good to the Hungarian immigrants, and they have reciprocated in kind. Their native talents and their natural desire to excel, combined with the unique opportunities offered by this unusually tolerant land, have brought the best out of the Hungarian immigrants and their descendants. And thus they have made discoveries and achieved goals that they could never have made and achieved within the confines of their much-loved but small homeland, with its limited opportunities. And this process of achievement is still continuing, with perhaps many surprises in the remaining years of our millennium.

Notes

Chapter One

1. Concerning American research on Hungary and Hungarian immigration to the United States see Dégh (1966), 551–56; Vardy (1975), 91–121; Bődy (1976), 1–6; Puskás (1977), 151–69; Vardy and Vardy (1981), 67–123; Vardy (1982c), 165–73; and Vardy and Vardy (1984), 79–124.

2. On Hungary of today and on the recent past see *Hungary* (1931); *Ezeréves* (1940); *Inf Hung* (1968); Kovrig (1970); and Sinor (1978).

3. On the origins and history of the Hungarians see Kosáry (1941); Sinor (1959); Macartney (1962); Kosáry and Vardy (1969); Dienes (1972); Ignotus (1972); Pamlényi (1973); Somogyi and Somogyi (1976); and Sisa (1983).

4. Puskás (1975), 5.

5. On the fate of the Hungarians in the surrounding states see Janics (1982); Illyés (1982); Cadzow, Ludanyi and Elteto (1983); and Borsody (1985).

Chapter Two

1. On these early Hungarian contacts with America see Pivány (1927); Quinn-Cheshire (1972); and Polányi-Striker (1953), 311–42.

2. Márki (1893), 49–94, quotation from p. 61.

3. Quoted by Pivány (1927), 18–19.

4. On Kováts and Pollereczky see Eszenyi (1975); Pók-Pivay and Zachar (1982); and Zachar (1980), 293–310.

5. Johnson (1851), 244.

6. Benyovszky (1790); and Jókai (1888).

7. Concerning Bölöni-Farkas see the two recent English versions of his work, edited respectively by Schoeneman (1977) and Kadarkay (1978). Quotations are from the Kadarkay version, p. 215.

8. Haraszthy (1844). Concerning Haraszthy see Fenyő (1983), 169–88; and Szente (1978), 110–24. See also Katona (1971), 51–94; and Király and Barany (1977).

9. Haraszthy (1962).

10. Wagner (1965), 90–97. See also Gál, I. (1971), 95–119.

11. On Kossuth see Deak, I. (1979). Concerning Kossuth's contacts with the United States see Horváth (1928), 231–42; Komlos (1973); Széplaki (1976); and Spencer (1977).

12. Quoted in Komlos (1973), 103, 100.

13. Lawrence's letter dated January 15, 1852, in Lawrence (1883), 88–89, as quoted in Jánossy (1940), 1:365.

14. Concerning some of these notable émigrés see Richter (1917); Biró (1922), 695–97; Ács (1941); Madden (1949); Sziklay (1953); Konnyu (1965); Gál, E. (1971); Anderle (1973), 687–709; Konnyu (1975); Konnyu (1976); Gellén (1977), 149–53; Xantus (1979); and Vassady (1979), 21–46.

15. Kende (1927), 1:57–64, 74–76, 122–23, 134–37; Taborsky (1955), 13–15.

16. On the role of the Hungarians in the Civil War see Pivány (1913); Kende (1927), 1:328–68; Vasváry (1939); Lengyel (1948), 73–93; Ács (1964); and Juhász (1979), 46–57.

17. Čapek (1920), 155.

18. Kaufman (1911); Vasváry (1939), 12–13.

19. Kuné (1911).

20. Estván (1864); Pogány (1961).

21. Kretzoi (1965), 61–92; Kretzoi (1974), 680–98.

22. *Pesti Napló,* January 12, 1865. Cf. Kretzoi (1974), 686.

Chapter Three

1. Concerning emigration from Hungary during the five decades before World War I see Kanyar (1957), 41–54; Virág (1971), 189–99; Puskás (1975), 65–103; Rácz (1977), 117–54; Rácz (1980); Puskás (1982a); Puskás (1982b); and Vardy (1983a), 189–216, the latter being a more detailed exposition of this topic.

2. *Dillingham Report* (1911), 357; Rácz (1980), 81, 127–28; Puskás (1975), 19.

3. On immigration and repatriation statistics see Thirring (1904); Löherer (1908); *MSKOKV* (1918); and Gould (1980), 41–112. Puskás (1982a), 27, claims that 38 percent returned, while Rácz (1980), 82–84, 230, puts this at 25 percent, of which one-fifth came back again. I tend to agree with Rácz.

4. *RNL,* 10:295, 13:200; Balogh (1902); and Macartney (1969), 721–39.

5. Cited in Fishman (1966), 4–5. On the Slovaks see Polányi (1976), 245–70; Stolarik (1976), 81–102; Stolarik (1980), 5–137; and Fejős (1980), 293–327.

6. Rácz (1973), 5–33.

7. In comparison with the economic causes, other considerations played only insignificant roles in the so-called "new immigration." Cf. *Dillingham Report* (1911), 309. On official contemporary United States views see Kramár (1978).

8. Puskás (1975), 18.
9. On this peasant migration see Rácz (1965), 2:432–83.
10. *MSKOKV* as cited in Puskás (1975), 26.
11. Rácz (1980), 88. See also Szászi (1970), 109–19; and Szászi (1972), 66–67.
12. Rácz (1980), 85.
13. Rácz (1980), 92–101; *Dillingham Report* (1911), 367–69.
14. *MSK* 67 (1918), 70. In United States statistics the ratio is 72.2 percent men and 27.8 percent women, probably the result of illegal immigration. Cf. *Dillingham Report* (1911), 376.
15. *MSK* 67 (1918), 8–9.
16. *RNL,* 10:219.
17. *Dillingham Report* (1911), 380.
18. Fermi (1968), 53–59.
19. Szász (1922), 225–88.
20. Cited in Fishman (1966), 4–5.
21. Szász (1922), 227, 275–88.

Chapter Four

1. On this ability to postpone rewards see Benkart (1975), 4–8, and the sources cited there.
2. Dinnerstein (1979), 134. See also Sarna (1981), 256–68, which contradicts this assertion.
3. For example see Prpić (1973), 263–86, quotation from p. 266. This view, which is prevalent in many traditional publications, is contradicted by the contemporary *Dillingham Report* (1911), 309, as well as by the examination of the emigration-immigration of the so-called "dominant" nationalities.
4. Lorant (1964), 213–14; and Novak (1978).
5. For this United States Labor Commission Report see the *Bulletin of the Bureau of Labor,* no. 72 (September 1907):474–82. For a contemporary Hungarian observation see *AMN Diszalbum* (1910), 41–42.
6. Kőrösfőy (1941), 87.
7. *AMN Diszalbum* (1910), 41.
8. For an interesting discussion of this custom see Vázsonyi (1978), 641–56; and Vázsonyi (1980), 89–97.
9. *AMN Diszalbum* (1910), 41–42; Bilkei (1910), 79.
10. Vázsonyi (1978), 656.
11. Puskás (1982a), 126–32; Puskás (1982b), 185–202. See also the contemporary description by Steiner (1906), 213–24.
12. Vecoli (1965), 404–17; Stolarik (1980), 27–29; Puskás (1982), 130–32.
13. Bodnar, J. (1977), 65, 160.

14. Puskás (1982a), 133–37; Puskás (1982b), 203–7.

15. Bell (1976), 48–54.

16. Gutman (1973), 553.

17. *AMN Diszalbum* (1910), 74–75.

18. Registry of the Magyar Reformed Church of Homestead, Pennsylvania. Cf. Puskás (1982a), 140.

19. On these organizations and associations see *Verhovayak* (1936); *Rákóczi* (1913); *Rákóczi* (1938); *Jub Em* (1940); *Am Beteg* (1942); *AMN Album* (1950). See also Kende (1927), 1:128, 134–37, 2:9–17, 83–91, 150–67, 260–62; Lengyel (1948), 158–78; and Puskás (1970), 528–68.

20. Kende (1927), 2:71; Lengyel (1948), 159.

21. *Verhovayak* (1936), 44–46.

22. Hoffmann (1911), 139.

23. On the tendency to overemphasize the Socialists among the immigrants see Kovács, J. (1977), 7–92. Although, to a lesser degree, this is even true of Puskás's above-cited works.

24. On these early efforts to organize the Hungarians see Kende (1927), 2:150–67; quotations from pp. 151 and 156.

25. Ibid., p. 167.

26. Vasváry (1950), 72–73, 19–100; Vardy (1982a), 174–75.

27. On these cultural activities and self-culture societies see Kende (1927), 2:281–303; and Szendrey (1983), 191–220.

28. On Károlyi's tour see Vassady (1982), 39–64.

29. Kende (1927), 2:292–98.

30. Lengyel (1948), 172–73.

Chapter Five

1. Concerning the role of the churches in Hungarian-American life see Benkart (1975), 133–219; Puskás (1970), 549–54; Puskás (1982a), 182–215; and Puskás (1982b), 250–284.

2. Quoted by Vasváry (1950), 64. See also Zombori (1977), 326–27.

3. *Szabadság Naptára* (1931), 63.

4. Kende (1927), 2:371–74.

5. Török (1978), 49–388; Kende (1927), 2:374–91.

6. Török (1978), 449–60.

7. Marchbin (1940), 168–69; Török (1978), 208–11; and Bődy and Boros-Kazai (1981), 16–18.

8. Török (1978), 422–25.

9. Concerning Mindszenty's visit see Somogyi (1974); Kótai (1975); and Csonka (1976), 178–212.

10. Kende (1927), 2:386.

11. Ibid., 384–90. See also Puskás (1982b), 541–42.

12. Török (1978), 422–44.

13. Kalassay L. (1939); Kalassay, S. (1942); Vasváry (1950), 64–65; Komjáthy (1962); and Révész (1965).

14. Hanák and Mucsi (1978), 420.

15. Kende (1927), 2:402–28; Puskás (1982a), 197–201; Puskás (1982b), 265–569.

16. Takaró (1940), 57–61.

17. Kende (1927), 2:428–30.

18. *Jub Em* (1940), 50; Puskás (1982b), 547–50.

19. Concerning Ligonier and its institutions see the various issues of the *Bethlen Naptár* (Bethlen Almanac) published every year since 1922. See also *Jub Em* (1950), 332–33; and Vardy and Vardy (1981), 75–79.

20. On the Lutherans see Kende (1927), 2:434–36; Vasváry (1950), 65; and Papp (1981), 201–3.

21. Concerning Carpatho-Ruthenian (Byzantine Catholic) immigrants see Warzeski (1971); Warzeski (1973), 263–86; and Máyer (1977), 169–204.

22. For a contemporary Hungarian view see Kende (1927), 2:391–402.

23. Concerning recent developments see Shereghy (1978).

24. Warzeski (1971), 199; and Kende (1927), 2:401–2.

25. Papp (1981), 206–7; Bődy and Boros-Kazai (1981), 13–14.

26. Jelinek (1972), 214–22; Braham (1960), 3–23.

27. Lengyel (1948), 193.

28. Vasváry (1950), 65.

29. Souders (1922), 85–87; Kende (1927), 2:437; Kautz (1946); and Gerzsányi (1978).

30. Graham (1977).

Chapter Six

1. On the development of the Hungarian-American press see Nagy, I. (1943), 7–18; Taborsky (1955); and Puskás (1982b), 284–302.

2. For an overly critical assessment see Park (1922), 74–76, 207–10, 347–52, 430–32.

3. For these categorizations see Puskás (1970), 454–55.

4. Souders (1922), 138–42; Taborsky (1955), 34, 100–105; Puskás (1982b), 610–11.

5. Kende (1927), 2:30–35.

6. On these early papers see ibid., 128–33; and *AMN Diszalbum* (1910), 56–59.

7. Concerning the *Szabadság* see Kende (1927), 2:189–203; Kőrösfőy (1941), 20–24; Park (1922), 73–76, 347–52. Park's extremely

critical views are based on information supplied by Eugene S. Bagger, alias Ernő Szekeres.

8. Taborsky (1955), 22. For two contradictory views on Kohányi see Kende (1927), 2:189–203, and Park (1922), 348–50.

9. Kende (1927), 2:197.

10. Kőrösfőy (1941), 22.

11. According to Ayer (1933), by 1932 the *Szabadság* had 42,784 subscribers.

12. Taborsky (1955), 95. On the history of the *Népszava* see Berkó (1910), 24–34; and Gáspár (1950), 131–57.

13. Concerning these subsidies see Benkart (1975), 80–86, 109–10; and Kovács, J. (1977), 29. On Hungarian revisionism see Király, Pastor and Sanders (1982); Vardy (1982b), 361–90; and Vardy (1983b), 21–42.

14. On the leftist Hungarian-American press see Kovács, J. (1977), 19–44.

15. According to its statement of ownership and circulation, by April 1, 1926, the *Új Előre* had 30,654 subscribers. No doubt this is a greatly inflated figure, belied both by Ayer's figures for 1923 and 1933 as well as by the known circumstances of the paper's publication. As acknowledged to me by several past and current editor-publishers of Hungarian-American papers, this tendency to inflate circulation figures was done regularly to impress the rivals.

16. Deák, Z. (1982).

17. Taborsky (1955), 26, 34; Németh (1975), 13–54.

18. These negative features are overemphasized by Parks (1922). For a more balanced view see Puskás (1982b), 299–302.

19. On this rivalry see Kende (1927), 2:266–70.

20. The author has a large collection of these calendars.

21. *Szabadság Naptára* (1931). The contributors included such noted Hungarian-Americans as Géza Kende, Árpád Tarnóczy, László Pólya, Joseph Reményi, Edmund Vasváry, Sándor Tóth, János Walkó, and many others.

22. Ibid., 140, 170.

23. These almanacs changed their titles slightly almost from year to year.

24. Taborsky (1955), 50–51. The author has a sizable collection of these memorial albums.

25. Already cited as *AMN Diszalbum* (1910).

26. Ibid., 345–404.

27. Already cited as *AMN Album* (1950).

28. Ibid., 59–74, 131–57.

29. Already cited as Kőrösfőy (1941).

30. Ibid., 7–18, 20–24.

32. Káldor (1937–39).

Chapter Seven

1. Concerning "American Action" see Benkart (1975), 59–101; Benkart (1980), 468–69; and Vassady (1982), 41–42.

2. For the most recent summary of developments during World War I see Puskás (1982b), 303–15. See also Barany (1967), 140–72.

3. Pivány (1921), 62.

4. *AMN 25 Jub* (1924).

5. Vardy (1982b); and Vardy (1983b).

6. On interwar Hungarian immigration statistics see Thirring (1931), 433–39; Benkart (1980), 470; and Puskás (1981), 738–39.

7. Puskás (1982b), 311, 319; Vardy (1982b), 190.

8. Cukor (1917).

9. *AMN 25 Jub* (1924).

10. During the 1950s the author had spent his youth and his early adult life in the Buckeye neighborhood and had experienced firsthand both the positive and the negative aspects of being the "citizen" of one of the most famous of "Little Hungaries." See also Éles (1972); Pap (1973), 155–78; and Papp (1981), 223–57.

11. On the notion of "ethno-class" see Gordon (1964), 51–53.

12. Fermi (1968), 53–59.

13. Beynon (1936), 427. See also Beynon (1934), 600–10.

14. Lengyel (1948), 239.

15. Cited by Fishman (1966), 4–5.

16. Pivány (1943).

17. *AMN Album* (1950), 147–48.

18. Nagy, I. (1939), 9–21; Vardy (1976b), 239–41; and the proceedings of the two world congresses cited as *Magy Vil* (1929), and *Magy Vil* (1938).

19. Concerning this struggle for the second generation see Puskás (1982b), 388–99.

20. *Verhovayak* (1936), 47, 77–79.

21. Kosáry (1941); expanded by the present author, Kosáry and Vardy (1969).

22. *AMN Album* (1950), 72–150. This feat was repeated in 1981 on the fiftieth anniversary of the first flight. Cf. *MHKK* (1983), 130.

23. On these collections see Vardy and Vardy (1981), 75–79; and Kolar and Vardy (1981), 127–35.

24. Balogh, J. E. (1945), 50.

25. Beynon (1936), 423–34.

26. Puskás (1982b), 392–93.

27. Szilassy (1979), 139.

28. Vardy (1982a), 175.

29. Nadányi (1942); Nadányi (1943); and Roucek (1943), 466–77, the latter being strongly critical of Eckhardt and his movement.

30. Szilassy (1979), 142; Vardy (1982a), 175–76.

Chapter Eight

1. *AMN Album* (1950), 96–97.

2. Ibid., 79–82.

3. *HEAEG* (1980), 494.

4. See the report on the AHF in *AMN Album* (1950), 98–100; and Vardy (1982a), 175.

5. Kosa (1957), 512–13; Váraljai-Csocsán (1974), 133–231; Nagy, K. (1982), 55, 137.

6. The first extensive, vibrant, if controversial study on postwar Hungarian emigration was done by Kázmér Nagy. Cf. Nagy, K. (1974); Nagy, K. (1982).

7. On the 56-ers see Gleitman and Greenbaum (1960), 62–76; Gleitman and Greenbaum (1961), 351–65; Soskis (1967), 40–46; Weinstock (1969); and Markowitz (1973), 46–59.

8. Balázs (1958).

9. In discussing the developments of the postwar decades in "Hungarian-America" the author had relied heavily on his own experiences and on those of his friends and acquaintances. A considerably different view is presented by Éles (1975), who represents the views of the interwar political elite in Hungary. The three generals were Gyula Kovács, Kornél Oszlányi, and Sándor Magyarossy.

10. See the "Regent's" own report in Kisbarnaki-Farkas (1969).

11. On these military-based organizations see Nagy, K. (1982), 62–66; and Rektor (1980), 234–333.

12. Concerning these associations see Vardy (1982a), 176–77.

13. Nagy, K. (1982), 61–63, 155–58.

14. On these Quixotic efforts see chapter 10, below.

15. *AMN Album* (1950), 35–37; Kovács, I. (1966), 301–14; Nagy, K. (1982), 70–74, 160–62.

16. *AMN Album* (1950), 37.

17. Nagy, K. (1982), 90–94.

18. Vardy and Vardy (1983), 3–14.

19. Nagy, K. (1982), 94–95.

20. *AMN Album* (1950), 128.

21. This three-fold segmentation is basically the author's perception of Hungarian-American society in the 1970s and early 1980s.

22. Weinstock (1969), 41.

Chapter Nine

1. Weinstock (1969), 15.
2. Bodnár, G. (1981).
3. Ibid., 10.
4. This assessment is based largely on the experiences of the author and those of his friends and acquaintances. On Hungarian-American education see also Vardy-Huszar (1974), 39–56; Bodnár, G. (1975); and Somogyi (1978).
5. On the Cleveland community see Sári-Gál (1966); Éles (1972); Pap (1973), 155–74; Éles (1975); Sári-Gál (1978); and Papp (1981).
6. Somogyi (1983), 17–18.
7. *Krónika*, I–XXIII.
8. Concerning this "Hunglish" speech see Bakó (1965), 211–24; Dégh and Vázsonyi (1971); and Vardy and Vardy (1981), 86–87. An example of a successful family of Old Immigrants is the case of the Jánossy family. Cf. *Jánossys* (1979).
9. On the Crown affair see Vardy (1982a), 185–87; and Simontsits (1983).
10. This discussion of Hungarian-American politics and political trends is based on the author's earlier study on this topic. Cf. Vardy (1982a), 171–97.

Chapter Ten

1. *AMN Album* (1950), 128. The reference here is probably to the *Magyar Jövő*, soon to be replaced by the *Amerikai Magyar Szó* (1952), and perhaps to the more moderate *Az Ember*.
2. The author has a complete collection of the *Végvár*, and samples of both the *Szabad Magyarság* and the *Magyar Szabadság*. For an inside view on the history of these papers, by a former editor, see Somody (1979), 255–74.
3. For two extensive, but incomplete, lists see Németh (1975), and Mildschütz (1977).
4. No adequate summary of Hungarian-American publishing activities exists. The brief discussion by Béládi (1982), p. 336, is totally inadequate.
5. *Élet és irodalom* (February 18, 1983).
6. See for example the poet Tibor Flórián's observations in the *Kanadai Magyarság* (June 15, 1974).
7. Gellén (1978), 83–84.
8. On interwar Hungarian-American poetry see Csorba (1930); Gellén (1978), 81–97; and Vardy-Huszar (1982), 14–15.
9. Szarvas (1928); Szarvas (ca. 1936).

10. Concerning Hungarian literature abroad see Béládi (1982), which, however, is much stronger on Western Europe than on North America (pp. 323–445).

11. For a critical summary of this phenomenon see Komoróczy (1976a), and Komoróczy (1976b), 259–303. For an opposing view see Badiny-Jós (1976).

12. On Hungarian-American historical research, libraries, and archival collections see Vardy and Vardy (1981), 67–123; Vardy (1982c); and Vardy and Vardy (1984).

13. Concerning university-level programs see Vardy (1973), 102–32; Vardy (1975), 91–121; Vardy (1977a), 49–62; and Vardy (1983c), 165–73.

14. Fermi (1968), 53–59, 111–16.

15. This discussion of the Hungarian contribution to the American film industry is based on Lengyel (1948), 206–15, 271–73; and Birnbaum (1982).

16. Lengyel (1948), 209.

17. Ibid., 213.

18. Ibid., 271.

19. Ibid., 273.

20. Ibid., 213.

References

Ács, Tivadar. 1941. *New Buda*. Budapest.
———. 1964. *Magyarok az észak-amerikai polgárháborúban, 1861–65*. Budapest.
Amerikai Betegsegélyző és Életbiztosító Szövetség ötven éves története. Edited by János Walkó. 1942. Pittsburgh. Cited as *Am Beteg*.
Amerikai Magyar Népszava aranyjubileumi albuma. 1950. New York. Cited as *AMN Album*.
Amerikai Magyar Népszava jubileumi diszalbuma, 1899–1909. Edited by Géza D. Berkó. 1910. New York. Cited as *AMN Diszalbum*.
Amerikai Magyar Népszava 25 éves jubileumi szám. Edited by Géza D. Berkó. 1924. New York. Cited as *AMN 25 Jub*.
Anderle, Adam. 1973. "A 48-as magyar emigráció és Narciso Lopez 1851-es kubai expedíciója." *Századok* 107, no. 3:687–709.
Ayer, N. W. 1933. *American Newspaper Annual and Directory*. Philadelphia.
Badiny-Jós, Ferenc. 1976. *Mah-Gar a Magyar!* Buenos Aires.
Bakó, Elemér. 1965. *On the Linguistic Characteristics of the American Hungarian*. Basel.
Balázs, Béla. 1958. *A középrétegek szerepe társadalmunk fejlődésében*. Budapest.
Balogh, Pál. 1902. *Népfajok Magyarországon*. Budapest.
Balogh, J. E. 1945. *An Analysis of Cultural Organizations of Hungarian Americans in Pittsburgh and Allegheny County*. Ph.D. diss., University of Pittsburgh.
Barany, George. 1967. "The Magyars." In *The Immigrants' Influence on Wilson's Peace Policies*. Edited by Joseph P. O'Grady. Lexington, Ken., pp. 140–72.
Béládi, Miklós. 1982. *A határontúli magyar irodalom*. Budapest.
Bell, Thomas. 1976. *Out of This Furnace*. Pittsburgh.
Benkart, Paula K. 1975. *Religion, Family and Community among Hungarians Migrating to American Cities, 1880–1930*. Ph.D. diss., Johns Hopkins University. Baltimore.
———. 1980. "Hungarians." *HEAEG*, 462–71.
Benyovszky, Mauritius. 1790. *Memoires and Travels*. Edited by W. Nicholson. London.
Berend, Ivan T., and Ránki, György. 1974. *Hungary: A Century of Economic Development*. New York.
Berkó, Géza D. 1910. "Az Amerikai Magyar Népszava tíz éves története." *AMN Diszalbum*, 24–34.

Beynon, Erdman Doana. 1934. "Occupational Success of Hungarians in Detroit." *American Journal of Sociology* 39, no. 5:600–610.

————. 1936. "Social Mobility and Social Distance among Hungarian Immigrants in Detroit." *American Journal of Sociology* 41, no. 4:423–34.

Bilkei, Ferenc. 1910. *Magyar ember Amerikában.* Székesfehérvár.

Birnbaum, Marianna D. 1982. "The Hungarians of Hollywood. Image and Image-Making." Unpublished manuscript.

Biró, Lajos. 1922. "A honvágy halottja." *Pásztortűz* 2, 695–97.

Bodnár, Gábor. 1975. *Külföldi magyar oktatás 1974-ben. A cserkészet a magyar oktatásért.* Garfield, N.J.

————. 1981. *70 Jahre des ungarischen Pfaadfinderbundes.* Garfield, N.J.

Bodnar, John. 1977. *Immigration and Industrialization. Ethnicity in an American Mill Town.* Pittsburgh.

Bődy, Paul. 1976. "Hungarian Immigrants in North America: A Report on Current Research." *Immigration History Newsletter* 8, no. 1:1–6.

Bődy, Paul, and Boros-Kazai, Mary. 1981. *Hungarian Immigrants in Greater Pittsburgh, 1880–1980.* Pittsburgh.

Borsody, Stephen. 1985. *Hungary and the Hungarians: The Partition of a State and a Nation.* New Haven.

Braham, Randolph L. 1960. "Hungarian Jewry: An Historical Retrospect." *Journal of Central European Affairs* 20 (April):3–23.

Cadzow, J. F., Ludanyi, A and Elteto, L. J., eds. 1983. *Transylvania: The Roots of Ethnic Conflict.* Kent, Ohio.

Čapek, Thomas. 1920. *Čechs (Bohemians) in America.* Boston.

Csonka, Emil. 1976. *A száműzött bíboros.* München.

Csorba, Zoltán. 1930. *Adalékok az amerikai magyar irodalom történetéhez.* Pécs.

Cukor, Mór. 1917. "Polgárosodjunk." *Amerikai Magyar Népszava* (December 17).

Deak, Istvan. 1979. *The Lawful Revolution. Louis Kossuth and the Hungarians, 1848–1849.* New York.

Deák, Zoltán, ed. 1982. *This Noble Flame. An Anthology of a Hungarian Newspaper in America, 1902–1982.* New York.

Dégh, Linda. 1966. "Approaches to Folklore Research among Immigrant Groups." *Journal of American Folklore* 79, no. 314:551–56.

————. 1978. "Two Letters from Home." *Journal of American Folklore* 91, no. 361:808–22.

Dégh, Linda, and Vázsonyi, Andrew. 1971. "Field Report on Hungarian Ethnic and Language Research in the Calumet Region." Unpublished manuscript.

Dienes, István. 1972. *The Hungarians Cross the Carpathians.* Budapest.

Dillingham Report. 61st Congress, 3d Session, Senate Document. no. 748. 1911. *Reports of the Immigration Commission. Emigration Conditions in Europe.* Presented by Mr. Dillingham. Washington, D.C.

Dinnerstein, Leonard, et al. 1979. *Natives and Strangers: Ethnic Groups and the Building of America.* New York.

Dreisziger, N. F., et al. 1982. *Struggle and Hope: The Hungarian-Canadian Experience.* Toronto. Best work on Canadian-Hungarian history.

Éles, Géza Szentmiklósy. 1972. *Hungarians in Cleveland.* M.A. thesis, John Carroll University, Cleveland.

————. 1975. *Two Hungarian Immigrations: Victims of Misconception.* Unpublished typescript.

Eszenyi, László. 1975. *Faithful unto Death.* Washington, D.C.

Estván, Béla. 1864. *War Pictures from the South.* London.

Eszterhás, István. 1978. *Száműzött a szabadság igájában.* Cleveland.

Az ezeréves Magyarország. 1940. Budapest. Cited as *Ezeréves.*

Fejős, Zoltán. 1980. "Kivándorlás Amerikába a Zemplén középső vidékéről." *A Herman Otto Múzeum Évkönyve* 19 (Miskolc):293–327.

Fenyo, Mario D. 1983. "Haraszthy: A Hungarian Pioneer in the American West." In Vardy and Vardy, *Society in Change,* pp. 169–88.

Fermi, Laura. 1968. *Illustrious Immigrants: The Intellectual Migration from Europe, 1930–41.* Chicago; 2d ed. 1971.

Fishman, Joshua A. 1966. *Hungarian Language Maintenance in the United States.* Bloomington, Ind.

Gál, L. Éva. 1971. *Újházi László a szabadságharc utolsó kormánybiztosa.* Budapest.

Gál, István. 1971. "Széchenyi in the U.S.A." *Hungarian Studies in English* 5:95–119.

Gáspár, Géza. 1950. "Az Amerikai Magyar Népszava története. Ötven év kulisszatitka." *AMN Album,* 131–57.

Gellén, József. 1977. "Colonel Prágay's Unknown Letter to American Statesmen." *Hungarian Studies in English* 11:149–53.

————. 1978. "Immigrant Experience in Hungarian-American Poetry before 1945." *Acta Litteraria* 20, no. 1–2:81–97.

Gerzsányi, László. 1978. *An Analysis of the Hungarian Baptist Mission in Cleveland, Ohio, in Light of Programs Introduced between 1973 and 1977.* D.D. diss., Southern Baptist Theological Seminary.

Gleitman, Henry, and Greenbaum, Joseph J. 1960. "Hungarian Socio-Political Attitudes and Revolutionary Action." *Public Opinion Quarterly* 24, no. 1:62–76.

————. 1961. "Attitudes and Personality Patterns of Hungarian Refugees." *Public Opinion Quarterly* 25, no. 3:351–65.

Glenn, A. S. 1913. *Amerikai levelek.* Budapest.

Gordon, Milton M. 1964. *Assimilation in American Life: The Role of Race, Religion and National Origin.* New York.

Gould, J. D. 1980. "European Inter-Continental Emigration. The Road Home: Return Migration from the U.S.A." *Journal of European Economic History* 9, no. 1:41–112.

Billy Graham in Hungary. 1977. Budapest. Cited as *Graham.*

Gutman, Herbert G. 1973. "Work, Culture and Society in Industrializing America, 1815–1919." *American Historical Review* 78 (June):531–88.

Halácsy, Dezső. 1944. *A világ magyarságáért.* Budapest.

Hanák, Péter, and Mucsi, Ferenc, eds. 1978. *Magyarország története, 1890–1918.* Budapest.

Haraszthy, Ágoston. 1844. *Utazas Éjszak-Amerikában.* 2 vols. Pest.

———. 1862. *Grape Culture, Wines, and Wine-Making, with Notes upon Agriculture and Horticulture.* New York.

Harvard Encyclopedia of American Ethnic Groups. Edited by Stephan Thernstrom et al. 1980. Cambridge, Mass. Cited as *HEAEG.*

Hungarian Ethnic Heritage Study of Pittsburgh. 1981. Study Director Paul Bődy. Pittsburgh. Cited as *HEHSP.*

Hoffmann, Géza. 1911. *Csonka munkásosztály. Az amerikai magyarság.* Budapest.

Horváth, Jenő. 1928. "Amerika és a magyar szabadságharc." *Századok* 61, no. 7–8:231–42.

Hungarians in America. A Biographical Directory of Professionals of Hungarian Origin in the Americas. Edited by Tibor Szy. 1966. New York. Cited as *Hungarians* (1966).

Hungarians in America. A Biographical Directory of Professionals of Hungarian Origin in the Americas. Edited by Desi K. Bognar. 1972. Mt. Vernon, N.Y. Cited as *Hungarians* (1972).

Hungary. A Friendly Gift to the Rotarians of Every Part of the World. 1931. Budapest. Cited as *Hungary.*

Ignotus, Paul. 1972. *Hungary.* New York.

Illyés, Elemér. 1982. *National Minorities. Change in Transylvania.* Boulder–New York.

Information Hungary. Edited by Ferenc Erdei et al. 1968. Oxford. Cited as *Inf Hung.*

Janics, Kálmán. 1982. *Czechoslovak Policy and the Hungarian Minority, 1945–1948.* New York.

Jánossy, Dénes. 1940–1948. *A Kossuth-emigráció Angliában és Amerikában, 1851–1852.* 2 vols. in 3. Budapest.

Jánossy, Gustav S. 1979. *Jánnossys.* Unpublished manuscript and newspaper clippings. Gardena, Calif.

Jelinek, Yeshayahu. 1972. "Self-Image of First Generation Hungarian Jewish Immigrants." *American Jewish Historical Quarterly* 61 (March):214–22.

Johnson, Joseph. 1851. *Traditions and Reminiscences Chiefly of the American Revolution in the South.* Charleston, S.C.

Jókai, Mór. 1888. *Gróf Beynyovszky Móric életrajza.* Budapest.

Jubileumi Emlékkönyv. Edited by Sándor Tóth. 1940. Pittsburgh. Cited as *Jub Em.*

Juhász, László. 1979. *Magyarok az újvilágban.* München.

Kadarkay, Árpád, ed. 1978. *Bölöni-Farkas Sándor. Journey in North America.* Santa Barbara.

Kalassay, Louis A. 1939. *The Educational and Religious History of the Hungarian Reformed Church in the United States.* Ph.D. diss., University of Pittsburgh.

Kalassay, Sándor. 1942. *Az amerikai magyar reformátusság története, 1890–1940.* Pittsburgh.

Káldor, Kálmán, ed. 1937–1939. *Magyar Amerika írásban és képben. Amerikai magyar úttörők és vezető férfiak arcképes életrajza. Magyar egyházak, egyletek, közintézetek története és működése.* 2 vols. St. Louis.

Kanyar, József. 1957. "Kivándorlás Somogyból, 1901–1910." *Somogyi parasztság, somogyi nagybirtok* (Kaposvár), 41–54.

Katona, Anna. 1971. "Hungarian Travelogues on Pre–Civil War America." *Hungarian Studies in English* 5:51–94.

———. 1973. "Nineteenth-Century Hungarian Travelogues on Post–Civil War U.S.A." *Hungarian Studies in English* 7:35–52.

Kaufman, W. 1911. *Die Deutschen im amerikanischen Bürgerkrige.* München.

Kautz, Edvin L. 1946. *The Hungarian Baptist Movement in the United States.* M.A. thesis, University of Pittsburgh.

Kende, Géza. 1927. *Magyarok Amerikában. Az amerikai magyarság története, 1583–1926.* 2 vols. Cleveland. The most comprehensive old-time history by a Hungarian-American journalist. The third volume, for the period 1914–1926, was finished but never published.

Kerek, Andrew. 1978. "Hungarian Language Research in North America. Themes and Directions." *Canadian-American Review of Hungarian Studies* 5, no. 2 (Fall):63–72.

Király, Béla K., and Barany, George, eds. 1977. *East Central European Perception of Early America.* Lisse, The Netherlands.

Király, Béla K.; Pastor, Peter, and Sanders, Ivan, eds. 1982. *War and Society in East Central Europe. VI. Essays on World War I. A Case Study of Trianon.* New York.

Kisbarnaki-Farkas, Ferenc. 1969. *Az altöttingi országgyűlés története.* München.

Kolar, Walter W., and Vardy, Agnes H., eds. 1981. *The Folk Arts of Hungary*. Pittsburgh.

Komjáthy, Aladár. 1962. *The Hungarian Reformed Church in America. An Effort to Preserve a Denominational Heritage*. Ph.D. diss., Princeton Theological Seminary.

Komlos, John H. 1973. *Kossuth in America, 1851–1852*. Buffalo, N.Y.

Komoróczy, Géza. 1976a. *Sumer és magyar?* Budapest.

———. 1976b. "On the Idea of Sumero-Hungarian Linguistic Affiliation: Critical Notes on a Pseudo-Scholarly Phenomenon." *Annales Universitatis Scientiarum Budapestinensis de Rolando Eötvös Nominatae* 17 (Budapest):259–303.

Konnyu, Leslie [Könnyǔ, László]. 1962. *A History of Hungarian American Literature*. St. Louis.

———. 1965. *John Xantus: Hungarian Geographer in America*. Köln.

———. 1967. *Hungarians in the U.S.A. An Immigration Study*. St. Louis.

———. 1975. *Xantus János geográfus Amerikában, 1851–1864*. St. Louis.

———. 1976. *Acacias. Hungarians in the Mississippi Valley: A Bicentennial Album*. Ligonier, Pa.

Kőrösfőy, John, ed. 1941. *Hungarians in America. Az amerikai magyarság aranykönyve*. Cleveland.

Kosa, John. 1957. "A Century of Hungarian Emigration, 1850–1950." *American Slavic and East European Review* 16 (December):501–14.

Kosáry, Dominic G. 1941. *A History of Hungary*. Cleveland–New York; reprinted New York, 1970.

Kosáry, Dominic G., and Vardy, Steven B. 1969. *History of the Hungarian Nation*. Astor Park, Fla.

Kótai, Zoltán, ed. 1975. *Mindszenty József—Cleveland, Loraine, Barberton, Akron 1974*. Cleveland.

Kovács, Imre, ed. 1966. *Facts about Hungary, The Fight for Freedom*. New York.

Kovács, József. 1972. *Társadalmi és nemzeti haladás gondolata az amerikai magyar sajtóban*. C.Sc. diss., Budapest.

———. 1977. *A szocialista magyar irodalom dokumentumai az amerikai magyar sajtóban, 1920–1945*. Budapest.

Kovalovszky, Miklós. 1981. "Észak- és Dél-Amerika magyar szobrásza." *Magyar Hirek* 34, no. 17–18 (August 22):45.

Kovrig, Bennett. 1970. *The Hungarian People's Republic*. Baltimore.

Kramár, Zoltán. 1978. *From the Danube to the Hudson. U.S. Consular and Ministerial Dispatches on Immigration from the Habsburg Monarchy, 1850–1900*. Foreword by S. B. Vardy. Atlanta.

Kretzoi, Miklósné. 1965. "The American Civil War as Reflected in the Contemporary Hungarian Press." *Hungarian Studies in English* 2:61–92.

————. 1974. "Az amerikai polgárháború a magyar sajtóban 1861–1865 között." *Századok* 108, no. 3:680–98.

A . . . Magyar Találkozó Krónikája. 1962–1984. Vol. 1 edited by Béla Béldy; vols. 2–23 edited by János Nádas and Ferenc Somogyi. Cleveland. These are the proceedings of the annual "Hungarian Congress" with the dotted space signifying the specific number. Cited as *Krónika.*

Kuné, Julian. 1911. *Reminiscences of an Octogenarian Hungarian Exile.* Chicago.

Lawrence, Abbot. 1883. *Memoir of Abbot Lawrence.* Edited by Andrew Hamilton. N.p. For private distribution.

Lengyel, Emil. 1948. *Americans from Hungary.* Philadelphia; repr. Westport, Conn., 1974. Up to the appearance of Puskás's recent works (1982a and 1982b) this was the best summary of Hungarian-American history. It is still useful today.

Löherer, Andor. 1908. *Az amerikai kivándorlás és visszavándorlás.* Budapest.

Lorant, Stefan. 1964. *Pittsburgh: The Story of an American City.* New York.

Macartney, C. A. 1962. *Hungary: A Short History.* Chicago.

————. 1969. *The Habsburg Empire, 1790–1818.* New York.

Madden, H. W. 1949. *Xantus: Hungarian Naturalist in the Pioneer West.* Palo Alto.

Magyar Hirek Kincses Kalendáriuma 1983. 1982. Budapest. Cited as *MHKK.*

Magyar Statisztikai Közlemenyek. 1918. Budapest. Cited as *MSK.*

A Magyar Szent Korona Országainak kivándorlása és visszavándorlása, 1899–1918. 1918. Budapest. Cited as *MSKOKV.*

A Magyarok Világkongresszusának tárgyalásai. Budapesten 1929 augusztus 22–24. Edited by Sándor Krisztics. 1930. Budapest. Cited as *Magy Vil I.*

A Magyarok II. Világkongresszusának tárgyalásai. Budapesten, 1938 augusztus 16–19. 1938. Budapest. Cited as *Magy Vil II.*

Marchbin, Andrew A. 1940. "Hungarian Activities in Western Pennsylvania." *Western Pennsylvania Historical Magazine* 23, no. 3 (September):163–74.

Márki, Sándor. 1893. "Amerika és a magyarság." *Földrajzi Közlemények* 22 (March):49–94.

Markowitz, Arthur A. 1973. "Humanitarianism versus Restrictionism: The United States and the Hungarian Refugees." *International Migration Review* 7, no. 1 (Spring):46–59.

Máyer, Mária. 1977. *Kárpátukrán (Ruszin) politikai és társadalmi törekvések, 1860–1910.* Budapest.

Nadányi, Paul. 1942. *The "Free Hungary" Movement.* New York.

————. 1943. *Hungary at the Crossroads of Invasions.* New York.

Nagy, Iván. 1939. *Az amerikai magyarság.* Pecs.

————. 1943. *A külföldi magyar sajtó.* Budapest.

Nagy, Kázmér. 1974. *Elveszett alkotmány.* München.

————. 1982. *Elveszett alkotmány. A hidegháború és a magyar politikai emigráció 1945–1975 között.* London.

Novak, Michael. 1971. *The Rise of the Unmeltable Ethnics. Politics and Culture in the Seventies.* New York.

————. 1978. *The Guns of Lattimer.* New York.

Pamlényi, Ervin, ed. 1973. *A History of Hungary.* Budapest.

Pap, Michael S., ed. 1973. *Ethnic Communities of Cleveland: A Reference Work.* Cleveland.

Papp, Susan M. 1981. *Hungarian Americans and Their Communities of Cleveland.* Cleveland.

Park, Robert E. 1922. *The Immigrant Press and Its Control.* New York.

Pivány, Eugene [Jenő]. 1913. *Hungarians in the American Civil War.* Cleveland.

————. 1921. "Az amerikai magyarságról." *Új Magyar Szemle,* January, 56–72.

————. 1927. *Hungarian-American Historical Connections from Pre–Columbian Times to the End of the American Civil War.* Budapest.

————. 1943. *Egy amerikai küldetés története.* Budapest.

Pogány, András H. 1961. *Béla Estván: Hungarian Cavalry Colonel in the Confederate Army.* New York.

Pók-Pivny, Aladár, and Zachar, József. 1982. *Az amerikai függetlenségi háború magyar hőse.* Budapest.

Polányi, Imre. 1964. "A kivándorlás kérdéséhez. Az északi megyékből szlovák anyanyelvűek kivándorlása, 1870–1914." *A Szegedi Tanárképző Főiskola Tudományos Közleményei* 1:245–69.

Polány-Striker, Laura. 1953. "Captain John Smith's Hungary and Transylvania." In Bradford Smith, *Captain John Smith: His Life and Legend.* Philadelphia, pp. 311–42.

Prpić, George J. 1971. *The Croatian Immigration in America.* New York.

————. 1973. "The Croatian Immigration in Pittsburgh." In *The Ethnic Experience in Pennsylvania.* Edited by John E. Bodnar. Lewisburg, Pa., pp. 263–86.

Puskás, Julianna. 1970. "Magyar szervezetek Amerikában az 1880-as évektől az 1960-as évekig." *Történelmi Szemle* 13, no. 4:528–68.

————. 1975. *Emigration from Hungary to the United States before 1914.* Budapest. Repr. from *Etudes Historiques* 2:65–103.

————. 1977. "Some Recent Results of Historical Researches on International Migration." *Acta Historica* 23:151–69.

————. 1981. "A magyarországi kivándorlás sajátosságai a két világháború között, 1920–1940." *Magyar Tudomány* 88, no. 10:735–45.

————. 1982a. *From Hungary to the United States, 1880–1914.* Budapest.

————. 1982b. *Kivándorló magyarok az Egyesült Államokban, 1880–1940.* Budapest.

Quinn, David B., and Cheshire, Neil M. 1972. *The Newfound Land of Stephen Parmenius.* Toronto.

Rácz, István. 1965. "A parasztok elvándorlása a faluból." In *A parasztság Magyarországon a kapitalizmus korában, 1848–1914.* Edited by István Szabó. 2 vols. Budapest, 2:432–83.

————. 1973. "Attempts to Curb Hungarian Emigration to the United States before 1914." *Hungarian Studies in English* 7:5–33.

————. 1977. "Emigration from Hungary to the U.S.A." *Magyar Történeti Tanulmányok* 10 (Debrecen):117–54.

————. 1980. *A paraszti migráció és politikai megítélése Magyarországon, 1849–1914.* Budapest.

Emlékkönyv a bridgeporti (Conn.) Ráckóczi Magyar Betegsegélyző Egylet 25 éves jubileumára, 1888–1913. Edited by Vince Troll. 1913. New York. Cited as *Rákóczi* (1913).

Rákóczi Aid Association Golden Jubilee Book—Rakóczi Segélyző Egyesület Arany Jubileumi Könyve, 1888–1938. Edited by László Lakatos. 1938. Bridgeport, Conn. Cited as *Rákóczi* (1938).

Rektor, Béla. 1980. *A Magyar Királyi Csendőrség oknyomozó története.* Cleveland: Árpád Könyvkiadó Vállalat.

Richter, August P. 1917. *Die Geschichte der Stadt Davenport und des County Scott.* Davenport, Iowa.

Révai Nagy Lexikona. 1910–1935. 21 vols. Budapest. Cited as *RNL.*

Révész, Imre. 1956. *History of the Hungarian Reformed Church.* Translated by George Knight. Washington, D.C.

Roucek, Joseph S. 1943. "The 'Free Movements' of Horthy's Eckhart and Austria's Otto." *Public Opinion Quarterly* 7 (Fall):466–77.

Roucek, Joseph S., and Eisenberg, Bernard, eds. 1982. *America's Ethnic Politics.* Westport, Conn.

Sári-Gál, Imre. 1966. *Az amerikai Debrecen. Képek a clevelandi magyarság életéből.* Toronto.

————. 1978. *Clevelandi Magyar Múzeum. Riportok, versek, fényképek a clevelandi magyarság életéből.* Toronto.

Sarna, Jonathan D. 1981. "The Myth of No Return: Jewish Return Migration to Eastern Europe, 1881–1914." *American Jewish History* 71, no. 2 (December):256–68.

Schoeneman, Theodore, and Schoeneman, Helen Benedek, ed. and tr. 1977. *Journey in North America by Alexander Bölöni Farkas.* Philadelphia.

Shereghy, Basil, ed. 1978. *The United Societies of the U.S.A. 1903–1978. A Historical Album.* McKeesport, Pa.

Simontsits, Attila L., ed. 1983. *The Last Battle for St. Stephen's Crown.* Toronto.

Sinor, Denis. 1959. *History of Hungary.* New York.

————, ed. 1978. *Modern Hungary. Readings from the New Hungarian Quarterly.* Bloomington, Ind.

Sisa, Stephen. 1983. *The Spirit of Hungary. A Panorama of Hungarian History and Culture.* Toronto.

Somody, István. 1979. *Szemben a sorssal.* Astor Park, Fla.

Somogyi, Ferenc, ed. 1974. *Our Hero. Loyal to God, to Church and to Country. Visit of Cardinal Mindszenty to Cleveland, 1974.* Cleveland.

————, ed. 1978. *Emlékkönyv. A clevelandi magyar nyelvoktatás, 1958– 1978.* Cleveland.

————. 1983. *A Magyar Társaság három évtizedének vázlatos története.* Cleveland.

Somogyi, Ferenc, and Somogyi, Lél. 1976. *Faith and Fate. A Short Cultural History of the Hungarian People through a Millennium.* Cleveland.

Soskis, Philip. 1967. "The Adjustment of Hungarian Refugees in New York." *International Migration Review* 2, no. 1 (Fall):40–46.

Souders, David A. 1922. *The Magyars in America.* New York; repr. 1969.

Spencer, Donald S. 1977. *Louis Kossuth and Young America: A Study in Sectionalism and Foreign Policy, 1848–1852.* Columbia, Mo.

Steiner, Edward A. 1906. *On the Trail of the Immigrant.* New York.

Stolarik, M. Mark. 1976. "From Field to Factory: The Historiography of Slovak Immigration to the United States." *International Migration Review* 10 (Spring):81–102.

————. 1980. "Slovak Migration from Europe to North America, 1870– 1918." *Slovak Studies* 20:5–137.

Szász, József. 1922. "A magyarság Amerikában." *Gazdaságpolitikai Szemle,* June, 225–88.

Szabadság Naptára az 1931-ik esztendőre. 1930. Cleveland.

Szántó, Miklós. 1970. *Magyarok a nagyvilágban.* Budapest.

————. 1982. "A kivándorolt magyarság a hetvenes évek végén." *A Magyar Hirek Kincses Kalendáriuma 1982.* Budapest, pp. 35–40.

Szarvas, Pál [Indian]. 1928. *Heti strófák.* Pittsburgh.

————. ca. 1936. *Heti strófák.* Detroit. Not identical with above.

Szászi, Ferenc. 1970. "A kivándorlás hatása a Szabolcs megyei paraszttársadalomra, 1886–1914." *Magyar Történeti Tanulmányok* 3 (Decebren):109–19.

————. 1972. *Az Amerikába irányuló kivándorlás Szabolcs megyéből az első világháborúig.* Nyíregyháza.

Szécskay, György. 1947. *Őszi tarlózás ötven éves mezőn.* Pittsburgh.

Szendrey, Thomas. 1983. "Hungarian-American Theatre." In *The Ethnic Theater in the United States.* Edited by Maxine S. Seller. Westport, Conn., pp. 191–220.

Szente, Péter. 1978. "Egy elfelejtett amerikás magyar: Haraszthy Ágoston." *Századok* 112, no. 1:110–24.

Széplaki, Joseph. 1975. *The Hungarians in America, 1583–1974: A Chronology and Fact Book.* Dobbs Ferry, N.Y.

————. 1976. *Louis Kossuth: The Nation's Guest.* Ligonier, Pa.

Sziklay, Andor. 1953. *Koszta Márton esete.* Washington, D.C.

Szilassy, Sándor. 1979. "Az amerikai magyarság a második világháborúban." *Új Látóhatár* 30, no. 1–2 (June 15):138–43.

Taborsky, Otto Árpád. 1955. *The Hungarian Press in America.* MSLS diss., Catholic University of America, Washington, D.C.

Takaró, Géza. 1940. "Az egyetlen út: A Tiffini Egyezmény története." *Jub Em,* 57–61.

Thirring, Gusztáv. 1904. *A magyarországi kivándorlás és a külföldi magyarság.* Budapest.

————. 1931. "Hungarian Migration of Modern Times." In *International Migrations.* Edited by Imre Ferenczi and Walter F. Wilcox. 2 vols. New York, 1929–1931, 2:411–39.

Török, István. 1978. *Katolikus magyarok Észak-Amerikában.* Youngstown.

Tóth, Sándor. 1940. "A lancesteri magyar tanszék." *Jub Em,* 125–33.

Váraljai-Csocsán, Eugene. 1974. "La population de la Hongrie en XXe siècle." *Révue de l'Est* 5, no. 4 (October):133–231.

Vardy, Steven Bela. 1973. "Magyarságtudomány az észak-amerikai egyetemeken és főiskolákon." *Krónika* 12:102–32.

————. 1975. "Hungarian Studies at American and Canadian Universities." *The Canadian-American Review of Hungarian Studies* 2, no. 2 (Fall):91–121.

————. 1976a. *Modern Hungarian Historiography.* Boulder–New York.

————. 1976b. "A magyarság összefogásának és tudományos tanulmányozásának kisérletei 1920-tól 1945-ig." *Krónika* 15:239–50.

————. 1977a. "Az amerikai magyarságtudomány kifejlődése, nehézségei, és feladatai." *Valóság* 20, no. 8 (August):49–62.

————. 1977b. "The Development of East European Historical Studies in Hungary prior to 1945." *Balkan Studies* 18, no. 1:53–90.

————. 1981. "The Hungarian Community of Cleveland." *Hungarian Studies Review* 8, no. 1 (Spring):137–43.

————. 1982a. "Hungarians in America's Ethnic Politics." In *America's Ethnic Politics.* Edited by Joseph S. Roucek and Bernard Eisenberg. Westport, Conn., pp. 171–96.

————. 1982b. "Trianon in Interwar Hungarian Historiography." In Király-Pastor-Sanders, *War and Society,* pp. 361–89.

————. 1982c. "Az amerikai-magyar történelemkutatás úttörői." *Magyar Hirek* 35, no. 3 (February 6):12–13.

————. 1983a. "The Great Economic Immigration from Hungary; 1880–1920." In Vardy and Vardy, *Society in Change,* pp. 189–216.

————. 1983b. "The Nature of Interwar Hungarian Irredentism: The Impact of the Treaty of Trianon upon the Hungarian Mind." *Hungarian Studies Review* 10, no. 1–2 (Fall):21–42.

————. 1983c. "Az észak-amerikai magyarságtudomány mai helyzete." *Hungarológiai oktatás régen és ma.* Edited by Judit M. Róna. Budapest, pp. 165–73.

Vardy-Huszar, Agnes. 1974. "Alsó és középfokú magyarságtudományi oktatás Észak-Amerikában." *Krónika* 13:39–56.

————. 1982. "Az amerikai magyar irodalom kezdetei: Pólya László költői arcképe." *Magyar Hirek* 35, no. 2 (January 23):14–15.

————. 1983. "Magyarságtudomány Pittsburghben: Eredmények és lehetőségek." *Hungarológiai oktatás régen és ma.* Edited by Judit M. Róna. Budapest, pp. 174–81.

Vardy, Steven B., and Vardy-Huszar, Agnes. 1981. "Research in Hungarian-American History and Culture: Achievements and Prospects." In Kolar and Vardy, *Folk Arts,* pp. 67–123.

————. 1983. *Society in Change: Studies in Honor of Béla K. Király.* Edited by Steven Bela Vardy and Agnes Huszar Vardy. Boulder–New York.

————. 1984. "Historical, Literary, Linguistic and Ethnographic Research on Hungarian-Americans: A Historical Assessment." *Hungarian Studies* 1:79–124.

Vassady, Bela, Jr. 1979. "Kossuth and Újházi on Establishing a Colony of Hungarian 48-ers in America, 1849–1952." *Canadian-American Review of Hungarian Studies* 6, no. 1 (Spring):21–46.

————. 1982. "The 'Homeland Cause' as Stimulant to Ethnic Unity: The Hungarian-American Response to Károlyi's 1914 American Tour." *Journal of American Ethnic History* 2, no. 1 (Fall):39–64.

Vasváry, Edmund {Ödön]. 1939. *Lincoln's Hungarian Heroes. The Participation of Hungarians in the Civil War, 1861–1865.* Washington, D.C.

————. 1950. "Az amerikai magyarság története." *AMN Album,* 59–74.

Vázsonyi, Andrew [Endre]. 1978. "The Cicisbeo and the Magnificent Cuckold: Boardinghouse Life and Lore in Immigrant Communities." *Journal of American Folklore* 91, no. 360:641–56.

————. 1980. "A főburdos és a csodaszarvas." *Valóság* 23, no. 3 (March):89–97.

Vecoli, Rudolph J. 1964. "Contadini in Chicago: A Critique of *The Uprooted." Journal of American History* 51 (December):404–17.

Verhovayak Lapja. Verhovay Fraternal Insurance Association, 1886–1936. Edited by József Daragó. 1936. Pittsburgh. Cited as *Verhovayak.*

Virág, Ferenc. 1971. "Adalékok a kivándorlás Békés megyei történetéhez." *Békési Élet,* pp. 189–99.

Wagner, Ferenc S. 1965. "The Start of Cultural Exchanges between the Hungarian Academy of Sciences and the American Philosophical Society." *Hungarian Quarterly* 5, no. 1–2 (April-June):90–97.

Warzeski, Walter C. 1971. *Byzantine Rite Rusins in Carpatho-Ruthenia and America.* Pittsburgh.

———. 1973. "The Rusin Community in Pennsylvania." In *The Ethnic Experience in Pennsylvania.* Edited by John E. Bodnar. Lewisburg, Pa., pp. 263–86.

Weinstock, S. Alexander. 1969. *Acculturation and Occupation: A Study of the 1956 Hungarian Refugees in the United States.* The Hague.

Xantus, John. 1979. *Letters from America.* Translated and edited by Theodore Schoenman and Helen Benedek Schoenman. Detroit.

Zachar, József. 1980. "Pollereczky János őrnagy az amerikai forradalmi függetlenségi háborúban." *Hadtörténelmi Közlemények* 83, no. 2:293–310.

Zombori, István. 1977. "A mult századi Amerika magyar szemmel. Ismeretlen kézirat a Kossuth-emigrációból." In *A Móra Ferenc Múzeum Évkönyve, 1976–1977.* Szeged, pp. 325–64.

Bibliographical Aids

Bakó, Elemér. 1973. *Guide to Hungarian Studies*. 2 vols. Stanford.

Horecky, Paul L. 1969a. *East Central Europe. A Guide to Basic Publications*. Chicago.

————. 1969b. *Southeastern Europe. A Guide to Basic Publications*. Chicago.

————. 1976. *East Central and Southeast Europe. A Handbook of Library and Archival Resources in North America*. Santa Barbara.

Mildschütz, Koloman. 1977. *Bibliographie der ungarischen Exilpresse, 1945– 1975*. Ergänzt von Béla Grolschammer. München.

Németh, Mária. 1975. *Külföldi magyar nyelvű hírlapok és folyóiratok címjegyzéke és adattára, 1945–1970. II. Nem szocialista országok*. Budapest.

Széplaki, Joseph. 1977. *Hungarians in the United States and Canada: A Bibliography*. Foreword by S. B. Vardy. Minneapolis.

Index